30 TALES TO GIVE YOU

Goosebumps®

R.L. STINE

SCHOLASTIC INC.
New York Toronto London Auckland Sydney
Mexico City New Delhi Hong Kong Buenos Aires

The *Goosebumps* book series created by Parachute Press, Inc.

12 11 10 9 8 7 6 5 4   5 6 7 8 9/0

Printed in the U.S.A.   23

This edition created exclusively for Barnes & Noble, Inc.
2004 Barnes & Noble Books

ISBN 0-7607-5680-5

First compilation printing, July 2004

Contents

TALES TO GIVE YOU
Goosebumps®

THE HOUSE OF NO RETURN

We were afraid to go too close to the house. So we stayed down at the street, staring up at it. Staring across the bare, sloping front yard.

No grass would grow in that yard. The trees, gnarled and bent, were all dead. Not even weeds sprouted in the dry, cracked dirt.

At the top of the sloping yard, the house seemed to stare back at us. The two upstairs windows gaped like two unblinking black eyes.

The house was wide and solid-looking. Built of bricks. Many years ago, the bricks had been painted white. But now the paint was faded and peeling. Spots of red brick showed through like bloodstains.

The window shutters were cracked. Several had fallen off. The beams of the front porch tilted dangerously. A strong wind could blow the porch over.

No one lived there. The house had been empty for years and years.

No one *could* live there.

The house was haunted. Everyone in town said it was.

Everyone knew the legend of the house: If you spent the night inside it, you would never come out.

That's why we brought kids there. That's why we dared them to go inside.

You couldn't join our Danger Club unless you stayed inside the house — by yourself — for an hour.

Staring up at the house, bathed in a haze of pale moonlight, I shivered. I zipped my windbreaker up to my chin and crossed my arms over my chest.

"How long has he been in there, Robbie?" Nathan asked me.

Lori and I both raised our wrists to check our watches. "Only ten minutes," I told Nathan.

"Fifty minutes to go," Lori said. "Think he'll make it?"

"Doug is pretty brave," I replied thoughtfully, watching the moon disappear behind a cloud. "He might last another five minutes!" I said, grinning.

Lori and Nathan snickered.

The three of us felt safe down here by the street.

Poor Doug probably didn't feel too safe right now. He was shut inside the dark house. Trying to stay there an hour so he could join our club.

I turned and saw a light rolling silently over

the street, coming toward us. A white, ghostly light.

My breath caught in my throat.

It's a car, I realized, as it floated closer. A car with only one headlight. The first car we'd seen on this street all night.

The beam from the headlight washed over my two friends and me, forcing us to shield our eyes. As it passed, we turned back to the house — and heard a shrill scream.

A wail of terror.

"Here he comes!" Nathan cried.

Sure enough, Doug burst out through the front door. He stumbled off the crumbling porch and came tearing across the dead, bare yard.

His hands waved wildly in front of him. His head was tilted back, and his mouth was frozen open in one long, high shriek of fright.

"Doug — what did you see?" I called. "Did you really see a ghost?"

"S-something touched my *face*!" he wailed. He ran right past Nathan, Lori, and me, screaming his head off.

"Probably only a spiderweb," I murmured.

"Robbie — we've got to stop him!" Lori cried.

"Doug! Hey — Doug!" We called his name and chased after him, our sneakers slapping loudly on the pavement.

Waving his arms frantically and screaming, leaning into the wind, Doug kept running.

We couldn't catch him. "He'll run home," I said breathlessly. I stopped and leaned over, pressing my hands against my knees, trying to catch my breath.

Up ahead, we could still hear poor Doug's frightened wail.

"Guess he doesn't join the club," I said, still breathing hard.

"What do we do now?" Nathan asked, glancing back at the house.

"I guess we find another victim," I replied.

Chris Wakely seemed like a perfect victim.

His family had moved to town last summer, and Chris started in my sixth-grade class in September. Chris had pale blue eyes and very short, white-blond hair. He was kind of shy, but he seemed like a really nice guy.

One day after school, I saw Chris walking home and I hurried to catch up with him. It was a windy October day. All around us, red and yellow leaves were falling from the trees. It looked like it was raining leaves.

I said hi to Chris and started telling him about our club. I asked if he'd like to join.

"It's only for brave people," I explained. "In order to join, you have to spend an hour at night inside the house on Willow Hill."

Chris stopped walking and turned to me,

squinting at me with those pale blue eyes. "Isn't that house supposed to be haunted?" he asked.

I laughed. "You don't believe in ghosts — do you?"

He didn't smile. His expression turned serious. The light seemed to fade in his eyes. "I'm not very brave," he said softly.

We started to walk again. Our sneakers crunched on the leaves strewn over the sidewalk. "We'd really like you to join the club," I told him. "You're brave enough to spend one hour in an empty house, aren't you?"

He shrugged and lowered his eyes. "I — I don't think so," he stammered. "I've always been afraid of monsters and things," he admitted. "I believed there was a monster living under my bed until I was eight!"

I laughed. But his expression remained solemn. He wasn't kidding.

"When I go to a scary movie," Chris continued, "I have to duck under the seat when the scary parts come on."

Lori and Nathan came running up to us. "Are you going to do it?" Nathan asked Chris. "Are you going to join the club?"

Chris shoved his hands deep into his jeans pockets. "Did you guys spend an hour in the house?" he asked.

I shook my head. "We don't have to," I told

him. “We started the club, so we don’t have to go in the house. We already know we like danger. New members have to prove themselves.”

Chris chewed thoughtfully at his lower lip. We turned the corner and kept walking. The house was up the hill, at the end of the block.

We stopped in front of it and stared across the bare front yard. “See? It doesn’t look scary at all in the daytime,” I said.

Chris swallowed hard. “Needs a paint job,” he muttered. “And how come all the trees died?”

“No one to take care of them,” Nathan said.

“How about it, Chris?” I urged. “We really need new members.”

“Yeah,” Lori agreed. “A club isn’t much fun with only three kids in it.”

Chris had his eyes on the house. He kept his hands jammed into his jeans pockets. I thought I saw him shiver. But it might have been the wind rustling his jacket.

“W-will you come in with me?” he asked.

“No way,” I replied, shaking my head.

“We can’t,” Lori told him. “The idea of the club is to show how brave you are.”

“We won’t come in,” Nathan said. “But we’ll wait out front for you.”

“Come on, Chris,” I urged. “Do it. It’ll be fun! It’s almost Halloween. Get in the spirit!”

He swallowed a couple of times, staring up at the house. Then he shook his head. “I really don’t want to," he murmured in a low voice, so low I could barely hear him. "Guess I'm kind of a scaredy-cat."

I started to plead with him. But I could see he was really embarrassed. So I didn't say any more.

Chris waved good-bye and hurried off toward his house. Lori, Nathan, and I watched him until he disappeared around the corner.

"Now what?" Nathan asked.

We held a club meeting at my house two nights later. It was a pretty boring meeting. None of us could think of another cool kid to join our club. And we couldn't think of anything fun to do.

"Halloween is Saturday," I moaned. "We should be able to think of something scary to do."

"What are you going to dress up as?" Lori asked Nathan.

"Freddy Krueger," Nathan replied. "I already bought the metal fingernails."

"Weren't you Freddy Krueger last year?" I asked him.

"So? I *like* being Freddy Krueger!" Nathan insisted.

"You and every other kid in school," Lori muttered.

Lori planned to dress as a vampire. And I had my monster costume all ready.

"We need more club members," Lori said, sighing. "You can't have a club with just three people."

"Chris would be perfect," I replied. "If only he weren't such a scaredy-cat."

"You know," Nathan started, rubbing his chin thoughtfully, "it would be really good for Chris to get over his fears."

"Huh? What do you mean?" I asked.

"I mean we could help Chris out," Nathan replied, smiling. "We could help him be brave."

I still didn't understand. "Nathan — what are you saying?"

His smile grew wider. "We could *force* him to go into the house."

I called Chris later that night and invited him to go trick-or-treating with us. He said yes. He sounded grateful to have some kids to go around with. He had only been at our school two months, and he hadn't made many friends.

The three of us met at my house on Halloween. Nathan clicked his long metal nails and kept cackling and grinning like Freddy Krueger. I was a very cool monster, with eyeballs on springs popping from my purple head. Lori kept talking in a weird vampire voice.

"Where's Chris?" Nathan asked, looking around. "Is he meeting us here?"

"Yeah. Where is he?" Lori demanded.

We were all a little tense. We were playing a mean trick on Chris. But we knew he'd feel good about things by the end of the night.

The doorbell rang, and we all ran to answer it. Chris stood in the porch light, his face an ugly green. He raised both hands to show them to us. They were covered in green, too.

"What are *you* supposed to be — a pea pod?" I joked.

Chris looked hurt. "No. I'm a corpse."

"Very scary," I said. I handed out trick-or-treat bags. "Let's get going." I led the way down the driveway and up the street.

We stopped at several houses and collected candy. It was a cool, windy night with a tiny sliver of a moon. Gusts of wind kept fluttering our costumes and making our trick-or-treat bags fly up.

We were approaching the house on Willow Hill. I had a heavy feeling in my stomach. My hands suddenly felt ice cold.

I hope Chris can stay in the house for a whole hour, I thought. He's such a nice guy. I'd really like him to be in the club.

Such a nice guy. And we were about to do such a mean thing to him.

But he'll quickly get over it, I told myself. And he'll be glad we made him test his bravery.

The eerie house came into view. I saw Chris glance at it, then quickly turn to cross the street. He didn't want to go near it. Especially on Halloween night.

But Nathan and I grabbed him by the arms.

Chris cried out in surprise. "Hey — let go! What are you guys doing?"

Chris struggled to pull free. But Nathan and I were much bigger than him, and stronger.

Lori led the way over the bare, dirt yard, up the sloping hill to the dark, silent house. Chris tried to swing both arms, tried desperately to break free. But Nathan and I dragged him onto the tilting porch, up to the front door.

"No! Please!" Chris pleaded. "Please — don't do this! Don't!"

I turned to him. Even under the green makeup, I could see the terror on his face. The poor guy was totally freaked!

"Chris, you'll be okay," I said softly, soothingly. "Go inside. It'll be fun. We'll wait for you. I promise."

"You'll be proud of yourself," Lori told him, helping to push him up to the door. "And then you'll be in our club."

Lori started to push open the heavy door. Nathan and I moved to shove Chris inside. But to my surprise, he reached out and grabbed my arm.

"Come in with me — please!" he begged, his eyes wide with fright. "Please! I'm too scared! I'm just too scared!" He held on tightly to my arm. "Let's all go in together — okay?"

I glanced at Lori and Nathan. "No way," I replied. "You've got to prove your bravery, Chris. See you in an hour."

We gave him a hard shove inside the house. Then we slammed the heavy door behind him.

"He seems so . . . scared," Lori said, her voice muffled by the vampire fangs.

"He'll be okay," I said. "Let's wait for him down by the street."

We took our places at the bottom of the driveway, and waited.

And waited.

We checked our watches after ten minutes. After twenty minutes. After half an hour.

"Chris is doing great!" I whispered, my eyes on the dark windows of the house. "I didn't think he'd last *two* minutes."

"He's a lot braver than I thought," Nathan said from behind his Freddy Krueger mask.

We huddled close together, staring up at the house as the wind shook the trees all around us. Heavy clouds rolled over the moon, covering us in darkness.

We waited ten minutes more. Then ten minutes more.

"He's going to do it," I said, checking my watch again. "He's going to stay in there for a whole hour."

"Let's really give him a big cheer when he comes out," Lori suggested.

As the hour ended, we counted off the last thirty seconds out loud, one by one. Then we took a few steps up the driveway, eager to congratulate

Chris and welcome him to the Danger Club.

But the front door didn't open. The house remained dark and silent.

Ten more minutes passed.

"I think he's showing off," I said.

No one laughed. We kept our eyes raised to the house.

Ten more minutes. Then ten more.

"Where *is* he?" I cried shrilly.

"Something is wrong," Lori said, taking the plastic vampire fangs out of her mouth. "Something is wrong, Robbie."

"Chris should be out of there by now," Nathan agreed in a trembling voice.

I felt a chill run down my back. All of my muscles were tightening in dread. I knew my friends were right. Something bad had happened inside that house. Something very bad.

"We have to go in there," Lori urged. "We have to find Chris. We have to get him out."

All three of us exchanged frightened glances. We didn't want to walk up that driveway. We didn't want to go inside that dark house.

But we didn't have a choice.

"Maybe we should wait a few more minutes," I suggested, trying to stop my legs from shaking. "Maybe he doesn't have a watch. Maybe he's — "

"Come on, Robbie." Lori gave me a hard tug. "Chris isn't coming out. We have to go get him."

The wind swirled around us, fluttering our costumes as we made our way up to the front door. I started to open the door, but my hand was so sweaty, the doorknob slid under my grasp.

Finally, Nathan and I pushed open the heavy door. The rusty hinges creaked as we opened the door and peered into the solid blackness.

"Chris?" I called. "Chris — you can come out now!" My voice sounded tiny and hollow.

No reply.

"Chris? Chris? Where are you?" All three of us began calling him.

The floor groaned and creaked beneath us as we took a few steps into the living room. The wind rattled the old windowpanes.

"Chris — can you hear us? Chris?"

No reply.

A loud crash made all three of us cry out.

The front door had slammed behind us.

"J-just the wind, guys," I choked out.

It was much darker with the door closed. But it didn't stay dark for long. Pale light flickered at the top of the stairs. It looked at first like dozens of fireflies clustered together.

I gasped as the light flared brighter. And floated down the stairs, like a shimmering cloud.

"Let's get out!" I cried.

Too late.

The shimmering cloud spread around us. And inside it I saw two frightening figures — a ghostly man and woman, hazy and transparent except for their red, glowing eyes.

Their terrifying eyes sparkled like fiery coals as they circled us, floating silently.

I can see right through both of them! I realized. This house really is haunted.

"Wh-where's Chris?" I managed to blurt out.

The man's voice was a dry whisper, the sound of wind through dead leaves. "Your friend? He went out the back door," the ghost replied. "About an hour ago."

"We didn't want to let him go," the woman whispered, her red eyes glowing brighter. "But he made a bargain with us." She snickered, a dry, dead laugh. "He promised that if we let him go, three kids would come in to take his place."

"And here you are," said the ghostly man, flashing an ugly, toothless smile. "Here you are."

"Don't look so frightened, kids," the woman rasped, floating closer. "You might as well make yourselves at home. You're all going to be here — *forever*!"

TEACHER'S PET

Do you like snakes?

If you're in Mr. Blankenship's class, you *have* to like snakes — or you're in *major* trouble!

Let me start at the beginning, on the first day of school last September. Benjy, my best friend, was shouting to me from my front porch. "Becca, move it! We'll be late!"

I grabbed my black denim jacket and tucked my ponytail under my New York Yankees baseball cap. I hurried, even though I knew Benjy would never leave without me.

Benjy and I had walked to school together every day since kindergarten. Some people think it's weird that a girl and a guy are best friends. But Benjy and I don't care. We've always liked to do the same sort of stuff — like play basketball and baseball, and cook. (Benjy would kill me if he knew I told anyone about that!)

Benjy and I were starting sixth grade. At our

school, sixth-graders get to do great stuff — like go on a camp-out for a whole week!

We were supposed to have Ms. Wenger this year, the coolest teacher in the whole school. Ms. Wenger is the kind of teacher who takes the whole class in-line skating so that when someone falls down, she can talk to us about gravity!

Benjy and I figured this would be just about the best school year ever.

So you can imagine our surprise when we walked into our classroom and saw the teacher writing his name on the board. The teacher wasn't Ms. Wenger. It was a man named Mr. Blankenship.

Benjy and I both groaned in disappointment. Mr. Blankenship was a strange-looking dude. He was really, really tall and really, really skinny. And he was almost completely bald.

His clothes were pretty bad, too. Especially the weird turtleneck sweater he was wearing with the beige, brown, and black diamonds all over it.

He greeted Benjy and me at the door and asked our names.

"I'm Becca Thompson," I said.

"Benjy Connor," Benjy said.

"I'm just getting things together right now. Why don't you two join the others and take a tour around the room?" Mr. Blankenship suggested.

The room looked pretty dull — not cool the way Ms. Wenger would have done it. Mr. Blankenship had set up the typical stuff — reading corner, computer corner, and a corny "Welcome Back" bulletin board.

The only unusual things were the five or six glass tanks placed around the classroom. I walked over to one of the tanks and pressed my nose up against the glass. Not much to see — some rocks, a pile of dried grass, a stick, and . . .

"*Aaagh!*" I uttered a shriek.

Then I just stood there, pointing at the long, skinny, hissing creature. I hate snakes. I can't help it. I just hate them!

I hate those tiny, black eyes that sort of stare right through you. That's what scares me the most — those eyes.

I wanted to turn away from the snake's angry glare, but I couldn't. I seemed to be paralyzed. Frozen stiff. And my heart was pounding so hard, I thought it was going to pop out of my chest!

It was Benjy who broke the snake's spell over me. He came over and shoved me out of the way to get a better view. "Oh. A snake," he said calmly. But I knew that Benjy is just as afraid of snakes as I am.

"I see you've met one of my little pals," Mr. Blankenship said to us, smiling. "We're going to study snakes this year. Fascinating creatures. Fascinating."

Leaning over the cage, Mr. Blankenship turned to me. "Did you know that snakes can live for months without food? Of course, they'd much rather swallow a tasty little mouse instead. Watch."

He reached into a smaller cage hidden behind a bookshelf and grabbed a small white mouse by the tail. The mouse tried to wriggle free, but Mr. Blankenship held tight to its slender pink tail.

He dangled the thrashing, wriggling mouse over the snake's tank for a few seconds. Then he dropped it right next to the snake.

I didn't want to watch. But I couldn't help myself.

The snake snapped open its jaws, and swallowed the little white mouse — whole! I let out a groan as I watched the pink tail slide past the snake's teeth like a spaghetti noodle.

I felt really sick to my stomach. But there was no way I was giving Mr. Blankenship the satisfaction of knowing he had totally grossed me out.

"Who's next?" Mr. Blankenship asked, rubbing his long, slender hands together. "Who's hungry?"

That's when I realized that *all* of the glass cages in the room were filled with Mr. Blankenship's slimy, slithering, hissing little "pals."

Benjy and I tried to like Mr. Blankenship's class. But it wasn't easy. For one thing, he kept adding more and more snakes. Soon, one entire wall was filled with glass tanks.

The snakes slithered silently, their black eyes

following Mr. Blankenship. "There are more snakes than kids in here!" I whispered to Benjy one day.

It seemed as if Mr. Blankenship could talk about nothing else! In science, we studied about the hatching of snake eggs. For history, we read stories about ancient beliefs in serpents. For geometry, we made chalk drawings of snakeskin patterns.

One enormous glass cage behind Mr. Blankenship's desk stood empty. Benjy and I wondered what he planned to put in there. "A giant python!" Benjy guessed.

I shuddered. I didn't want to think about it.

Every time I peered into a glass cage and saw a snake staring back at me, I panicked. I knew the snakes hated being cooped up in those tanks. Something in their eyes told me that if they ever got out, they would go for the first human they saw.

I hoped it wasn't me!

One night I was lying in bed, trying to get to sleep. Pale moonlight washed over my room from the open window. I saw a shadow move against the wall.

Uttering a frightened gasp, I clicked on my bed-table lamp.

And saw a snake slithering out of my backpack on the floor.

How had it escaped from its tank? How had it crept into my backpack?

Frozen in terror, I watched it slither over my shag rug, making its way to my bed.

I screamed and forced myself to sit up. I tried to scramble away. But I felt something warm and dry curl around my arm.

"Uh-uh-uh-uh — !" I was making this weird gasping sound. I felt something like a rope tightening around my ankle. Another snake slithered over my pillow. Two more snakes crawled over my pajama legs.

"Helllllp!" My frantic plea escaped my lips in a hushed whisper.

The snakes tightened themselves around me, curling around my waist, my arms, my legs. One of them slithered through my hair.

I started to shudder and shake. I shook so hard, I woke myself up.

What a horrible nightmare!

Mr. Blankenship and his room full of snakes were ruining my life. But what could I do?

The next day I tried to switch my seat to one far away from the snake tanks. But the tanks were everywhere, on the shelves, on the tables, stacked along the window ledges. Every day there seemed to be more of them.

I tried hard not to think about the snakes around the room. I tried to concentrate on our geography lesson — the snakes of New Mexico.

But just as Mr. Blankenship began to discuss the heat of the desert, I heard a *thud.* Then Melissa Potter let out a shrill scream.

"I'm sorry!" she cried. "I bumped a cage. I let out one of the mice!"

"Where? Where did it go?" Mr. Blankenship cried excitedly.

"There it goes!" Benjy cried, pointing. The little white mouse scampered across the floor. Kids screamed and laughed.

But Mr. Blankenship had a serious, angry expression on his face. "Grab it! Grab it — quick!" he shouted.

"It's over there!" shouted Carl Jansen, pointing to the window in the corner. Mr. Blankenship always left that window open so his snake pals could get fresh air.

Mr. Blankenship dived across the room. The mouse scuttled onto the window ledge. Mr. Blankenship grabbed for the tail. Missed. The mouse vanished out the window.

Our teacher turned beet-red. Even the top of his bald head was red. "Now look what you've done!" he screamed at Melissa. "You let a perfectly good snake dinner get away!

"You will all have to be taught to be more careful," Mr. Blankenship bellowed. "Perhaps an extra homework assignment will help you remember. I want three pages on the feeding habits of the eastern diamondback rattler. And I want it tomorrow!"

"What is his problem?" I whispered to Benjy.

"Becca!" Mr. Blankenship shouted. "I heard that! *You* will write a *ten*-page essay!"

"But — but — !" I sputtered.

"And you will clean the snake cages for the next two weeks!" Mr. Blankenship added.

I clamped my hand over my mouth to keep myself from getting in even worse trouble. But I was so angry, I could have let *all* the mice out of their cages!

Which gave me a great idea. "Benjy," I whispered when Mr. Blankenship had turned away. "After school. My house. Get ready for Operation Mouse Rescue."

Later, after school, Benjy and I worked out all of the details. Operation Mouse Rescue would take place on Thursday night, after our parents went to play bridge.

The plan was simple. Simple, but excellent. Benjy and I were going to sneak into school and set all of the white mice free. We could just picture Mr. Blankenship's face when he arrived Friday morning and found the mice scampering all over the room.

Thursday seemed to stretch on forever. I barely heard a word Mr. Blankenship said. I was too busy watching the clock, waiting for the bell to ring.

I know I ate dinner with my family — but don't ask me what we had. All I could think about was Operation Mouse Rescue.

Finally, my parents said good-bye, left all the right phone numbers, and drove off to their bridge tournament. It didn't take long before Benjy gave me our secret signal — a single ring of the telephone.

My heart pounding, I pulled on my black jeans and dark jacket and raced up the block to Benjy's house. He was waiting for me at the bottom of the driveway.

"What took you so long?" he demanded. "You're not wimping out — are you?"

"No way!" I replied, although I suddenly felt as if *I* had white mice fluttering around in my stomach. "Let's go."

Half walking, half jogging, we made our way to school. It was a cool, breezy night. The trees shivered, shedding fat brown leaves. Shadows twisted and bent over our path as we crept up to the dark school building.

"Around the back," I whispered.

The school seemed so much larger, so much scarier at night, bathed in total blackness.

We found our classroom. Benjy clicked on his flashlight.

"No — turn it off!" I instructed. "Someone may see us."

He obediently clicked off the light. We spotted

the open window, the window in the corner that Mr. Blankenship always leaves open.

My hands felt cold and wet as I grabbed the stone window ledge and pulled myself up. Inside the room, I turned and helped pull Benjy in.

"It — it's so dark," he whispered, huddling close to me. "Can't we turn on the flashlights?"

"Okay," I whispered back. "But keep the light down on the floor."

Our circles of yellow light swept over the floor. Slowly, we made our way to the table that held the mice cages. The floorboards creaked under our sneakers.

I glanced nervously around the room. Tiny lights flickered in the blackness. It took me a long moment to realize they weren't lights. They were glowing snake eyes.

"They — they're all watching us," I whispered to Benjy. "The snakes — they're — "

So many glowing eyes. So many snakes! All around us. Staring. Staring.

I forgot to watch where I was going. I stumbled over a chair.

"Ow!" I cried out. I tried to catch my balance, but fell against a table.

A glass tank toppled to the floor with a shattering *crash*. I glanced down in time to see two snakes slither onto the floor. They uncurled in the trembling light of my flashlight. Then moved quickly toward my legs.

"Benjy — help!" I thrashed out my arms. I turned to run. And knocked over another snake cage.

A long black snake rolled silently onto the floor, arched itself up, opened its jaws, and shot its head toward me.

"Run!" I shrieked. "Benjy — the snakes are out!"

"How — ?" Benjy started.

I jumped as a snake slithered between my feet.

We turned to run — but stopped as our lights played over the enormous, empty glass case.

Which wasn't empty anymore.

A giant gray-and-black cobra glared into the shaking lights. The cobra arched its head up, opened its jaws, and hissed at us, its red eyes gleaming excitedly.

When did that snake get in there? I asked myself. The cage was empty this afternoon!

"R-run!" I stammered, grabbing Benjy's shoulder.

But neither of us could move. We stood staring in frozen horror as the enormous cobra rose up. Lifted itself up. Out of the cage.

It stood over us, at least six feet tall. Its eyes glowing. Its thick tongue flicking across its open jaws.

And as it rose up, its skin shifted and stretched. Its head tilted up. Its body grew wide. Grew arms. Legs.

And we recognized him. We saw him. We knew him.

We knew we were staring at Mr. Blankenship.

The snake was Mr. Blankenship!

"Noooooooooo!" Did that terrified howl escape *my* throat? Or was Benjy howling like some unearthly creature?

I only knew that we turned and ran. Dived out through the open window. Into the dark night. And kept running. Running till we were safe at home. Safe. Safe from snakes. Safe from the biggest snake — Mr. Blankenship.

But safe for how long? Safe till we had to return to school the next morning?

Trembling with fright, Benjy and I hesitated at the classroom door on Friday morning. What would Mr. Blankenship do to us now that we knew his horrible secret? What would he say?

He smiled as Benjy and I entered, and didn't say a word. The day went by like any other day. He didn't say a word about what had happened the night before.

Until the final bell rang that afternoon. He dismissed the rest of the class, then turned to Benjy and me. "I want you two to stay," he said sternly. He moved quickly to block the doorway.

We were alone with him now. He closed the door and moved toward us, rubbing his slender hands together, his dark eyes glowing excitedly.

*　*　*

Mr. Blankenship isn't such a bad guy. He made us a deal. He said he wouldn't tell anyone we broke into the school. And he promised not to harm us as long as we didn't tell anyone his secret.

Of course Benjy and I quickly agreed.

There's just one part of the deal that I hate.

We have to bring in white mice and feed him every afternoon.

I really hate the way the mice wriggle and squirm as I hold them up by their pink tails.

But what choice do I have?

A deal's a deal.

"Here you go, Mr. Blankenship. Open wide."

STRAINED PEAS

My life changed forever the day Mom brought the new baby home from the hospital. My little sister is no ordinary baby.

If only she were.

I sat on the front steps with Mrs. Morgan, waiting for Mom and Dad to bring the baby home. Mrs. Morgan had stayed with me and Dad while Mom was in the hospital.

I thought about the new baby. Hannah. A little sister.

Yuck.

I sighed and tapped a stick against the brick steps.

"Stop fidgeting, Nicholas," Mrs. Morgan scolded. "Why don't you read your comic book until your parents get home?"

I opened my *Iron Man* comic book and picked up where I'd left off. Iron Man has cornered a bad guy disguised as a kindly doctor. "Unmask yourself!" says Iron Man.

Iron Man rips the mask off the doctor's head, revealing the hideous face of a mad scientist. Iron Man gasps. "The Mark of Evil!" he cries. "Dr. Destro!"

Iron Man has never seen Dr. Destro before, but he recognizes the bad guy by the birthmark on his face — the Mark of Evil.

I heard a car coming and glanced up. Dad's dark green Volvo chugged down the street and pulled into our driveway. Mom sat in the passenger seat, waving to me and smiling brightly.

Mrs. Morgan gave me a little shove. "Go on," she said. "Go meet your new sister!"

Ugh, I thought. I *was* glad to see Mom, though. I dragged myself over to the car.

Dad opened the car door. Mom stepped out, carrying a little bundle in her arms. She bent down and said, "Look, Nicholas. Isn't she adorable?"

I looked at the crumpled red face in my mother's arms. A thin fuzz of dark hair covered her head. She had blue eyes and tiny, wet red lips. No teeth. She waved a wrinkled fist in the air, then stuffed it into her mouth.

I didn't think she was so adorable. I thought she was kind of ugly.

But then I nearly choked. On Hannah's cheek was a tiny, brown, heart-shaped birthmark.

I pointed to the birthmark and gasped, "The Mark of Evil! Just like Dr. Destro!"

"Cut it out, Nicholas," Dad said sternly. "This is no time for your crazy comic book talk."

He turned his back on me to gawk at Hannah.

"She's perfect," Dad said, giving Mom's shoulders a squeeze.

How could he be so stupid? I picked up my comic book and pointed to the mark on Dr. Destro's face.

"Look!" I cried. "Hannah has a birthmark like Dr. Destro's! It's a sign of evil!"

Mom smiled vaguely at me. "Don't be silly," she said. She carried the baby inside, and the rest of us followed her.

Soon Grandma and Grandpa came over, and Aunt Julie and Uncle Hal. They oohed and ahhed every time Hannah burped, or hiccupped, or cooed. It was disgusting.

"Look at that — she blew a bubble!"

"She's a genius!"

"Dori, darling, let me hold her for a few minutes," Grandma begged Mom.

But Mom said, "Let Nicholas hold her. He's her big brother, after all."

"No," I said, backing away. "That's okay."

"Oh, come on, Nick. You'll like it." Mom smiled and put Hannah in my arms. She showed me how to hold her. Hannah burped. Everyone laughed.

As I held her, I thought, she's sort of cute, I guess. Maybe I got a little carried away with that Mark of Evil stuff. After all, comic books don't come true. And Hannah's just a baby.

But like I said, she was no ordinary baby.

I swear I saw something glint in her dark blue eyes.

That little heart-shaped birthmark on her cheek seemed to darken.

Then Hannah opened her mouth wide — and threw up all over me.

"Ugh!" I cried. I was covered with milky white glop.

Mom quickly took the baby.

Hannah started crying. "Poor little Hannah," Mom said.

Poor little Hannah! *I* was the one she threw up on!

And she did it on purpose. I knew she did.

That night, the howling began.

A horrible sound woke me up. A loud, screeching wail.

I sat up in bed, shaking. My eardrums rattled in my ears.

What was that noise?

I got out of bed to see what was going on. Mom was walking Hannah up and down the hallway, patting and shushing her. But Hannah didn't stop screaming. She sounded like some kind of wild animal in pain.

"Mom — what's wrong with her?" I asked.

"Nothing," Mom replied. "It's just a normal baby sound. Go back to sleep."

I didn't get any sleep. Hannah never stopped crying.

That's no normal baby sound, I thought. No one can tell me that terrifying screech is normal.

Hannah's wailing continued, night after night. Each night was worse than the last. Wild screams that even the neighbors could hear. Monstrous screams. When Hannah started crying, the neighborhood dogs threw their heads back and howled along with her.

I could swear I saw her birthmark grow, just a little.

A few months passed. Hannah learned to crawl early. Mom and Dad thought that meant she was smart. I knew better.

She had a mission. She wanted to be an only child.

She wanted to get rid of me.

The crying didn't get rid of me. The puking didn't get rid of me.

But Hannah had other tricks up her little terry-cloth sleeve.

One morning before school I found Hannah in my room, chewing on something. She held a bit of paper in her hand. When she saw me coming, she tried to stuff it into her mouth. I snatched it away from her.

"Oh, no!" I cried. "My math homework!"

Or what was left of it. Mostly just my name and the date. Covered with drool.

Hannah had eaten my homework.

She swallowed and smiled that evil smile.

Ha-ha, her smile seemed to say. Gotcha.

"Mom!" I called. "Hannah ate my homework!"

Mom swooped in and picked up Hannah. "She *what*? Is she all right?"

"Mom! What about my homework?"

Mom frowned at me as if she just realized what I was telling her.

"Nicholas, you didn't do your homework, did you? And now you're trying to blame it on Hannah!"

"Mom, I'm telling the truth! Give Hannah an X ray. You'll see my homework in her stomach!"

Mom shook her head. "Nicholas, what's wrong with you lately?"

Later that day, when my teacher asked me where my math homework was, I told her my baby sister had eaten it.

She kept me after school.

That's what I got for telling the truth.

"Nicholas! Get in here! I want to talk to you!" Dad called.

I was playing in the backyard when his voice boomed at me from an upstairs window.

I found Dad in my parents' bedroom. At least I *thought* it was their room. It was where their room was supposed to be. Only it didn't look much like their room anymore.

Normally, my parents' room was white. I mean WHITE. White rugs, white walls, white curtains, white bedspread. I wasn't allowed to play in there, or eat, or do anything. They were always worried about all that white stuff.

The room wasn't white anymore. It was multicolored. Paint splashed everywhere.

"Nicholas," Dad said. "You are in big trouble. Huge trouble."

Little jars of paint from my paint set littered the floor. Red, blue, green, yellow, and black paints were splashed all over the white rug, the white curtains, the white bedspread, the white walls. And in the middle of it all, splattered with blood-red paint, Hannah sat laughing her evil laugh.

"You have one minute to give me an explanation for this, Nicholas," Dad said. "Go."

"I didn't do it," I said. "Hannah did it."

Dad laughed sarcastically. "Hannah did it? Hannah took your paint set, brought it all the way to our room, opened the jars, and splattered paint all over everything?"

"Yes," I said.

"Nicholas, go to your room."

"But, Dad — I didn't do anything wrong!"

"Oh, no? Go to your room and think about it until you can see what you did wrong."

"Dad — Hannah did it! She did it on purpose —

to get me in trouble! You're playing right into her hands!"

Dad gave me his stony glare. He pointed to my room.

I went. There's no fighting Dad's stony glare.

She's a monster, I thought. She's really a monster.

But she won't get away with this. I'll find a way to convince them, somehow. I'm not leaving this family. *She* is.

The next day, when I came home from school, I heard terrible screams from the kitchen.

I ran in. Hannah sat in her high chair, screaming with laughter. My mother stood beside her. Mom, Hannah, the floor, the walls — all covered with green slime.

Green slime oozed out of the corner of Hannah's mouth.

Hannah had spewed green slime everywhere.

"She's a monster!" I shouted. "This is proof!"

Mom ignored me. "Hannah, you naughty girl!" she said. "Strained peas all over the kitchen!"

Hannah banged her spoon on her high-chair tray. More green stuff splattered on the wall.

All right. It wasn't exactly green slime. But it was close enough. Strained peas. They're green, and they're slimy.

Mom said, "Nicholas, get a sponge and help me clean this up."

"Why do I have to clean it? *She* made the mess!"

“Nicholas, I’m tired. Just help me out, please.”

I stared at Hannah’s pea-covered face. Something was different. Her eyes. Her eyes — were brown!

“Mom!” I cried. “Hannah’s eyes changed colors! I told you she had evil powers!”

Mom just laughed. “Most babies are born with blue eyes,” she explained. “Sometimes their eyes change after a few — ”

“Mom, that’s impossible! People’s eyes don’t change color!”

“Yes, they do, Nicholas. Some babies — ”

I grabbed her by the arms and tried to shake some sense into her. “Mom — you’re losing it. Hannah’s brainwashing you! She’s trying to get rid of me! We’ve got to send her back — before it’s too late!”

“Nicholas, that’s enough! You’ve been jealous of Hannah from the beginning. It’s time for you to get over all of this and start acting a little more mature!”

I felt like tearing my hair out. Why wouldn’t my parents believe me? How could I get them to see what Hannah was doing?

Mom started cleaning the strained peas from Hannah’s face. The birthmark seemed to glow like a tiny spark.

The worst was still to come.

I was sitting in the den, watching TV. Minding my own business. Then I heard a creeping sound.

Creep, creep, creep. The sound of little knees scraping against the rug.

Oh, no, I thought. Here she comes.

I turned around to look. Hannah was crawling toward me — clutching a pair of scissors in her tiny fist!

She crawled closer, closer, that evil gleam in her eye, the birthmark pulsing on her face.

She was going to stab me!

"NO!" I yelled. I backed away. She kept crawling toward me, the scissors gleaming.

This is it, I thought. My baby sister is going to kill me.

"Nicholas!" My mom stood in the doorway. Then she ran to Hannah and snatched the scissors away from her.

"Thanks, Mom. You saved my life!" I cried.

"How could you *do* this?" Mom said. "How could you let Hannah carry around such a sharp object! She could have been seriously hurt!"

"*She* could have been hurt! Mom, she was going to kill me!"

"Nicholas, this is ridiculous."

"Mom, she's trying to get rid of me! She wants to be an only child!"

"I think that's what *you* want, Nicholas," Mom said. "I think we need to have a long, long talk."

"I'm not making this up, Mom! Why won't you believe me? You always trusted me before — until Hannah came along!"

The phone rang. Mom picked up Hannah and stormed off to the kitchen to answer it.

A few minutes later, I heard Mom cry out, "Oh, no! No! I don't believe it!"

I hurried to the kitchen to see what was wrong.

Mom was crying. She said, "All right, Dr. Davis. We'll be there this afternoon."

She hung up the phone and cried some more. She gripped the wall as if she thought she'd faint. Then she stopped crying and stared at Hannah with a new, weird look on her face. A look of horror.

At last, I thought. She believes me!

The doctor must have called to warn us that Hannah is a monster!

"That was the hospital," Mom said in a slow, hoarse voice. "They said . . . they said — "

"That Hannah's a monster!" I finished for her.

Mom turned sharply to me. "Nicholas, stop it!" She scooped Hannah up and hugged her tightly, crying.

"I can't believe it," she said. "I love her so much. But she's not really our baby."

"What?" I was afraid I hadn't heard her right. It seemed too good to be true. Had Mom just said Hannah was not really our baby?

"Our real baby and Hannah were switched at birth," Mom said through her tears. "Hannah is someone else's child."

Hannah wasn't my sister at all. Her real parents

were probably monsters, too. It explained everything.

"Yippee!" I shouted. I was free! Free from Hannah's evil! Everything would be okay now. We'd get my *real* baby sister, and she'd be cute and normal like other babies. She wouldn't try to get rid of me. She wouldn't be a monster.

Mom started crying harder than ever. She carried Hannah upstairs to her room and shut the door.

I felt a little bit sorry. Mom was really upset. I knew Dad would be, too.

But they'll be happier when we get our real baby, I thought. And so will I.

Dad came home from work early. We bundled Hannah up and took her to the hospital. A nurse introduced us to a woman who held a baby Hannah's age. Hannah's real mother. She had a tiny heart-shaped birthmark on her cheek, just like Hannah's.

Monster Mom, I thought, even though she didn't look like a monster at all.

The nurse gave my mother the new baby. It seemed weird to call the new baby Hannah, so Mom decided to name her Grace.

When we got home, the first thing I did was check Gracie for birthmarks. She was clean. No birthmarks anywhere.

She was a sweet baby, blond, blue-eyed, smiling, and rosy-cheeked. She looked like an angel. She smiled and cooed at me.

I watched Gracie carefully the first day. Just to be sure.

She didn't cry like an animal. She didn't spew peas or try to stab me. She did nothing but gurgle and coo.

By the end of the day, I thought, she's normal! She's not a monster. She's not out to get me. She's even cute!

Everything is going to be okay now.

Mom put Gracie to bed. I sneaked into her room to play with her for a few minutes.

I tickled her. She giggled. I tickled her again. This time she didn't giggle so much. So I tickled her one more time.

She opened her mouth and croaked, "If you tickle me again, kid, I'll rip your arm off!"

Her eyes bulged as she uttered a deep growl.

"Aaaauuugh!" I wailed. "A monster!"

I ran from the room, screaming my head off. And as I was leaving, I heard the baby cackle, "I'll get rid of you, creep. Just wait till I can walk!"

STRANGERS IN THE WOODS

"This ruins everything, Lucy," wailed Jessica when I called her to deliver the bad news. "I can't believe you're getting shipped off to . . . what's the name of that town, anyway?"

"Fairview," I said, with a long, very sad sigh. I twisted the phone cord around and around my finger. "I could just *cry*."

I'm not usually so depressed. Actually, Jessica says I'm annoyingly happy most of the time.

But finding out that I'd be spending six weeks this summer with Great-Aunt Abigail in her boring farm town was enough to put me in a bad mood forever. I mean, there's *nothing* in Fairview but tractors and cows and cornfields.

I hoped that something exciting had happened to Fairview since my last visit to Great-Aunt Abigail's two summers before. But when Dad pulled the car into town, the place looked even duller and drabber than I remembered. One grocery, a hardware store, a gas station, and a tiny library.

We bumped our way down Great-Aunt Abigail's long dirt road and pulled up in front of 25 Butterfly Lane, her small, redbrick house. I climbed out of the car and looked around. Fields and forests as far as I could see.

Great-Aunt Abigail came running out, dressed in her usual flowered housedress and sneakers. She looked a little different than I remembered, a little older, a little more wrinkled, a little skinnier.

We all greeted one another. Then Mom and Dad followed Great-Aunt Abigail into the house to have tea.

I started to let my dog Muttster out of the car so that he could explore the yard. But the big brown mutt pulled back, his tail between his legs.

"Muttster — what's your problem?" I asked. He acted like a big scaredy-cat, whimpering and huddling in the backseat.

When I finally coaxed him out with a doggie pretzel, he started barking really loud, and running around and around in circles.

The thing you have to know about Muttster is that he *never* barks. He's really well-behaved. That's why he was being allowed to stay in Fairview with me while Mom and Dad went off on their big trip to Asia.

I should have known that something was terribly wrong as soon as Muttster started barking.

But I didn't guess. I just figured the big dog was excited.

Then when Great-Aunt Abigail came outside to see what all the fuss was about, Muttster really went crazy — growling and snapping like a mean old junkyard hound.

"Oh, dear, Lucy," she said nervously. "Why is he doing that? Maybe you should put him in the yard."

I didn't want to tie him up. But Muttster was just going ballistic! So I tied him to a huge oak tree and ran back to the porch to say good-bye to my parents.

"Honey, I'll miss you," Mom said. "You won't be able to call us because we'll be moving around so much. But we'll call when we can and send lots of postcards."

After a lot of hugs and kisses, my parents were off on their trip. I waved sadly, until their car disappeared down the long driveway.

What a boring summer this is going to be, I thought glumly.

I had no idea how *wrong* I was.

Great-Aunt Abigail did her best to cheer me up. "I have a surprise for you, dear," she said. "Your favorite cookies."

Cookies? I'd almost forgotten that Great-Aunt Abigail made the best peanut-butter fudgies in the world.

I took a cookie off the tray she offered. Still warm and soft from the oven. I bit into it eagerly. It was chewy and fudgey and peanut buttery — but something was wrong. Something didn't taste right.

Was it too salty? Were the ingredients different?

How weird, I thought. Great-Aunt Abigail's cookies are always perfect.

I could see her watching me eagerly, so I finished the cookie and pretended to love it. Then I jammed a few cookies in my pocket and threw on my denim jacket. "I'm taking Muttster for a walk," I called out. "Just to relax him."

"Have fun, dear," she said. "But stay out of the woods, okay?"

That's weird, I thought. She never warned me away from the woods during my other visits.

Muttster and I had a nice walk in the sloping, green fields. At times, the dog seemed as calm and playful as always. But then he would start barking excitedly again — for no reason at all.

I couldn't get to sleep that night. Maybe it was because Muttster had to spend the night outside as punishment for his constant barking. At home, he *always* slept at the foot of my bed.

I tried reading a book, but that only made me feel more awake. So I gazed out the window and counted the stars.

And that's when I saw the frightening lights.

In the purple night sky. Six lights, forming a circle.

At first, I thought they were super-bright stars because they were up in the sky. But then I realized they were moving, lowering slowly to the ground.

As I stared with my mouth hanging open in amazement, the lights hovered over the woods on the other side of Great-Aunt Abigail's cornfield. I felt their light washing over me — brightening my whole room, bright as daylight.

Then, slowly, the circle of lights lowered into the woods. And it became dark again.

A cold shudder shook my body. What had I just seen?

I crept down the hall to Great-Aunt Abigail's room and called softly outside her closed door. But she has always been a sound sleeper. She didn't wake up.

Back in my room, I could hear Muttster down in the yard, barking furiously. I shut the window tight. How would I ever get to sleep?

"Do you know what those lights are out in the woods?" I asked Great-Aunt Abigail as I sat down to breakfast.

She narrowed her eyes at me. I thought I saw her cheeks go pink. "Lights? What lights, dear? How do you want your eggs?"

"Scrambled, please. There were about six lights, all in a circle. They were so weird."

"Don't worry, dear. I'm sure it's just reflections or something. Have you fed Muttster?"

Why is she so eager to change the subject? I wondered. Why does she seem so nervous?

Her scrambled eggs tasted different, too. Not as fluffy and fresh-tasting as in the past.

After I ate, I took Muttster his breakfast, a bowl of dry dog food. Then I sat on the lawn, talking to the dog, and staring at the woods — hoping to see something, *anything*, that might explain those lights.

Thinking about those lights made me feel strange. You know how your stomach feels after you've eaten five slices of pizza? That was it, only more nervous and fluttery.

My stomach felt even funnier after Great-Aunt Abigail and I took a drive to the hardware store. Did I say "drive"? It was more like a roller coaster ride!

To my shock, my usually careful great-aunt drove like a maniac! We almost clipped the mailbox on the way out of the driveway. Then she kept weaving from lane to lane and whizzing right through stop signs. I held on to the dashboard, too terrified to scream.

I got my voice back when we finally pulled over on Main Street. "Aunt Abigail!" I cried breathlessly. "Is there something wrong with the car? Why are you driving like this?"

"Like what?" she replied innocently.

The only thing more frightening than the drive to town was the drive back to the house! By the time we returned, we'd gone through two red lights, terrorized a farmer on his tractor, and missed a parked car by an inch!

Great-Aunt Abigail didn't seem to notice that anything was wrong.

My heart still in my mouth, I leaped out of the car and staggered over to Muttster. He wagged his bushy brown tail and licked my face, as if I'd been gone for ten years!

But he stopped in mid-lick when Great-Aunt Abigail climbed out of the car. "GRRRRRRRR," he growled ferociously, straining at his leash.

What is going *on* here? I asked myself.

Why does everything seem so different — so *wrong*?

I saw the eerie lights again that night. And the next night, too. Bigger and brighter than ever. Hovering in a circle over the woods.

As I pressed my face up against the window to watch them, I suddenly had a frightening thought. They looked just like the lights of the alien spaceship in my favorite movie, *Attack of the Pod People*.

I tried desperately to come up with another explanation for the lights. Streetlights? Not in Fairview. A plane? A plane couldn't hover like that. And I'd *never* seen a plane with lights that bright.

I felt a chill down my back as I realized there was no other explanation. Aliens had invaded Fairview. And they were landing in the woods near my great-aunt's house!

Wrapping my arms around myself to stop the chills, I found myself thinking about Great-Aunt Abigail. She seemed so different, so changed.

Had the aliens taken over Great-Aunt Abigail's mind? Just like in the *Pod People* movie?

I could hear Muttster start to bark down in the yard. Dogs have a sixth sense, I knew. Muttster sensed that Great-Aunt Abigail was possessed by an alien. That's why he had been barking and growling at her.

Suddenly gripped with fear, I turned away from the window.

Was I next? Would the aliens come after me next?

I had to get out of there. Run away. But where?

Mom and Dad were thousands of miles away. Should I call my best friend, Jessica, back home? She'd think I was joking. Besides, how could she help?

I needed someone closer. The police!

Trying not to make a sound, I crept down the

stairs to the phone in the kitchen. Great-Aunt Abigail — or *whoever* she was — had gotten there first.

She had her back to me. She couldn't see me. But I could hear her: "Don't worry, my niece doesn't know. Yes, yes, I told her to stay away from the woods. And she won't know anything until it's all over tomorrow night."

My palms started sweating, and I got that itchy feeling under my arms I always get when I'm really nervous.

"All over?"

Until *what* was all over? The alien invasion? Until Muttster and I had been taken off to some weird planet where they'd put us in cages?

I had to get back to my room — and fast. I turned back to the stairs. But the floorboards creaked loudly beneath me.

Great-Aunt Abigail whirled around to face me.

I gasped, and my mouth dropped open in horror.

My great-aunt's face was glowing green!

"Lucy — what are you doing up?" Great-Aunt Abigail demanded. She took a few steps toward me. I suddenly realized I was *terrified* of her.

"Uh . . . just going back to b-bed," I stammered, backing away.

I hurried up the stairs, my entire body trembling. I closed the bedroom door tightly and waited. Waited to hear Great-Aunt Abigail pad up the stairs and go into her room.

I knew I couldn't spend another minute in the house. I couldn't stay there with an alien from outer space.

Frantically, I pulled on jeans and a sweatshirt. I had to get to the police. I had to tell them about the aliens.

But would they believe me?

They will if I go to the woods and see the aliens first, I decided.

I know, I know. I wasn't thinking clearly. But I was having a major panic attack. And it seemed like the best idea at the time.

I sneaked silently down the stairs and out the back door. I should have woken up Muttster and brought him with me to the woods. But I was so out of my mind with fear, I didn't even think of him.

I ran across the backyard, heading to the woods. Nothing but darkness ahead. No lights hovering in the sky.

What was waiting for me in that darkness? Were there really aliens there? I needed to get a glimpse of them. Just a glimpse, so I could describe them to the town police.

The woods were dark, steamy, and wet. It was like plunging through a thick jungle. There was no path, so I had to push my way through, stumbling over fallen logs and marshy ground.

As I made my way, I kept hearing rustling noises on both sides of me.

Was I being followed? Was I being watched?

As I stopped to catch my breath, a light appeared up ahead. Swallowing hard, I moved toward it. The trees thinned out, and I found myself in a large clearing.

What were those sounds? Voices? Human voices?

Or alien voices?

I gasped as the bright lights washed over me. The white beam blinded me, captured me in a harsh spotlight.

I shielded my eyes as the light hovered over me, closing in, covering me, holding me helpless.

"Bring her here," I heard a deep voice order.

I felt hands tugging me.

I tried to pull away. But my captor was too strong.

"You can't take over my brain!" I shrieked. "I won't let you!"

"Cut the lights," another voice ordered.

The harsh lights dimmed to black. I could see smaller lights all around.

As my eyes adjusted to the darkness, I saw a man walk toward me. He wore a baseball cap and a long-sleeved Polo shirt over jeans.

"Young lady, I don't know what you're screaming about," he said. "But you can't just wander on to a film set. You just ruined a shot that took three hours to set up."

Film set? I opened my mouth to reply. But no sound came out.

"We asked the people in town to stay out of the woods," the man said sternly. "We're finishing our movie tomorrow. Then we'll be out of here."

"M-movie?" I took a deep breath, trying to get myself together. Suddenly, I heard dogs barking.

"The dogs are ready," a young woman carrying a clipboard announced. She raised a dog whistle to her lips. She blew into it. It made no sound that I could hear. But the dogs immediately barked louder.

That explains why Muttster has been barking all the time, I told myself. He keeps hearing the dog whistle from the woods.

Everything made sense now. Great-Aunt Abigail warning me to stay out of the woods. The bright lights. My great-aunt saying on the phone that it would all be over tomorrow night.

"I-I'm sorry," I told the man. "Really. I'm so sorry."

I felt like a total jerk.

I ran all the way home. Great-Aunt Abigail was waiting for me at the back door, her face tight with worry. "Lucy, where did you go? Where have you been? I was about to call the police."

I told her how sorry I was. And then the words just burst out of me. "I saw the lights. And Muttster was acting so strange. And your skin was green. And you drove so wildly. And the cookies were wrong. And — and — "

Great-Aunt Abigail wrapped me in a hug and held me till I stopped trembling. When I finally backed away, she was chuckling. "I guess my green mint julep facial mask would give *anyone* the creeps!" she declared.

I laughed, too.

"I should have told you about the movie folks," Great-Aunt Abigail said, shaking her head. "But I figured they'd be gone by tomorrow."

I started to say something. But she raised a hand to stop me. "I have more to explain," she said, frowning. "I have a confession to make, Lucy. I lost my glasses just before you arrived. And I've been trying to get along without them."

"That's why your driving was so wild?" I cried.

She nodded. "And that's why my cooking may have been a little off. It's so hard to see the ingredients."

We hugged each other again and shared a good laugh. "I can't believe you thought I was an alien from outer space!" Great-Aunt Abigail said. "You've seen too many movies!"

She was right. I felt like such a fool.

We had some hot chocolate. It didn't taste quite right, but I didn't complain. Then I made my way upstairs to go to sleep.

The night had grown cool, and I love sleeping

with the windows open. So I went to the linen closet to get an extra blanket.

As I pulled open the door, Great-Aunt Abigail's glasses tumbled out.

Terrific! I thought. Now she won't have to buy new ones.

I picked them up and carried them down the hall to her room. "Aunt Abigail?" I called.

The door was open a crack. I pushed it open and stepped inside. She stood with her back to me. "Aunt Abigail — look. I found your — "

My words choked in my throat as she turned to face me.

And I saw the four slimy tentacles waving at her sides. Her skin glowed bright green in the light from the dresser top. And her three fat, black lips made sucking sounds as she unrolled a long blue tongue.

"You found my glasses!" she croaked, reaching out all four tentacles toward me. "Thanks, Lucy."

GOOD FRIENDS

Jordan and his best friend, Dylan, hopped off the school bus and walked up Oak Street. "Want to ride bikes?" Jordan suggested.

"Yeah, okay," Dylan replied. "But I have to do my homework first."

Jordan rolled his eyes. Dylan was the only sixth-grader he knew who always did his homework the second he got home from school.

Jordan dropped his backpack on the front lawn and crossed the street. "Can't you do it later?" he asked.

Dylan kicked a pebble across the sidewalk. "No way. My mom will have a cow," he muttered.

Jordan sighed and pushed his bangs out of his eyes. "Then just tell her you did your homework in school, Dylan. She won't be home for hours. She won't know if you did it or not."

Dylan bit his bottom lip. "I don't know, Jordan," he said, lowering his voice. "What about — ?" He pointed toward his house.

"Who? Richard?" Jordan asked, making a face. "Will you forget about him already? Your older brother is a total jerk!"

Dylan shot a nervous glance toward the house. "Sshh! He'll hear you!"

Jordan folded his arms across his chest. "So what?" he demanded loudly. "Everyone knows Richard is a total jerk!"

Dylan gasped. "Come on, Jordan," he pleaded. "Be quiet! He'll *pound* me!"

Jordan shook his head. He couldn't believe Dylan was so scared of his brother. Richard was fourteen, and big and strong. But so what?

"Just forget about him, will you?" Jordan said. "Come on. Let's ride."

They rode their bikes around the neighborhood for a while. Then they stopped in Dylan's driveway to shoot some hoops. Dylan kept staring up nervously at his brother's bedroom window.

"I hope he leaves us alone today," he said to Jordan. "Ever since my mom put him in charge after school, Richard has been worse than ever. He acts like he's the king of the house."

"Oh, he's King all right," Jordan snickered. "King of the Jerks!"

Dylan laughed nervously and glanced back up to the window.

"Would you forget about him already?" Jordan said. "Come on, let's play. Show me your best slam dunk!"

Dylan dribbled the ball on the driveway. He was just about to shoot — when The Pest came skipping across the street.

The Pest was Ashley, Jordan's seven-year-old sister. Ashley plopped down on the sidewalk in front of Dylan's house and began playing with her Barbie dolls and talking to herself.

"Jaclyn, your hair is long and pretty like Barbie's!" Ashley said.

Jordan and Dylan exchanged glances, then cracked up. "Your sister is talking to her imaginary friend again," Dylan said, rolling his eyes.

"You're *sad*!" Jordan called out to his sister. "You're really *sad*!"

Ashley shot Jordan an angry look. "Shut up, dummy!" she screamed at him. "Jaclyn and I think that *you're* sad!"

"Where *is* Jaclyn?" Jordan demanded. "How come Dylan and I can't *see* Jaclyn? How come it looks like you're talking to yourself again?"

Ashley ignored her brother. "Don't pay any attention to them, Jaclyn," she said. "They're just acting dumb."

Dylan shook his head. "Come on, Jordo," he said softly. "Let's just play."

Jordan made a face at his sister, then grabbed the ball and took a jump shot. The ball hit the rim and bounced off.

"Hahaha!" Ashley burst out laughing. "Did you

see that, Jaclyn?" she cried. "Jordan missed an easy one."

"Ashley — get lost!" Jordan cried angrily. "And take your imaginary friend with you!"

Ashley dropped her dolls and ran up to him. "I told you, Jaclyn isn't imaginary!" she screamed. "She's real!"

"Oh, yeah?" Jordan shot back. "Then if Jaclyn is real, where is she standing?"

"Right here," Ashley replied, pointing to her left.

Jordan lobbed the ball at high speed in that direction. "Think fast, Jaclyn!" he shouted.

Ashley gasped. "No! Stop it! You'll hurt her!"

Jordan laughed and moved closer to his sister. "How come Jaclyn didn't catch the ball?" he teased.

"Because . . . because . . . you threw it too fast!" Ashley stammered.

"Where is she now?" Jordan demanded. "Let me try it again. This time, I'll aim for her head!" He and Dylan both laughed.

"You leave us alone! I'm telling!" Ashley whined. "Come on, Jaclyn. Let's go." She turned to leave.

"Come on, Jaclyn!" Jordan mocked in a whiny voice, trying to imitate his sister.

"Shut up, Jordan!" Ashley cried.

"Shut up, Jordan!" Jordan repeated.

"Cut it out!"

"Cut it out!" Jordan grabbed the air and pretended to hold somebody. "Hey, look, Ashley — I've got Jaclyn! She's my prisoner!"

Ashley balled her hands into fists. "Let her go! Let her go!"

"Hey, Dylan, bring me that rope from the garage. Let's tie Jaclyn to that tree!" Jordan cried, grinning.

Ashley screamed. "No! Stop! Jordan, let her go!"

Jordan kept laughing. "Wait! Maybe Jaclyn would like to help us practice our jump shots! We can hang a net on her head and use her face as a backboard!"

"I'm telling! I really am!" Ashley declared. She picked up her dolls and angrily ran down the driveway and across the street.

"Do you see what I have to put up with?" Jordan said, shaking his head.

Dylan started to answer. But an angry voice interrupted, shouting from the window above them. "Hey — loser!"

Jordan and Dylan raised their eyes to the upstairs window.

Dylan's brother, Richard, stuck his head out. "Dylan, did you do your homework yet?" he called down. "You'd better have it finished — or I'm telling Mom!"

Dylan nervously rolled the ball between his hands. "Just ignore him," Jordan whispered.

Dylan lifted the ball and tossed it up to the net. The ball missed the backboard completely.

Richard burst out laughing. "You really *are* a loser, Dylan! I could make that shot blindfolded. Who taught you how to play? Did your best friend, Jordan, teach you how to shoot like that?"

Jordan's face grew red. He opened his mouth to say something nasty. But Dylan's eyes pleaded with him not to.

"Please, Jordan," Dylan begged in a whisper. "Just ignore him! Please!"

"What did you say?" Richard shouted down from the window. "Are you talking to me, loser?"

Dylan cleared his throat. "No. Just leave me alone. I did my homework already. So just leave me alone."

Richard shook his head. "Try shooting with *both* hands!" he called down. Then he slammed the window shut with a loud thud.

Dylan hugged the ball tightly to his chest. His face was white. "He thinks he's so great," he muttered, his voice trembling.

"What a jerk!" Jordan exclaimed. "Why do you let him boss you around like that?"

Dylan shrugged. "Because he can beat me up," he admitted.

"Well, if he were my brother, I'd tie him to his

bed at night and tape his mouth shut!" Jordan said seriously.

Dylan laughed. "You always have the *best* ideas, Jordan!"

"What are good friends for?" Jordan replied.

Later, Dylan sat at his desk, slumped over his math book.

"I've got it!" Jordan cried suddenly, startling him.

"You've got what?" Dylan asked.

"The perfect trick to play on Ashley!" Jordan announced with a mischievous grin.

Dylan smiled and lowered his pencil. "What is it?" he asked eagerly. "Your tricks are always the coolest!"

"Thanks!" Jordan replied proudly. "Okay, here it is. You know how scared Ashley is of Axel and Foley, right?"

Dylan nodded. "Yeah. I don't like Richard's pet tarantulas much, either."

"Well," Jordan continued, grinning, "what if Axel and Foley somehow got loose?"

Dylan's eyes widened. "I don't know — "

"Oh, come on!" Jordan insisted. "Ashley would freak! I'll run up to her and scream, 'The spiders are loose! The spiders are loose! Run for your life!' Then, when Ashley runs out screaming, I'll tell her that I saw Axel swallow Jaclyn up whole!"

"Well . . ." Dylan hesitated. His friend's plans always scared him a little.

"Dylan, come on! It's perfect! Look at her!" Jordan pointed out the bedroom window. "My dopey sister is playing catch with her invisible friend right there in the front yard for everyone to see!"

Dylan peered out the window. "She does look pretty stupid," he admitted.

"Okay, so let's sneak into Richard's room, and — "

"Jordan, I don't know if this is such a good idea," Dylan said. "Richard will pound me for sure if we touch his spiders."

"Oh, stop worrying so much!" Jordan replied impatiently. "He'll never know! He's down in the den right now watching television. We'll be real quiet. No problem!"

Dylan peered out the window again and watched Ashley playing catch with her imaginary friend. "Okay. Let's do it," he agreed.

Jordan led the way to Richard's room. They crept inside and made their way to the tarantula tank.

"Go ahead," Jordan urged, whispering. "Pick them up. Hurry."

Dylan picked up the two tarantulas, one in each hand. They felt warm and hairy. They kind of tickled.

Tiptoeing silently, they made their way downstairs, sneaking past Richard in the den. Jordan pushed open the front door. They crept down the front steps and onto the driveway.

"This is going to be awesome!" Jordan whispered as they crept up behind Ashley.

Dylan held the tarantulas high above his head.

Ashley didn't hear them coming. She was laughing, calling out to her invisible friend, "Nice throw, Jaclyn!"

They tiptoed closer, until they were right behind her. One more step, and . . .

"DYLAN!" a voice roared from the porch.

Jordan and Dylan whirled around.

"It's Richard!" Dylan gasped in horror. Jordan saw his friend's face go white.

Richard moved toward them quickly, glaring furiously at Dylan.

"What are you doing out here with my tarantulas?" Richard demanded.

"I . . . uh . . . well . . ." Dylan stammered.

"I *know* what you're doing!" Richard accused angrily. "You're playing with Jordan and Ashley again, aren't you?"

Dylan stumbled backward as Richard moved closer. "Well . . ."

"Do you know what an *embarrassment* you are?" Richard cried. "You're just such a weird kid! Always playing by yourself and talking to yourself!"

"But — but . . . " Dylan sputtered.

Richard took the tarantulas from Dylan's hands. "Dylan, you're too old for imaginary friends," Richard said. "Forget about Jordan and Ashley. Okay? They don't exist. They're just in your mind. Imaginary friends are for babies!"

HOW I WON MY BAT

I guess you're admiring my swing, right? And you're admiring the baseball bat I'm holding.

Maybe you're wondering how I got this bat.

There's a story behind it. That's for sure.

I was the power hitter on my junior high's baseball team. Our team went to the state finals every year, and I was the star.

You could read about me in the local paper all the time: "Michael Burns: He's Got the Power." "Michael Burns Wins It for Lynnfield . . . Again!"

That's me, Michael Burns. But now I wish I'd never even touched a baseball bat. Things are diferent now. I'm different.

How much time has gone by since the afternoon that changed my life? I'm not sure. But I can remember everything that happened as if it were yesterday. . . .

Baseball practice. We had just finished doing our warm-up exercises on the field. Coach Manning called out, "Hey, Mike! You're up at bat."

At the games, I always batted cleanup. Fourth in the lineup. That made sense. I was the best.

But this was only practice. And the coach liked to shuffle us around, to keep us on our toes.

I felt all my muscles go tight as I stepped up to the plate. You see, I had a problem. A big problem. I was in a real batting slump.

The last game we played, I struck out four times!

And the past few batting practices? Jimmy, the pitcher, would lob me the ball and I'd choke — swinging with everything I had as if they were fastballs.

Some power hitter, huh? I couldn't even connect. And everyone knew it. I was afraid my new nickname was going to be "Swing-and-Miss Mike!"

"Come on, Mike," Coach Manning called as I took a few practice swings. "Concentrate now. You know tomorrow's game with Lakeland is for first place."

"Yeah, Mike, don't mess up," Jimmy muttered from the pitcher's mound.

I hunched over the plate. The bat just didn't feel right. It felt heavy. Too heavy. "Relax," I told myself. "Just relax, and everything will be fine."

The pitch came. High. I let it go. "Strike!" Ron called from behind me.

I turned to him. "Since when does the catcher make calls?"

"Since when does the power hitter strike out every time?" he shot back.

Well, that did it. No way could I relax after that crack.

I tried to get my old swing back. But the bat felt even heavier. And I could see my teammates shaking their heads.

After about ten minutes of batting practice — where the best I could do was a little dribble right to the pitcher — the coach called in somebody else.

"Listen, Mike," he said, putting his heavy arm around my shoulder. "Why don't you go home and get some rest for tomorrow's game."

I thought he was being nice. But then he added in a sharp voice, "You'd better shape up, kid. This game is for all the marbles."

I trudged off the field feeling lower than a grounder to third.

"Hey, Mike. Hold up a second." I recognized the guy jogging toward me. It was Tom Scott, a local TV reporter.

School sports are a big deal in Lynnfield. But a TV reporter covering a practice? Wow!

"You feeling okay, Mike?" he asked me. "Are you doing anything to shake this slump?"

"I'm trying," I mumbled, feeling my face turn

red. "Really." I hurried into the locker room, feeling really embarrassed.

I showered and dressed in a hurry. I wanted to get out of there before the team finished practice. I knew I couldn't stand all the teasing I'd get.

A few minutes later, I stepped back outside and started toward the bike rack. I had my eyes on the ground, and I was deep in my unhappy thoughts. "I'd give *anything* to get out of this slump," I muttered to myself.

I didn't even see the strange-looking little man until I nearly tripped over him. "Oops. Sorry," I muttered.

He smiled at me. "I heard what you said. You just need a lighter bat," he said.

"Huh?" I squinted at him, startled.

The man wore a heavy, black wool suit. He had a tiny, round head, completely bald. His skin was so pale, he looked like a lightbulb!

Had this guy ever been outdoors?

"What did you say?" I asked him.

"You need a lighter bat," he repeated. His eyes were silvery. They crinkled as his grin grew wider.

I saw for the first time that he held a baseball bat in one hand. He raised it so that I could see it better.

It was shiny black wood. It had tape wrapped around the end. It looked as if it had been used before.

"It's very light — and very powerful," the man said. He let out a strange cackle, as if he had just told a joke.

"Wh-who are you?" I stammered, staring at the bat.

"I'm a sports fan," he said. With his free hand, he reached into his suit jacket pocket. He pulled out a business card and handed it to me.

It read: MR. SMITH, DIRECTOR. LYNNFIELD SPORTS MUSEUM.

I handed the card back to him. I stared at the bat. "You want to sell me this bat?"

He let out another cackle. He shook his shiny bald head. "I'll give it to you, Mike." His strange, silver eyes glowed excitedly.

Had I told him my name?

"It's a very good bat. You'll like it," he said. "Very powerful."

The bat didn't look very special to me. "You want to *give* it to me?"

He nodded. "Take it. Now. You just have to make one promise."

I knew there had to be a catch! "What promise?" I asked. Clouds rolled over the sun. The air turned cold. I felt a chill at the back of my neck.

"You have to promise you will return the bat to the museum — right after the game. You will not change clothes. You will not go home first. You will return it to me at the museum. Understood?"

He pushed the bat into my hands.

He's crazy! I thought. Why am I taking this bat? Am I *that* desperate to get over my batting slump?

Yes!

My hands wrapped around the bat. It didn't feel any different from the bat I had used that afternoon.

Then a chill passed through my body. Mr. Smith's ice-cold hand gripped my shoulder. "Remember," he said, "return the bat right after the game."

I nodded and slung the bat over my shoulder. Then I made my way to my bike and pedaled away as quickly as I could.

The next day was sunny and cool. A perfect day for baseball.

The locker room was noisy before the game. All the guys were talking and laughing. But I was sitting quietly, trying to psych myself up.

"Hey, Mike," Jimmy called, tossing me a water bottle. "We're behind you all the way. We're counting on you, man."

"Yeah." Ron gave me the thumbs-up. "We know you won't let us down."

I felt so nervous, the water bottle nearly slipped out of my hand. I took a long swig of water. "I can't strike out," I told myself. "I won't strike out."

And then it was time. We were up at bat.

In the dugout, Coach Manning called everyone to gather around for the new batting order. "I've made some changes," he began, staring right at me.

I knew what the coach meant, and so did everyone else. He was moving me from the cleanup spot. "Ron will bat fourth," he said, "and Mike will bat second."

Second? I could deal with that. I'd be able to show everybody that much sooner that I was still a winner.

Rick, the first guy at bat, hit a single.

My turn at the plate.

"I can't watch this," I heard Jimmy groan to Ron.

I picked up my new bat. All of a sudden it felt really light, just as the strange little man had said.

I carried it to home plate and took my stance.

This is weird! I thought. The bat started to tingle. Suddenly, I felt tiny vibrations all the way to my toes.

The pitch came — low and outside. "Strike!" called the umpire.

I let the second pitch go, too. Strike again.

I had to swing at the next one, no matter what. The bat tingled and vibrated in my hands.

The pitch was a fastball. I sucked in my breath and swung, trying to stay in control.

Crack!

The ball sailed high into the air. I shaded my eyes as I ran to first. But the ball flew so high, I couldn't see it. Was it going over the fence for a home run?

It was!

"It worked!" I shouted gleefully. "The bat worked!"

I jogged to second, my arms held high above my head in a victory sign. The third-base coach was grinning, waving me along.

My teammates charged over as I rounded third, cheering and thumping me on the back. Then I came home.

Lynnfield: 2. Two runs batted in for me.

The next inning, I hit an even higher home run.

Two innings later, I came to bat twice — and hit *two more* home runs!

That's the way it went every time I went to bat. I pounded out homer after homer. By the time I hit my seventh, the crowd was going *ballistic*!

Seven home runs broke the school record. And when I hit my ninth? That broke the state record!

The final score: Lynnfield: 19, Lakeland: 3. Not shabby. Not shabby at all.

Afterward, a crowd of people swarmed around me. Jimmy and Ron hoisted me on their shoulders, and Tom Scott, the TV guy, asked me questions while camera crews and photographers took pictures.

"Hey, Mike!" Ron waved me over after everything settled down. "We're all going to Pat's Pizza Place. You know, to celebrate. So come on, man — you're the star!"

I hopped on my bike. "Lead the way!" I cried, so excited about the game, I thought I might burst.

We rode off, still in our uniforms. The whole team was chanting, "Mike! Mike! Mike!"

It was a great feeling. But, suddenly, my heart sank. The bat! I had promised to return it right after the game. I had promised to deliver it back to Mr. Smith at the sports museum.

I slowed down, letting the other guys pass me by. They were still chanting my name as they disappeared around the corner. "Catch up with you later!" I called. I don't know if they heard me or not.

But I knew one thing for sure. I couldn't return the bat.

No way.

I had to keep it.

It was the greatest bat in the world. The bat had hit nine home runs in one game. I couldn't part with it. Promise or no promise — I had to keep it.

Standing over my bike, I gripped the bat in my hands, trying to decide what to do. My first thought was to ride home and hide the bat in my room. Mr. Smith didn't know where I lived. Chances are, he would never find me.

No. I decided that wasn't right.

I decided to go to the museum. To tell Mr. Smith the truth. That I *had* to have that bat. I'll offer to pay him for it, I decided. Any amount he wants. It's worth it.

I remembered the address from the business card. It took a long time to ride my bike there. The museum was in a strange part of town. Nobody on the streets. No cars. Nothing.

The museum was a low, gray building. Not too inviting. I parked my bike beside the entrance. Carrying the bat, I stepped inside.

What a cool place! I couldn't believe I'd never been there before. The enormous, bright room was filled with life-size sports displays.

Two players elbowed each other fiercely in a hockey display. The figures were made of wax or something. I couldn't *believe* their scary expressions.

I walked past a tennis display. A young man in tennis whites had his racket up, about to serve to another player. They looked so real, I expected to see the ball fly over the net!

I passed two high school basketball players going up for a rebound. Their muscles were straining. I could actually see beads of sweat running down their faces.

Cool, I thought, leaning on the bat as I studied the display. So cool!

The baseball display was under construction. Part of a diamond had been built, but there were no wax figures playing ball.

As I stared at the real-looking scene, Mr. Smith appeared from behind it. "Hello, Mike," he said, smiling. His bald head shone under the bright display lights. "Thanks for returning the bat."

I hesitated. "I . . . uh . . . can't return it," I stammered.

His silver eyes narrowed in surprise. "What?"

"I have to keep it," I told him. "It's the greatest bat in the world. I'll do anything to keep it, Mr. Smith," I pleaded.

He rubbed his pale chin. "Well . . ."

"Really," I insisted. "I really need this bat. I want to keep it forever!"

"Okay," he agreed. "You can keep it forever."

My mouth fell open. I was stunned. "You mean it? I can keep it?"

He nodded, smiling. "If that's what you want," he murmured. "Let me see your swing, Mike. Take a good swing, okay?"

I was so happy and grateful. I lifted the bat, started to show off my swing — and froze in a blinding flash of silver light.

And I've been standing here ever since. Frozen in place. The bat gripped tightly in my hands. About to take my best swing.

A lot of time has passed. I don't really know how much. I stare out at the cardboard backdrop, and I prepare to take my swing.

People visit the sports museum. They come over to the baseball display. And they stare at me.

They talk about how real I look. And what a great swing I have.

It makes me happy that they like my swing.

And, I guess I have one other thing to be happy about.

I get to keep the bat. Forever.

MR. TEDDY

"Mom, can I *please* get this teddy bear! Please? I'll never ask for another thing."

Willa clasped her hands together and gazed longingly at the stuffed teddy bear staring at her from the department store shelf.

Willa was a collector. She collected stuffed animals, dolls, posters, porcelain eggs — you name it. Every inch of her room was crammed with her collections.

"Mom, look at him!" Willa gushed. "Have you ever seen such cute little brown paws? And look at his big, round eyes. They're practically glowing."

Leaning on the counter, Gina, Willa's eleven-year-old sister, started to whine. "Mom! No fair! Willa already has enough stuffed animals to fill this whole store."

"So?" Willa shot back. "I can't help it if *your* room is bare, Gina."

Gina made a face at her older sister. "That's

because every chance you get, you beg Mom to buy you something else. 'Mom, get me this. Mom, buy me that,' " Gina mimicked.

"Girls! That's enough!" Mrs. Stewart cut them off. Willa and Gina glared at each other. "Willa, you're twelve. Aren't you getting too old for teddy bears?" her mother asked.

"I can't help it, Mom," Willa replied. "I want him. He's . . . not like any other stuffed animal I've ever seen."

"His eyes are weird," Gina commented.

"They are not!" Willa protested. But she knew Gina was right. She could almost feel the bear studying her with those huge eyes of his.

"Willa," her mother said. "There isn't any space left in your room. Where will you put it?"

"I'll put Old Bear on the shelf and sleep with this one," Willa replied.

Gina folded her arms. "What's wrong with Old Bear?"

"Nothing," Willa told her. "I just love this one." She pressed him against her cheek. "See how cuddly he is? Please, Mom?"

Mrs. Stewart hesitated. "Well . . ."

"Mom, that's not fair!" Gina wailed. "Willa's always getting stuff. What about my CD player?"

"Gina, a CD player costs a lot more than a teddy bear," her mother answered sharply. "That's something you can ask for on your birthday."

"Mom, please?" Willa said, still clutching the bear.

"Oh, all right," her mother said, sighing. "But this is *it*, understand, Willa?"

Willa threw her arms around her mother. "Oh, thank you, thank you, thank you, Mom."

On the other side of the counter, Willa could see Gina scowling at her.

"Sometimes I really hate you, Willa," Gina muttered.

Willa waved the teddy in Gina's face. "His name is Mr. Teddy, Gina," she announced. "And you'd better be nice to him."

As soon as Willa got home, she took Mr. Teddy up to her room to show him around. "Here we are," she announced, opening the door. Her room was done all in peach, her favorite color.

To the right of the door stood her dresser. On top of the dresser was her porcelain egg collection. Willa gently picked up each egg and told Mr. Teddy where it had come from. Next, she showed him all the rock star posters that covered her walls. Then she went through the two long shelves above the dresser crammed with stuffed animals.

When she finished with the animals, Willa took Mr. Teddy over to the doll collection in the other corner. Willa had been collecting dolls the longest, and had the biggest collection of anyone she knew.

Still clutching Mr. Teddy, Willa crossed the room to her bed. "Hello, Old Bear," she said. She reached onto the pillow and picked up her ragged old teddy bear — the one she'd slept with since she was a baby — and kissed him on top of his head. "You're going to sleep over here now," she said, crossing back over to the shelves. She pushed aside a stuffed unicorn to make room for Old Bear. "Sleep tight," she told him.

Gina poked her head into the room. "Who's in here?" she asked.

"No one," Willa replied.

"Then who were you talking to?"

"Nobody."

Gina's eyes lit up. "You were talking to your stuffed animals again, weren't you?" She started laughing at Willa.

"Shut up, Gina!" Willa snapped. "You're mad because you didn't get a CD player."

"I am not," Gina answered. "I'm mad because you have Mom wrapped around your little finger. Every time you ask for something, she buys it." She stormed out, slamming the door behind her.

Willa glanced down at Mr. Teddy. "Don't worry about Gina," she whispered, carefully placing him on her pillow. "I bet she wishes she had a special bear, too. But she doesn't. You're all mine, Mr. Teddy. All mine."

* * *

That night, Willa slept with Mr. Teddy hooked in her arm. At first it felt funny to sleep with something so soft and fluffy. All the fur on Old Bear had worn off a long time ago.

But Mr. Teddy seemed to be staring at her. Every time she turned or moved, she felt his big eyes watching her.

Willa woke up early the next morning. The sun had barely begun to rise. Outside, she could hear birds chirping.

Something didn't feel right. She lifted her head and stared down at her bed.

Where was Mr. Teddy?

She groped around her covers, but couldn't feel him anywhere. Where was he?

Willa pulled herself up, squinting in the dim light. Had Mr. Teddy fallen out of bed?

She peered down at the floor. Not there.

She shook her covers again, then leaned over to check underneath the bed. "Are you there, Mr. Teddy?" she called softly.

A sock and some dust balls stared back at her. Where could Mr. Teddy be?

Willa's eyes moved up her dresser, then over to the windowsill above the doll corner.

She caught her breath. Mr. Teddy sat propped up on the windowsill, staring back at her. His eyes seemed to be shining.

"Huh?" Willa murmured. "How did you get over there?"

She climbed out of bed and lifted him off the windowsill. "Mr. Teddy," she scolded. "What are you doing? Did you get up and move during the night?"

The bear's dark eyes glowed back at her.

"Stop staring at me like that!" Willa laughed. "You're giving me the creeps." She kissed the top of his head, then popped him back on her pillow.

"Maybe I woke up and put him there myself and don't remember," Willa said to herself.

At breakfast, she caught Gina staring at her. "What are *you* looking at?" she asked sharply.

"Nothing," Gina smirked.

"Did you come into my room last night?" Willa demanded.

"No," Gina replied, still smiling. "Why would I?"

The next night, before she fell asleep, Willa made sure Mr. Teddy was hooked firmly in the crook of her arm. It took her a long time to fall into a restless sleep.

She kept waking up and checking on Mr. Teddy. But he was always right where she left him, in the bend of her arm, watching everything with those big, dark eyes of his. In a funny way, Willa felt as if he were guarding her.

She woke up the next morning with a start. Immediately, she felt around for Mr. Teddy.

Gone again!

Willa glanced suspiciously at the windowsill. Not there, either.

She sat up in bed and began to search the room. Her eyes swept over the doll corner, the floor, then moved up the dresser.

"Hey, you!" Willa cried out when she spotted Mr. Teddy on top of the dresser.

"What's going on, bear? What are you doing over there?" She jumped out of bed and hurried over.

She gasped when she saw the two porcelain eggs. They lay smashed under the big teddy bear.

Mr. Teddy's eyes had an evil glow.

"Who did this?" Willa demanded. "Who broke these eggs?"

Willa tried to think. It couldn't be Mr. Teddy. He didn't climb the dresser and plop down on the eggs. No way.

So who *could* it be? The one person who was jealous of all her stuff.

"Gina!" Willa shouted furiously. "How could you *do* this?"

Willa stormed into Gina's room. Empty. Where was she?

Willa stomped back into the hall and stood at

the top of the stairs. "Gina! I'm going to get you for this!"

Her mother appeared at the bottom of the stairs. "Why are you shouting, Willa?"

"Where's Gina?"

"She left early for school," her mother said. "Remember? She has chorus practice."

Willa clenched her fists. "Wait till she gets home tonight," she growled. "She'll be singing a sad song when I get through with her!"

That afternoon Willa paced the front hall, waiting for Gina to return home. She paced back and forth, back and forth, checking out the window every time she passed it.

Finally she saw Gina coming up the front walk. She angrily pulled open the front door to greet her.

"I know it was you who smashed my porcelain eggs last night!" Willa uttered in a shaky voice. She blocked Gina's path.

Gina pushed her aside. "What are you talking about, Willa? Are you totally losing it?"

"You know what I mean," Willa insisted. She followed her sister to the stairs. "You broke my best eggs for no reason. Then you moved Mr. Teddy onto the dresser to make it look like *he* did it. What a sick, stupid joke."

Gina stopped. "I really don't know what you're talking about."

"Do too," Willa snapped.

It *had* to be Gina. Who else could it be?

"You're just trying to get me in trouble with Mom," said Gina. "Leave me alone, Willa. I'm warning you."

Later, when Willa went to bed, she shoved Mr. Teddy all the way under the covers. "I want you to stay down there tonight, okay?" she told him. She curled her body around his, then pulled her covers up to her neck.

Nobody could get Mr. Teddy out now, Willa thought. At least not without waking her up.

But Willa was wrong.

The moment she woke up the next morning, Willa reached under the covers for Mr. Teddy.

Gone again.

"Huh?" Willa sat up, wide awake. "What's going on?"

She let out a shriek when she saw her dresser. The drawers had all been pulled out and turned upside down. Her clothing had all been strewn in clumps and piles over the floor.

Angrily hurling herself out of bed, Willa kicked aside a pile of T-shirts. "Gina!" she shrieked. "I'm going to *murder* you for this!"

Glancing up, she saw Mr. Teddy. He grinned at her from the dresser top.

Willa grabbed him. "Why is this happening to me?" she screamed. "Tell me this is a dream!"

Mr. Teddy's eyes glowed brighter. Willa heaved him onto the bed.

She flew down the stairs and burst into the kitchen. Gina was eating a bowl of cereal. "Why did you do it, Gina?" Willa demanded, clenching her hands into tight fists. "Why? Why? Why did you sneak into my room, and mess it all up, and — "

Gina gazed up from her breakfast. "I haven't been near your room. Honest." A grin broke out on her face.

Willa let out a furious cry. "See, Mom? See? She's smiling."

Mrs. Stewart narrowed her eyes at Gina. "Have you been playing mean jokes on your sister?" she demanded.

"No! No way!" Gina screamed. "Why are you blaming me for something I didn't do? I just smiled because it's funny. But I didn't do anything! Really!"

Willa stared hard at Gina. "I know you're lying," she said softly. "You're a liar, Gina. A total liar."

"I am not!" Gina shouted. She scraped her chair back from the table and jumped up. "You're the liar!" she told Willa. "You're just trying to get me in trouble for no reason!" She turned and stormed out of the kitchen.

"Stay out of my room, Gina!" Willa called after her. "You'll be sorry! I mean it! I really do!"

* * *

That night before climbing into bed, Willa shoved her dresser up against her door. "There," she said, pressing Mr. Teddy's soft body against her arm. "That should keep Gina out of here. What do you think, Mr. Teddy?"

Mr. Teddy's round, black eyes glowed back at her.

She slept restlessly again that night. Feeling hot, she kicked off her covers. She turned onto one side, then the other. She had strange nightmares.

When she woke up the next morning, before she opened her eyes, she reached out for Mr. Teddy.

Gone.

Willa's eyes shot open.

She screamed.

The dresser had been pushed to the middle of the room.

She sat up, her heart pounding. "My — my room!" she murmured.

Swallowing hard, she stood up. And gazed around her room.

Her posters — they had all been ripped from the walls and crumpled onto the floor.

Willa's eyes moved to the shelves. To her stuffed animals. A cold, sick feeling spread through her stomach.

Nearly all of the animals had been pulled apart.

Shredded. Bits of them lay strewn across the room. A tail here. A piece of stuffing there.

Their eyes had been torn out of their heads. Their arms and legs ripped from their bodies.

Willa staggered to her doll corner. Every doll had been broken and torn apart. They lay in a heap of arms, scraps of clothing, broken heads, patches of hair.

"Hey!" Willa raised her eyes to the top of the shelf. Mr. Teddy stood there triumphantly, his eyes glowing happily. In one raised paw, he held an arm from one of her dolls.

"No!" Willa murmured. "No. Please — no!"

Mr. Teddy suddenly toppled forward. His outstretched arms reached for Willa's throat.

Willa let out a shriek and dived out of his way.

The bear landed on the floor with a soft thud.

Willa spun around. Tripping over parts of dolls and stuffed animals, she plunged out of her room. Down the stairs. Into the kitchen.

"Willa! What is it? What's wrong?" demanded her mother.

"Mom! Come up to my room!" she sobbed. "Everything I own! All my dolls, my animals. Gina wrecked it all!" she cried furiously.

"Huh?" Mrs. Stewart's face twisted in surprise. "Gina?"

"Yes! Gina!" Willa declared. "She broke into my room last night, Mom. She wrecked everything! Everything!"

"But that's impossible!" Willa's mother cried. "Gina wasn't home last night, Willa. Don't you remember? She had a sleep-over at Maggie's house."

Willa pressed her hands against her face. The room began to spin wildly.

That's right, she remembered. Gina wasn't home last night.

"Nooooo!" She backed out of the kitchen, hands against her cheeks, shaking her head.

She didn't want to believe it. It couldn't be. But there was no other explanation.

She ran blindly up the stairs. She grabbed Mr. Teddy off the floor. His eyes glowed up at her as Willa frantically ripped him to pieces.

"It *was* you, after all, wasn't it?" she cried, tearing off his arms, pulling out his white stuffing, letting it fly over the room. "It was you! You! You!"

With a cry of fury, Willa tore off Mr. Teddy's head. "I hate you!" she shrieked. She tossed the head out the open window. "Evil thing! Now you're gone! You can do no more evil!"

Gasping for breath, her heart thudding, Willa stumbled across the room and pulled raggedy Old Bear off the shelf. She hugged him tightly. "You're all I've got left, Old Bear. Everything else was destroyed by that evil thing."

She clutched Old Bear gratefully. "From now on, it's just you and me."

Willa didn't see the pleased smile form on Old Bear's mouth. She didn't see his eyes begin to twinkle merrily.

Next time, Old Bear thought to himself, *maybe you won't be so quick to get rid of me, Willa. Maybe you've learned your lesson. You can't put me away on a shelf. Not me.* I'm *your bear. And I'm going to be with you for the rest of your life.*

CLICK

My name is Seth Gold, and I'm twelve. My hobby is channel-surfing on the TV. At least, that *used* to be my hobby.

Why did I sit for hours, clicking from channel to channel with the remote control? I guess I loved the feeling of power it gave me.

A boring show? *Click* — on to the next. A loud commercial about sinus headaches? *Click* — on to something better.

Sometimes I tried to imagine what life was like when people had to get up and walk over to the TV every time they wanted to change the channel. But it was just too *awful* to think about.

One day, my dad came home from work carrying a package about the size of a shoebox. He plunked it down on the kitchen table. "Wait till you see this!" he exclaimed, removing the wrapping.

My four-year-old sister, Megan, shoved past

me. "What is it? What is it? Let me see!" she begged.

I read the big black letters on the box:

UNIVERSAL REMOTE

"I got a great deal on this," Dad explained. "I was on my way home from work, and I passed a little store I'd never seen before. It was going out of business. This thing was only six dollars. Great, huh?"

"What does it do?" I asked, pulling it carefully out of the box.

"It's just like our regular remote control, except it works everything," Dad explained. "It will work the TV, the VCR, the CD player. If we had a laser disc player, it would work that, too."

"Wow!" I exclaimed, excited. "Can I try it?"

"Sure, Seth," Dad replied. "Just put some batteries in it."

I took some AA batteries out of the kitchen junk drawer and loaded them into the chamber. Then I examined the remote. It was slender and black. It fit nicely into my hand. And it had a million buttons on it. This was going to be *awesome*!

I ran up the stairs to the den.

"Don't watch TV for too long!" my mother shouted after me. "You have homework — remember?" But I was already gone.

For the next hour, I fooled around with the new remote. It was really excellent. I could go back and forth between a videotape and the TV. I could play a CD while watching the Weather Channel with the sound turned off. It looked as if the weatherman were singing!

Megan wandered in. “I want to watch a cartoon tape,” she said.

“Not now,” I told her. “I’m busy.”

“But I *want* to!” she insisted.

“Not now, Megan! Beat it!”

“I’m telling!” she whined.

“You are not!” I cried, reaching to stop her.

To my surprise, she grabbed the remote control out of my hand. Then she pulled back her arm and flung the new remote across the room. It crashed into the radiator and fell to the floor.

“Now look what you did!” I shrieked angrily.

I picked up the remote from the floor and shook it. It rattled. It hadn’t rattled before. I clicked it at the TV.

Nothing happened.

“You jerk!” I cried. “Now we can’t watch anything!”

“Sorry,” Megan replied softly. She stuck her thumb into her mouth and backed slowly out of the room.

I sat down on the sofa and went to work on the remote. Using a quarter, I pried off the back and studied the insides. Not much in there except for a few chips and wires. I wiggled things as much as I dared, and then closed it up.

Holding it up to my ear, I shook it.

No rattle.

I pointed it at the TV. *Click*. It worked again!

Ten minutes later, I was busily channel-surfing when my mother stormed into the room. "Seth — I am very disappointed in you! I *told* you not to watch for long, and there are chores to be done in this house, and your sister tells me you won't let her have a turn, and — "

On and on she yelled, shaking her head. I tried to tune her out. But she was yelling louder and louder.

So I pointed the remote at her and pushed MUTE. It was a joke. Just a dumb joke.

But the most amazing thing happened. Mom was still yelling — but no sound came out. *I had really muted her!*

I pushed the button again. " — And your room is a mess, and your homework isn't getting done, and — "

Click. I muted her again. She continued yelling silently.

Awesome! This was really awesome! I could mute my own mother with the new remote control!

" — So you'd better start shaping up, mister," she finished. She turned and stormed out of the room.

"Wow!" I cried out loud. Sitting on the edge of the sofa, I stared at the buttons on the remote.

A few seconds later, our beagle, Sparky,

walked into the room. "Here, boy," I said. Sparky trotted over and started scratching himself behind the ear with his back leg.

I stared down at the remote again. I had to try it once more.

I saw a button labeled SLOW MOTION. I pointed the remote at Sparky, pressed the button, and held it.

Sparky started scratching himself very, very slowly. I could see his lips flapping as his head twisted slowly back and forth. His ears floated around in the air.

"Unbelievable!" I whooped. I let go of the button, and Sparky started scratching himself at normal speed again.

I can control the *world* with this remote! I told myself. I was so excited, I nearly dropped it again!

"Dinner!" Mom called from downstairs.

"Be right down," I shouted. I tucked the remote in my jeans pocket. I wasn't going to let it out of my sight. Then I charged down the stairs.

I was too excited to focus on eating my tuna casserole. I picked at my dinner, thinking about the remote, feeling it in my pocket.

My mother frowned as she cleared the plates. "Well, Seth," she said, "maybe you'll be more interested in dessert."

I glanced at the bowl. Chocolate pudding. My favorite.

Mom spooned it into plates, and I gobbled down my portion.

Then I had a *brilliant* idea. I quietly pulled out the remote and studied the buttons under the table. Ah — there it was: REWIND. I pushed the button and held it.

In rapid motion, Mom, Dad, and Megan *un*-ate their pudding!

I kept rewinding until Mom appeared with the bowl of pudding. Then I let the button go. "Well, Seth," she said again, "maybe you'll be more interested in dessert."

Then we all had pudding again!

"You bet," I said, gobbling down my second portion.

Ha! This was excellent! When I was done, I pushed REWIND again, and then one more time — until I'd had four dishes of chocolate pudding. I was stuffed!

The next morning, I carried the remote to school with me. I knew I shouldn't be messing around with it. But I couldn't help myself. It was too much fun.

After the first bell rang, it was time for the flag salute. I decided I had heard it enough times. So I muted it.

Everyone sat down. "And, now," said Ms. Gifford, "you're going to have a pop quiz in geography, you lucky people." She started passing out papers.

Oh, no! A pop quiz! I had been so busy with the new remote, I hadn't done the homework! I didn't know *anything* about South America!

I swallowed several times, thinking hard. Then I remembered the remote, and I relaxed. I had a plan.

Ms. Gifford finished passing out the papers. "Okay, everyone," she said. "You'll have twenty minutes. Good luck."

I took a quick glance at my test paper. It was full of questions I knew nothing about. The capital of Brazil? Not a clue.

But I wasn't worried. I doodled on my notebook while everyone else got busy answering the questions.

Nearly all the time had passed. "Thirty seconds left," announced Ms. Gifford.

I waited another fifteen seconds. Then I took the remote out of my pocket. I hit FREEZE-FRAME.

Everybody froze. Ms. Gifford stopped in the middle of a yawn, glancing out the window. Mickey Delaney froze in the middle of scratching his nose. Annie Schwartz, the best student in the class, froze in the middle of putting her pencil neatly down on the desk.

I stood up and strolled over to Annie's desk. I took my test paper with me. I peered over Annie's shoulder at her answers.

"San Salvador . . . okay. Andes Mountains . . .

okay . . ." I wrote all of Annie's answers onto my test sheet. Then I strolled back to my desk, sat down, and hit the FREEZE-FRAME button again.

Everybody snapped back into motion. "Okay, everyone," said Ms. Gifford. "Pencils down."

I set my pencil down, making a great show of looking exhausted. Then I passed my paper up to the front. This was really cool!

After the test, I looked for more ways to have fun. I fast-forwarded the teacher and the entire class for a while. I slow-motioned the principal when she came to talk to the teacher. Then I froze the whole class again.

When the teacher squeaked her chalk on the blackboard, I turned the volume way up. Finally, the bell rang for lunch. I couldn't wait to go down to the lunchroom — a whole new place to have fun.

The lunchroom was the usual zoo — everyone yelling and laughing, straw wrappers and juice boxes flying everywhere, kids falling off their chairs, dropping their lunch trays.

Mr. Pinkus, the lunchroom monitor, ran around yelling at everyone to sit down. I pointed the remote at him and froze him in his tracks.

Then I stepped into the food line. I took a cheeseburger, a salad, and two desserts.

"You can't have two desserts," said the lunchroom lady. "You know that."

I didn't even think twice. I pointed the remote

at her and punched the MUTE button. She continued to lecture me silently.

Quite pleased with myself, I continued down the line and picked up a carton of milk. Before I went to sit down, I pointed the remote at the lunchroom lady again and pressed MUTE to turn her voice back on.

Nothing happened.

I pressed the button again. She was still talking without making a sound. I banged the remote against my tray and tried again. But she still didn't get her voice back.

Well, it really isn't a tragedy if that lunchroom lady is muted for a while, I thought to myself. I never liked her anyway.

I figured the remote must need a little jiggling. I'd get it to work. I reached over to take another dessert.

But as I set the plate of pie down on my tray, my blood turned to ice. The remote wasn't there!

Breathing hard, I tried to think. Where was it? I had set it on the tray, hadn't I? I swallowed hard, feeling my panic rise.

"Freeze, Seth!"

I glanced up to see Danny Wexler, a big, freckle-faced, redheaded eighth-grader, standing a few feet away, pointing the remote at me!

"Danny — don't touch that!" I pleaded. "Don't press any buttons!"

Danny grinned at me. "Why not? Hey, why do

you have a remote control in school, anyway?" He moved his finger over the buttons, deciding which one to push.

"Don't touch it!" I begged. I dove for him and snatched it out of his hand.

"Hand it back, Seth," Danny growled. His eyes narrowed. His expression turned mean. He moved toward me with his hand outstretched.

In a panic, I hit the FREEZE-FRAME button.

And froze him.

I started to back away. But a girl's startled cry made me stop. "Hey, what's going on? Why is Danny frozen like that?"

Melissa Fink stood staring at us. I realized in horror that she could see Danny, could see what was going on. Other kids were starting to crowd around.

"What is that?" Melissa demanded. She tried to pull the remote out of my hand.

"Don't touch it!" I warned. "Please!"

"What is going on here?" A woman's voice burst in. I glanced up to see the principal. "What's all this commotion?"

She saw the remote in my hand. "Seth, let me see that."

In a total panic, I pushed FREEZE-FRAME and froze her.

The lunchroom filled with frightened shouts. "Seth froze the principal! Somebody — help! Seth froze the principal!"

A big crowd moved around me. I started to back away.

I pressed the FREEZE-FRAME button again to unfreeze the principal.

But it didn't work. She stayed still as a statue.

My brain was whirling. The whole room started to spin. The shouts and cries of the other kids made it hard to think straight.

What had I done?

What if I can't unfreeze her? I thought, my entire body trembling. What if I can't unfreeze Danny or Mr. Pinkus?

Would they stay like that forever?

I knew I was in trouble now. *Major* trouble.

"Get Seth!" someone shouted. "Get that thing away from him!"

I turned and ran for the lunchroom door. Kids came running after me. "Stop him! Stop him!" they shouted.

I turned back and pointed the remote at them. I started pushing buttons frantically.

I didn't know what I was doing. I was so frightened. So totally panicked.

My heart pounded. My stomach was doing wild flip-flops.

I pushed button after button.

None of them worked. None of them did anything.

"Stop Seth! Stop him!" The crowd continued to chase me.

I pushed another button. Another button.

Not working. Nothing worked. And then I pushed the button marked OFF.

"Hey — !" I cried out as the world went black.

I blinked several times. But the darkness didn't lift.

It was silent now. Silent and black.

I'm all alone, I realized.

No shouting kids. No kids at all. No school. No light.

No picture. No sound.

A faint glow in my hand made me raise the remote control. I brought it close to my face. A small red light blinked steadily.

Squinting into the blinking light, I read the words beneath it: BATTERY DEAD.

BROKEN DOLLS

"You broke my doll!" Tamara Baker screamed.

"I did not!" Neal, her seven-year-old brother, protested. "The arm fell off. It wasn't my fault!"

Tamara grabbed the doll from his hand. The slender pink arm fell to the floor. "That's the third doll you broke, Neal!" she cried. "Why can't you keep your paws off my doll collection?"

"Aw, you've got plenty more," her brother muttered, pointing to Tamara's shelves and shelves of dolls.

"You could at least say you're sorry," Tamara scolded.

"Sorry," Neal said softly. And then a grin spread across his face as he added, "NOT!" He turned and ran out of Tamara's room.

She angrily slammed her door. She replaced the broken doll on its shelf, shaking her head. Then she walked to the mirror to brush her hair.

Tamara studied her reflection. She was twelve, and her face was longer and thinner than ever before. That was fine with Tamara, who wanted to look older.

She had large brown eyes. They were her best feature. Her skin was tanned, her nose was small and straight and, best of all this year — no braces! Tamara smiled. She was satisfied, except for her hair!

Tamara's hair was a long, dark, wavy mass that had always refused to be put in any normal style. Tamara frowned and tugged at it. I have a bad-hair day *every* day! she thought glumly. She brushed it back and jammed a couple of barrettes in it.

"Tamara, are you coming?"

She heard her dad calling impatiently from downstairs. He hated waiting. He was taking the family to the crafts fair at the fairgrounds. And he insisted on getting there when the fairgrounds opened at ten A.M.

Tamara opened her door and stepped on something squishy. It made a squeaking sound, and Tamara jumped a mile. Then she spotted Neal peeking out his door, laughing his head off.

"I scared you! I scared you!" he crowed.

Tamara picked up the object. It was a bath toy inside a sock, placed just where Tamara would have to step. She aimed and threw it at Neal's laughing face. He bolted for the stairs, and she chased after him.

"Children! Children!" Mrs. Baker cried as the two circled around her. "Stop this right now!"

"She started it!" Neal claimed in his whiniest voice.

"Mom — he broke another one of my dolls!" Tamara said.

"Stop it! Just stop it!" their mother ordered. "Get in the car, both of you."

The car ride seemed to take forever. Tamara sat in the backseat with Neal. Neal had never been able to sit still for more than ten seconds. He squirmed and bounced and stretched his neck to see out all the windows at once. It drove Tamara crazy.

Once they were at the fairgrounds, Neal went wild. He wanted to see everything and be everywhere at once.

"Tamara," Mrs. Baker said, "your dad and I want to see the ceramics. But I don't want Neal around things that can break."

"Good thinking, Mom," Tamara replied, rolling her eyes.

"So why don't you take him for a half hour, and then meet your father and me at the information booth after that?" Mrs. Baker suggested.

"ME take Neal?" Tamara howled in horror. "What do I look like? A wild-animal trainer?"

"No," Neal giggled. "You look like the wild animal! Hahahaha!"

Tamara could see that she was trapped. "Okay, I'll do it," she grumbled. "Come on, you little monster."

Tamara held Neal's hand in a "grip of death" so he couldn't get away. She wished she had a pair of handcuffs. She strolled around looking at exhibits, ignoring Neal's nonstop chatter.

Tamara wasn't much of a crafts person. Her mom was the "craftsy" one. Mrs. Baker couldn't look at a simple T-shirt without wanting to put rhinestone studs on it.

Still, Tamara enjoyed walking through the booths. There were quilts, clay pots, lots of handmade jewelry, and carved wooden toys that got even Neal's attention.

"Wow! How does this wooden popgun work?" Neal asked.

Tamara wasn't too interested in popguns. She turned to the booth across the aisle.

And saw the dolls.

There were at least fifteen or twenty of them. And they were strikingly human looking.

The dolls all had different faces, different expressions. One looked sweet, another pouting. The next was crying. Another was asleep. On and on, like a quiet nursery.

Tamara stared from doll to doll. They were so real looking. She thought if she touched one, the doll would feel warm, not cold like a regular doll. She reached out . . .

"Do you like them?" a raspy voice called from right behind her.

Tamara jumped. She turned and faced the oldest woman that she had ever seen. Her withered face was lined with deep crags. Her white hair hung down stiff as straw. Her eyes were narrowed slits.

"Did you make these dolls?" Tamara asked.

"Every one, dearie."

"I've never seen dolls like these before. They're so *real*!"

"No two are the same," the old woman replied. "and they're perfect in every detail. Go ahead, take a closer look."

Neal padded over to Tamara. "I'm hungry," he whined.

"I'll get you something in a minute," Tamara snapped.

"Aren't you *precious*!" the old lady crooned at Neal. "Quite the little man. I think there may be a cookie around here for such a nice boy."

Neal perked up at the mention of a cookie. Tamara turned back to the doll she'd been studying. It was wearing a dark purple dress with white trim.

She picked it up. "Wow. It weighs as much as a real baby, too," she said. "That's incredible."

Tamara set the doll down and turned around. As she did, she thought she saw the old lady put her hand on Neal's head. The gesture was odd and formal, almost like a blessing.

Strangest of all was the look on Neal's face. He stood still. And quiet.

Tamara grabbed Neal's hand, harder than she intended, and pulled him away from the doll booth. "Come on. We've got to go," she said. "Thank the lady for the cookie."

"Thank you," Neal mumbled through a mouth full of crumbs.

Tamara and Neal met their parents, and the four of them walked around the exhibits together. They didn't go past the doll booth again.

When Mr. Baker had had enough, and Mrs. Baker had bought enough goodies to keep the entire family in puff-paint heaven through Christmas, they all piled into the family car and headed home.

Neal didn't squirm the way he had on the way to the crafts fair. In fact, he didn't do much of anything. He sat back in his seat, staring straight ahead.

Mrs. Baker noticed Neal's unusual quiet behavior as soon as they got home. She felt his forehead. "Ted, he's running a fever," she told her husband.

"Probably all the excitement today," Mr. Baker replied. "I'll get the baby aspirin. Neal, get into bed."

"I don't want to go to bed. It's daytime," Neal protested. But he went upstairs anyway.

Mrs. Baker got Neal into his pajamas and brushed her hand over his head lovingly. Tamara went upstairs just as Mrs. Baker pulled her hand away, chuckling.

"What have you gotten into, young man?" she asked, wiping something off her hand. "You've got some kind of goop in your hair."

"Dolly jelly," Tamara heard Neal mumble, before he drifted into a feverish sleep.

Later in the afternoon, Neal was covered in a light rash. His face was pale, washed out.

"Looks like an allergy, Marge," Mr. Baker decided. "What did he eat today?"

"Oh, Ted," Mrs. Baker replied, sighing. "What *didn't* he eat!"

Tamara felt bad that her brother was sick. She went to his room to sit with him for a while.

He looked so pale. As if his face were fading away.

She placed her hand on his forehead. It felt really hot. Neal was mumbling something in his sleep. She listened.

"No dollies. Don't want to be a dolly. No dolly jelly. No."

Dollies?

Tamara remembered the doll lady. The cookie.

Maybe the cookie had something in it that had made Neal sick.

She remembered watching the old woman place her hand on Neal's head. Dolly jelly . . .

"Mom, I'm going out for a little while, okay?" Tamara said, pulling on her jacket.

"Where are you going?"

"Just for a bike ride." Tamara hurried out the back door.

She jumped on to her bicycle and began pedaling furiously. The fairgrounds were a couple of miles away. And she didn't know how late the crafts fair stayed open.

She arrived at the fairgrounds just as the gates closed. "Well, I'm here," she told herself "*Now* what do I do?"

People were packing up their crafts. Closing their booths.

Tamara saw the doll lady step out from one of the crafts areas. She was carrying a box. Tamara watched carefully as the old woman took the box to a trailer marked EXHIBITORS ONLY.

Staying in the shadows, Tamara crept toward the trailer. She watched. The doll maker stepped out of the trailer. She kept walking back and forth, carrying one box at a time into the trailer.

Tamara waited until the old woman was out of view. Then she took a deep breath, and sneaked into the trailer.

Her heart fluttering in her chest, Tamara

searched the trailer. She kept remembering Neal mumbling about the dollies, and "dolly jelly."

Glancing at the trailer door, she opened several boxes marked "dolls" and peered inside. To her surprise, these were not the dolls she'd seen on display.

The faces on these dolls were completely blank.

Tamara shivered. There was something creepy about a doll without any face at all. The smooth white heads stared up at her like ghosts.

With a shudder, Tamara opened another box. This doll had a pale face, so pale she could barely make out its features. She touched the doll's smooth head and her hand came away smeared with the same goop that was in Neal's hair.

Dolly jelly.

"Ohh!" Tamara cried out as the doll's features darkened. Came clearer. And she recognized Neal's eyes. Neal's pointy nose. Neal's mouth.

"Wh-what's happening?" Tamara stammered out loud. She gaped at the doll in horror.

The features darkened some more. Neal's face was growing clearer on the doll head.

Then she remembered how pale her brother had looked, lying in his bed asleep. How his face had appeared to be fading away.

"What is the old woman doing?" Tamara wondered aloud, frozen in sudden horror. "I've got to stop her!"

"Sssssstop her," a voice said.

Tamara gasped and spun around. Was it the old doll maker?

No. No one was at the trailer door. Where did the sound come from?

The closet.

"Sssstop her," a tiny voice repeated.

Swallowing hard, Tamara pulled open the closet door with a trembling hand.

Dolls. Crammed into the shelves.

The dolls from the crafts fair.

But they couldn't be dolls because they were moving! Reaching out their tiny, pink arms to Tamara!

"No!" Tamara shrieked. "You can't be alive. You *can't* be!"

She shrank back from their outstretched arms. "Don't touch me! Don't!" she pleaded.

Neal. She had to help Neal.

Tamara snapped back to her senses. She slammed the closet door shut. Then she grabbed the doll with Neal's features and darted out of the trailer.

"Going somewhere, dearie?" The old doll maker grinned at Tamara.

"Stay away from me!" Tamara cried breathlessly. "I've got the doll. My brother's doll! And I'm going to the police!"

The old woman's eyes sharpened. "Why don't you come inside, and we'll talk about it?" she said softly.

"No way!" Tamara exclaimed. "I saw your dolls. I know what you're doing!"

The old lady started toward Tamara, walking slowly but deliberately. Her face was hard and evil. "You don't know what I'm doing," she said through clenched teeth. "Your world has no idea of my ancient arts."

Tamara suddenly felt dizzy. What did she mean "your world"? Just how old *was* this woman?

The doll maker reached into her sweater and pulled out a container. Tamara recognized the goop that Neal had called "dolly jelly."

"I think it's time for you to go away, dearie," the old lady said quietly. "Young people disappear so often in this century. You'll just be one more. . . ."

The doll maker smeared a dab of the greasy goop on her fingers. Then she moved toward Tamara, mumbling some kind of chant.

Tamara struggled to move. But she couldn't.

She felt like a bird being hypnotized by a snake. The old woman looked like a cold, unblinking snake, slithering closer . . . closer . . .

"No!" Tamara shrieked — and dove forward. The sound of her own voice gave her strength.

She grabbed the jar of goop from the old woman's hand. Then she spun around and started to run.

"Give that back!" the doll maker called after her.

Tamara saw a small wading pool at the edge of the fairgrounds. She raised the jar of goop — and heaved it into the pool.

"You fool!" the old woman wailed. "You fool! What have you done?"

Tamara stared in disbelief as the pool water began to bubble and hiss. Choking clouds of black smoke rose up from the pool. The water turned green, then blue, then red. It swirled up in angry waves. Then splashed down hard under the billowing black smoke.

When Tamara turned back, the old woman had vanished.

She heard happy shrieks and cheers from the trailer. Were the dolls celebrating in there?

She didn't have time to find out. She ran to her bicycle and started to jam the Neal doll into her bike pack.

But to Tamara's surprise, the doll no longer looked like Neal. Its face was smooth and blank.

With a shiver that shook her whole body, Tamara tossed the doll as far as she could. Then she furiously pedaled home.

"Tamara, where on earth have you been?" Mrs. Baker scolded. "And just *look* at you! You're a mess!"

"Sorry, Mom," Tamara mumbled. "I'll clean up for supper."

Neal popped into the kitchen. He grinned at

Tamara. "You look like you've been playing in the mud!" he exclaimed. "Piggy! Piggy!"

"Neal! You're all right!" Tamara cried joyfully. She dropped to her knees and gave him an enthusiastic hug.

"Do you believe it?" Mrs. Baker said. "All of a sudden, his fever dropped, and he was his old self again."

"His old bratty self," Tamara laughed, ruffling Neal's hair. "Well, that's just fine with me!"

Everything was back to normal. Tamara decided to forget about the old doll maker. And the frightening, living dolls.

She forced the old woman out of her mind — until one night a few weeks later.

Her parents had gone out. Tamara was babysitting Neal.

Someone knocked on the front door.

"Who's there?" Tamara called out.

No reply.

"Who's there?" she repeated.

Still no reply.

Tamara peered out through the front window. A dark, moonless night. She didn't see anyone.

Curious, she pulled open the front door. And found a package on the front stoop. "Hey — !" She stared out at the dark street.

Who delivered this?

She carried the box inside and started to unwrap the brown paper.

"Is it for me?" Neal came hurrying into the living room. "Is it a present? For me?"

"I don't know," Tamara told him, struggling to tear off the wrapping.

A plain box was inside. She pulled open the lid.

And stared at a doll. An ugly doll. A doll with strawlike white hair. A craggy, wrinkled face. Narrow, squinting eyes.

"Ohh." Tamara recognized the doll instantly. It was the old woman. The doll maker.

She's followed me, Tamara realized.

She's found me.

She's here in my house with all of her evil.

Tamara felt cold all over. Her breath seemed to freeze as she stared in horror at the ugly, frightening doll.

She nearly dropped the box. What am I going to do? What can I do?

The idea popped into her mind.

She handed the doll to Neal. "Bet you can't break this one!" she told him.

"Huh?" He gaped at the doll, then back at Tamara.

"I dare you to break this one!" Tamara said.

"You dare me?"

Tamara nodded. "Bet you five dollars you can't."

"It's a bet!" Neal replied. He went to work on the doll.

A VAMPIRE IN THE NEIGHBORHOOD

We knew there was something different about Helga the first time we saw her.

For one thing, she had that strange name. Helga. Such an old-fashioned name.

Helga looked old-fashioned, too. She wore the same black skirt to school every day. Old looking, and kind of worn, with no style at all.

My friend Carrie and I were sitting in the back of Miss Wheeling's sixth-grade class the first day Helga came to school. "Check her out, Maddy," Carrie whispered, motioning with her eyes.

I turned to the front of the room and stared at the timid-looking girl talking with Miss Wheeling. With her tight, black ringlets of hair and her pale gray blouse tucked into her black skirt, the girl looked as if she had stepped out of an old movie.

"This is Helga Nuegenstorm," Miss Wheeling announced. "She is new to our school, and I'm sure you will all make her feel at home."

Helga lowered her eyes to the floor. Her skin

was so pale, as if it had never seen the sunlight. And she was wearing lipstick. Black lipstick.

"She's weird," Carrie whispered.

"She's kind of pretty," I replied. "I've never seen anyone who looked like that."

Later, Carrie, Yvonne, Joey, and I took our usual table in the lunchroom. The four of us are really good friends. We have been friends for a long, long time. We sit together in the lunchroom every day.

"Did you see the new girl?" I asked. The four of us were tossing an apple back and forth across the table to each other.

"Isn't she weird?" Carrie asked.

Yvonne and Joey nodded. "She's so pale, but she wears that yucky black lipstick," Yvonne said.

"Maybe she isn't wearing lipstick," Joey joked. "Maybe those are her lips!"

"Do you know where she lives?" I asked, catching the apple and tossing it to Joey.

"She moved into the Dobson house," Yvonne replied. "I was walking by and saw her moving in."

Carrie, Joey, and I gasped in surprise. The apple fell out of Joey's hands and rolled away.

The Dobson house stood all by itself on the edge of Culver's Woods. The house had been empty forever.

"What a creepy old house," Carrie said. "Did you see Helga's parents?"

Yvonne shook her head. "No. It was kind of strange. I saw the moving men carrying in all this heavy, old furniture. And I saw Helga. But I didn't see any grownups."

"Weird," Carrie muttered again. Her favorite word.

I started to say something else. But I glanced up and saw Helga standing awkwardly in the lunchroom doorway. "I'm going to invite her to sit down with us," I announced, jumping up.

"Why, Maddy?" Joey asked.

"Maybe we can find out more about her," I replied. I hurried over to Helga. "I'm Maddy Simon," I told her. "I'm in your class. Want to sit with me and my friends?"

She stared back at me with her pale, gray eyes, the strangest eyes I've ever seen. *Ghost eyes*, I thought.

"No thank you," she replied. Her voice was soft and whispery. "I never eat lunch."

She's a vampire, we decided.

The four of us were always searching for vampires.

"Helga *has* to be a vampire," Carrie declared. "She never eats. She looks so old-fashioned. She keeps totally to herself. And she's as pale as death."

It was three nights later. We were crouched

across the road from the old Dobson house. Helga's house.

A long, low hedge stretched along the dark street. We hid behind the hedge, huddled together, whispering.

We couldn't help ourselves. We had to spy on her. We had to find out the truth.

The creepy old house rose up in front of us, pale in the light of the full moon. Behind the house, the trees of Culver's Woods shook and shivered in the wind.

"Where is Helga?" Yvonne whispered. "The house is totally dark."

"She's in there," I replied, my eyes on the black windows. "She's in there in the dark."

"Weird," Carrie whispered.

"I tried to talk to her in school today," Joey reported. "But she walked right past me. She wears those heavy, black shoes. But her footsteps didn't make a sound."

"Why would anyone move into this horrible old house?" Carrie asked. "It's so far from town. Nothing but woods all around."

"For privacy," I replied. "Vampires crave privacy."

The others giggled.

I thought I saw something move in the window. A gray shadow against the blackness. "Come on, guys," I whispered. "Let's take a closer look."

We crept across the road. The silence was eerie.

The only sound was the soft, steady whisper of the wind through the trees.

The old house seemed to grow darker as we approached it. We pushed through the tall weeds that blanketed the front lawn. Moving silently, we huddled beneath the big front window, pressing ourselves against the damp, moldy shingles.

"Give me a boost," I whispered to Joey. "So I can look in the window."

"Be careful, Maddy," Carrie warned. "Helga might see you."

I ignored her warning. I had to take a look. I was just so curious.

Joey and Yvonne helped lift me. I grabbed the stone windowsill with both hands and hoisted myself up just high enough to see in.

Then I stared in through the dust-smeared glass. Into a vast, dark living room. A pale square of moonlight poured into the room. I could make out a long couch, wooden and stiff looking. Two old-fashioned chairs.

I nearly toppled to the ground when I saw Helga.

"She's in there!" I whispered excitedly to my friends. "I can see her. Standing in the dark, in front of a tall mirror."

"Does she have a reflection?" Joey whispered. "Check it out, Maddy. Does she have a reflection?"

I narrowed my eyes, trying to focus on the darkness.

Vampires don't have reflections, I knew. Did

Helga have a reflection? "It's too dark to see," I told my friends.

Helga turned suddenly toward the window. She seemed to be staring right at me.

"Let me down! Quick!" I demanded. I slid to the ground.

"Did she see you?" Carrie asked, her dark eyes wide with excitement.

"I don't know," I told her. "I hope not."

"Why is she there in the dark?" Joey asked. "Did she have a reflection? Was she walking, or floating?"

Questions I couldn't answer.

"We'll come back tomorrow," I said.

The four of us met there every night. We hid behind the long hedge and spied on Helga's house. We peered into the windows. We crept around back and tried to see in through the kitchen.

Some nights we spotted a dim light in an upstairs window. Most nights, there were no lights on at all.

Some nights we saw Helga inside the house. Always alone. We never saw her parents. We never saw anyone else.

My friends and I became obsessed with Helga, with finding out the truth about her.

We tried to talk to her in school. But she stared back at us with those wintry, gray eyes and never even pretended to be friendly.

I invited her to come with us to the basketball game in the gym on Friday night. But she said she didn't like basketball.

We tried to get invited to her house. One day, Joey asked if he could come to her house and copy her history notes.

Helga said she wouldn't be home that night.

"Then how about tomorrow after school?" Joey insisted.

"It's not a good idea," Helga replied mysteriously.

She wore the same black skirt every day. She never changed her hairstyle. Her black ringlets hung down around that pale, pale face.

One day, on an impulse, I grabbed her hand. We were standing side by side in the hall at school, waiting to get into the auditorium.

I couldn't help myself. I reached out and squeezed her hand. I had to know what it felt like. I had to find out if it felt alive.

I jerked my hand back in shock when I felt how cold Helga's hand was. As cold as a winter day. As cold as . . . death.

She *is* a vampire! I decided.

She clasped her pale hands together and gazed at me with those frightening gray eyes. "It's so cold in here," she whispered. "Don't you think so, Maddy?"

It was the first time she had ever said my name, and it sent a shiver down my back.

* * *

That night, my friends and I met in front of Helga's house. Once again, pale moonlight washed over us. It was the only light except for a dim, orange glow in an upstairs window.

Crouching low behind the hedge, we stared up at the window. The shade was pulled. But we could see Helga's silhouette moving back and forth on the window shade.

"She's all alone in there," Carrie whispered. "No parents. No one."

"She's probably hundreds of years old," I whispered back.

"She doesn't look it!" Joey joked.

We giggled. But our laughter was cut short when the light in the window went off.

"She went to bed," Yvonne guessed. "Does she sleep in a coffin?"

"She must," I replied, gazing up at the dark window. Something fluttered low over the old house's sloping roof. A bat?

"All vampires sleep in coffins," Joey murmured. "Coffins filled with the ancient dirt from their graves."

"I want to see Helga's coffin," I whispered, standing up. I took a step toward the street, my eyes on the house.

"Maddy — come back," Carrie warned.

"I have to see Helga's coffin," I told her. "I have to know for sure."

We all wanted to know. That's why we spied on Helga every night.

I crept silently across the street and into Helga's front yard. Huddled closely together, the other three followed.

A twisted, gnarled old tree tilted up toward Helga's bedroom window. I grabbed a low branch and started to pull myself up.

The bark felt cold and rough against my hands. The slender branches shook as if trying to toss me off.

I clung tightly to the trunk and reached for a higher branch. Hoisting myself on to it, I peered through the leaves at the house.

Helga's bedroom window was still high above me. I glanced down and saw Carrie, Yvonne, and Joey. They had circled the tree and were peering up at me. Even in the darkness, I could see the tense expressions on their faces.

Up I climbed. Ignoring the scratch of the bark, the trembling of the branches.

Slowly, steadily, I pulled myself up. Until I was high enough to see into the bedroom window.

Holding tightly onto the trunk, I turned slowly. Lowered my head to see through a tangle of dark leaves. Gazed into the window —

— and saw Helga gazing back at me!

Her face gleamed, silvery in the wash of moonlight. Her gray eyes glowed evilly as she stared out at me, her ghostly face pressed against the windowpane.

Too startled to cry out, I started to slip. My hands slid off the trunk, and I lurched backwards.

"No!" I thrust out both hands. Grabbed the hard trunk — and held on.

"She saw me!" I called down to my friends. "Helga saw me!" I scrambled down, moving frantically, sliding and scraping down the rough trunk.

By the time I reached the ground, my three friends were already running around to the front of the house. "Wait up!" I called hoarsely.

Too late.

The front door swung open.

Helga moved quickly. Out the door. Down the front stoop. Across the weed-choked lawn to block our path.

"I know you've been spying on me!" she cried angrily. "You'd better quit it! I'm warning you!"

I stopped. Carrie, Yvonne, and Joey stopped, too. We moved together, watching Helga storm toward us.

She had her hands balled into tight fists. Her eerie eyes were narrowed at us, her face twisted in a frightening scowl.

My friends and I huddled there in the middle of the dark yard. The trees whispered and shook. The tall weeds swayed all around us.

And then the words just burst from my mouth. "Helga — are you a vampire?" I just blurted out the question, without even thinking. "Are you a vampire?"

She moved closer, her gray eyes glowing. "Yes," she whispered.

"Show us your fangs," I demanded.

A strange smile spread slowly over Helga's face. "No," she replied. "You show me *your* fangs."

I hesitated for a second. Then I lowered my fangs.

Then Carrie, Yvonne, and Joey lowered their fangs, too. Our fangs slid easily out over our lips, down to our chins.

We grinned expectantly at Helga. "Your turn," I said.

But to my surprise, Helga stumbled back and let out a frightened squeal. "I was just *joking*!" she cried. "I — I thought you were joking, too!"

"No way," I told her.

We weren't joking. We're vampires. Me, Carrie, Yvonne, and Joey — all four of us are vampires.

We were so disappointed about Helga. We had such high hopes.

But we knew what we had to do.

We formed a tight circle around her. Then we moved in.

The mystery about Helga had been solved. In a few minutes, she would be a vampire, too.

More TALES TO GIVE YOU Goosebumps®

THE WEREWOLF'S FIRST NIGHT

"What's the problem, Brian?" my dad asked, peering at me in the rearview mirror. "We've been on the road for four hours, and you haven't said two words. Aren't you excited?"

"Sure, Dad." I scrunched down in the seat of the car. That way, he couldn't see my face. He couldn't see that I was lying.

We were driving to Thunder Lake. We go to Thunder Lake every summer. It's a vacation resort, with cabins, a golf course, a big lake, and some other stuff.

Lots of families go there because they have a camp for the kids. The grown-ups dump their kids in the camp. Then they play golf or hang out in the clubhouse.

"Are you sure you're okay, Brian?" Dad asked.

"Leave him alone, honey," my mom said. "Brian's probably a tiny bit nervous about being in the teen camp this summer."

Nervous wasn't the right word. *Terrified* was more like it.

Dad cleared his throat. He always clears his throat before he gives me a pep talk. "Look at it this way, Brian. The teen camp will help you get over your shyness. You'll feel more grown-up being with older kids. Anyway, you belong there. You're twelve years old now. . . ."

That's right, I thought. I'm twelve years old. And I'd like to live to see *thirteen*!

"You're going to have a great time," Dad insisted.

"I know you're scared now," Mom told me. "But the time is coming when you won't be afraid of anything. Just wait and see."

Mom and Dad had it all wrong. Sure, the teen camp made me a little nervous.

But what made me afraid were the stories about Thunder Lake. Stories about creatures in the night. About howls and shrieks, and enormous footprints.

About werewolves living by the lake.

I've been hearing those stories since we started spending our vacations at Thunder Lake six years ago. I've been really scared ever since. And that really annoys my parents.

My parents think I'm a wimp.

So I keep my mouth shut about the stories.

But I'm still scared.

"There's the ten-mile sign!" Dad called out.

I sat up straight and stared out the window. Sure enough, the sign said THUNDER LAKE: TEN MILES.

Next came the five-mile sign.

Time was running out.

Finally I spotted the sign I'd been dreading: WELCOME TO THUNDER LAKE! A FAMILY RESORT. SWIMMING. HIKING. BOATING. GOLF. TENNIS.

And werewolves.

The teen camp had ten kids in it. A guy named Kevin was the only other twelve-year-old. He and I were the youngest.

Kevin had red hair and the whitest skin I've ever seen. The older guys made fun of him because his mother forced him to smear on lots of lotion to keep from getting sunburned.

I have brown hair and eyes, and my skin doesn't burn. So they don't joke about the way I look. But I'm short and sort of klutzy. And that's what they make fun of.

The three oldest guys were the toughest. Jake, Phil, and Don. They were all fifteen.

Jake had dark curly hair and a gold earring in one ear. Phil had beady blue eyes and always wore a red Bulls T-shirt. Don was short, wide, and mean.

"If I had the guts, I'd call him Fatso," Kevin whispered to me one day during a baseball game.

"Yeah," I whispered back. "But he'd sit on you and squash you to death."

When it was my turn to bat, I trotted to the plate. Don was the catcher. When he saw me he called, "Easy out!"

Then he grinned.

And I froze.

I'd never seen Don smile before. So I'd never seen his teeth.

But I could see them now.

They were the longest front teeth I'd ever seen in my life. And they were sharp.

Like fangs.

Like a wolf's fangs.

Then Don did something strange. He shut his mouth real quick and turned his head away.

Like he forgot he wasn't supposed to smile.

I swallowed and licked my lips. Every second I stood at the plate, I expected to feel his fangs stick into my leg.

When I struck out, Don grinned again. I couldn't believe it! His teeth looked normal. His fangs were gone!

But I knew I hadn't imagined them.

Then I remembered the stories about werewolves. They started out as humans. They didn't change into wolves all at once. But on the night of the full moon — total werewolf!

Could Don be a werewolf?

After the game, I told Kevin about Don's teeth. Then I waited for him to laugh. But he didn't.

"Man!" he said. "I heard all the stuff about this lake and families changing into werewolves. But I didn't really believe it. Are you sure it wasn't a trick?"

"I guess it could have been," I admitted. "But if he wanted to scare me, why did he try to hide the fangs?"

"Yeah," Kevin agreed. "We'd better be careful when the full moon comes."

Later, I looked up the dates of the moon on Mom's little pocket calendar.

Only four nights until the next full moon!

I wanted to tell Mom and Dad how afraid I was. Afraid Don would come after me. But I didn't want them to get on my case about being such a wimp.

So I didn't say anything. Not even when they went to play cards at the clubhouse and left me alone in the cabin.

I kept telling myself that there were no such things as werewolves. That Don was just a kid.

Everything was quiet for a while. Then I heard rustling outside the cabin.

My heart started pounding. But I told myself it was a squirrel.

The rustling grew louder.

My knees began to shake. I told myself it was a raccoon.

I heard a low growl right outside the door. Then scratching sounds, and another growl.

I told myself it was Don.

I shut off the lights and peered out the front window. The moon lit up the darkness. In the distance, I saw something red moving through the trees toward the lake.

A red Bulls T-shirt.

Phil! Running through the woods like a wild animal!

As soon as Mom and Dad came back, I told them. I didn't care how wimpy I sounded.

"Oh, Brian, don't you get it?" Dad asked. "The guys are just playing a trick on you. They know you're scared, and they're taking advantage of it!"

"I know it's hard not to be scared, dear," Mom said. "But it will all change soon. Trust me."

"Your mother's right," Dad agreed. "I'm surprised you fell for that trick, Brian. Don't you realize how easy it is for someone to sneak up to a cabin and make a few scary sounds?"

Okay, so it's easy to make scary sounds and growls.

But how easy is it to make wolf tracks?

Because that's what I found the next morning.

Not regular wolf tracks.

These paw prints were at least ten inches long!

I found them in the dirt around the cabin and followed them until they disappeared into the woods — at the exact spot where I'd seen Phil the night before.

Phil was a werewolf, too. No doubt about it.

A couple of nights later, the teen camp had a cookout by the lake. I didn't want to go. But since the moon wasn't full yet, I figured I'd be okay.

After we ate hamburgers and toasted marshmallows, we all sat around the campfire. Jake told a spooky story about some guy with a hook for a hand.

I didn't pay much attention. A guy with a hook for a hand didn't scare me. Werewolves did.

I kept my eyes on Don and Phil. The firelight threw weird shadows on their faces. It turned their eyes blood-red. I expected them to start growing fangs and claws any minute.

But nothing happened.

When the cookout was over, we started along the path toward the cabins. Suddenly, I realized I'd forgotten my new jacket. Mom would kill me if I left it out in the sand all night. So I ran back to get it.

The moon lit up the dark beach. I saw a figure kneeling in the sand. When he lifted his head to the sky, something glinted in the moonlight.

Jake's gold earring.

As I watched, Jake held his arms up toward the moon, opened his mouth, and howled.

The bloodcurdling howl of a wolf.

I knew no human could howl like that! I turned and ran up the path as fast as I could.

I caught up to Kevin. "Kevin, did you hear that howl?" I gasped. "It was Jake!"

As I raced up to him, Kevin quickly stuffed something into his mouth.

But he wasn't quick enough, because I caught a glimpse of it — a piece of hamburger meat. *Raw* hamburger meat.

The blood from the meat oozed down his chin.

Kevin was one of *them.*

One more night until the full moon. I was terrified. But I figured if I stayed in the cabin, I'd be safe.

Then I learned about the overnight trip. We'd hike to a campground, pitch our tents, and sleep under the sky.

On the night of the full moon!

No way, I thought. I had to get out of it! But how?

On the day before the overnight, I told Mom I had a sore throat. "I think it's my tonsils," I croaked.

"Brian," Mom said with a sigh. "You had your tonsils out two years ago."

How could I have been so dumb? Now, even if I really got sick, she'd never believe me.

Next I tried making myself sick by swallowing

too much water during swimming. All I did was choke a lot.

Then I tried rubbing what looked like poison ivy leaves on my face and arms. Nothing happened.

Finally, I decided to tell the truth. Well, not the whole truth. I knew my parents would never believe that. So I just told part of it.

"The guys are mean," I said. "I know they're going to do something awful to me. Please don't make me go on the overnight. Please?"

Dad crossed his arms. Then he cleared his throat. "Brian," he said, "if I let you stay in the cabin, it would be the worst thing for you. Maybe these guys have been a little rough on you. But if you let them know you're scared, they'll get even rougher."

"Your father's right," Mom told me. "You just have to be patient. Everything will be okay."

"But Mom!"

"That's enough, Brian," Dad said sharply. "I don't want to hear another word. You're going on the overnight — and that's that!"

So there I was stuck in the woods with at least four werewolves.

When it started to get dark and the stars came out, I ducked into my tent.

"Hey, Brian, what are you doing?" Kevin yelled. "Don't you want to eat?"

Yeah, right. What was on the menu — raw squirrel?

While the others ate, I stayed in my tent. Pretty soon, the campfire died down. The woods around the lake grew quiet.

Then I spotted a light through my tent. The bright orange light of the rising moon.

The full moon.

I scrunched down in my sleeping bag.

I crossed my fingers and hoped I'd been wrong all along. Maybe nothing would happen.

That's when I heard the first howl.

The hairs on the back of my neck stood up straight. My heart banged away like a hammer. I'd heard that savage howl before.

I had to get out of there! I had to make a run for it.

I wiggled out of my sleeping bag. Then I crawled across the tent and pulled the flap back a little. Peeking out, I saw Phil standing in front of his tent in his red T-shirt.

Except he wasn't Phil anymore.

Thick dark hair covered his face and arms. White fangs poked out of his mouth, gleaming like daggers. He raised his head to the moon and howled again.

Phil had become a werewolf.

As his howl died down, I lifted the flap a little more. Shadowy figures began to emerge from the other tents. Growling, snarling figures, with thick fur and sharp fangs.

My heart beat double time. I recognized them all. Don, Jake, Kevin, and the five other kids in the teen camp. Werewolves! Every one of them!

They huddled around Phil. Formed a pack.

Together they raised their furry heads and howled at the moon.

The sound turned my blood to ice water.

Before I could move, the werewolves turned their wild eyes on me! Their fangs glowed as they began moving toward my tent.

I squeezed my eyes shut. My whole body shook.

Raw squirrel wasn't on the menu. *I* was!

The growls grew louder. My eyes popped open. The werewolves were closing in!

I opened my mouth to scream in terror. But I couldn't make a sound.

I tried to stand, but my legs had turned to jelly. My heartbeat thundered in my ears.

The pack crept closer.

Closer.

Then, Phil's eyes met mine. He put his furry hands under his chin.

And he pulled off his mask.

My mouth fell open in surprise. Phil laughed and laughed. Then Jake, Kevin, Don, and the others took their masks off and began laughing, too.

"Welcome to teen camp, Brian!" Phil shouted

through bursts of laughter. "We pull this trick on a new kid every summer. But you were the best!"

"Yeah, you really fell for it hard!" Jake hooted. He pulled a little tape recorder out of his pocket and turned it on. First I heard a single howl. After a pause, the horrifying howling I'd heard just minutes before.

"A whole pack of wolves," Jake explained. "It's on a sound effects tape!"

Phil held up the old shoes he'd carved up to make wolf tracks. Don showed me the fake fangs he'd worn during the baseball game.

Kevin held out a plastic bag. "Ketchup and chopped-up spaghetti!" he said. "Looks like raw hamburger, doesn't it?"

Dad had been right. It was all a trick.

I sighed with relief and crawled out of the tent.

The guys all laughed and slapped me on the back. "No hard feelings. Right, Brian?" Kevin asked.

I opened my mouth to say no. But all that came out was a low rumbling sound, from deep in my throat.

"Hey, Brian, the joke's over," Phil said.

Another deep rumble escaped my throat.

I felt strange. Prickly. Itchy all over.

I glanced down and saw the shaggy fur growing on the backs of my hands.

My fingernails grew, stretching into pointed claws.

I rubbed the thick, bristly fur that covered my cheeks and chin.

Snapping my jaws, I let out a sharp growl. Then I raised my face to the full moon — and howled.

Still holding their masks, the other guys stared at me in horror.

I didn't blame them. I used to be scared of werewolves, too!

I let out another long howl. So this is what Mom meant when she said everything would change soon!

My stomach rumbled. I realized I was really hungry!

I snapped my jaws. My terrified friends all started to run.

But I knew they wouldn't get far. Four legs are faster than two!

I guess Thunder Lake is going to be fun after all! I told myself.

Then I started to run.

P.S. DON'T WRITE BACK

Camp Timber Lake Hills. My new sleepaway camp. My new, really cool, sleepaway camp.

I've been here for eight days now. In Bunk 14. And I'm having a totally awesome time.

The guys in my bunk like to horse around and play tricks on each other. They're the best.

But Sam is crabby. He's the camp director. Sam is huge. Over six feet tall with a stomach that explodes over his belt. His gray, bushy mustache is the only hair that grows on his head. He's totally bald. And he never smiles. Never.

There's lots to do here. But softball is my favorite. The guys in my bunk are the best softball players in the whole camp.

Not to brag or anything, but I happen to be the bunk's star hitter. And I'm only twelve — a year younger than everyone else in the bunk.

Home Run Dave. That's what they call me.

As I said, camp is pretty excellent.

There is one problem, though.

I've been here for over a week, and I haven't received a single letter from home.

That might not sound so strange. But last summer Mom and Dad sent four letters and a carton of pretzels. And that was on the second day.

This year, so far, nothing. Not even a crummy postcard.

So when Sam grumbled, "Mail Call!" this afternoon, I raced out of the bunk. I knew he'd have a letter for me today.

Or a package.

Something.

Sam dug through his mail pouch and pulled out a bunch of letters. "Don Benson! Mark Silver! Patrick Brown!"

The guys jumped up to claim their mail.

By the time Sam finished, Don held up six letters. "Hey, guys. How many did you get?"

Jeremy waved three letters in the air.

Patrick paraded around with the new *Mutant Rat-Man* comic his dad had sent.

I had nothing.

"I can't believe this," I muttered. "Mom promised she would write!"

I know it's no big deal. Really. I mean, there must be lots of kids at camp who don't get mail.

But my parents had *promised.*

Three days later and still no mail.

I asked Sam to check with the post office. He

said he would. The post office is run by Miss Mildred. She's been in charge of the town mail forever. And in fifty years, she's never lost a letter. At least that's what she says.

I started imagining all these crazy things. Maybe Mom and Dad sent my letters to the camp I went to last summer. Or maybe there had been an earthquake, and they couldn't leave the house.

Dumb things like that.

Anyway, I finally decided to call home and find out what was going on.

"Sam," I said after mail call that day, "I need to phone home."

Sam shook his head no. "No calls home unless it's an emergency," he barked.

"But it *is* an emergency!" I insisted.

"No calls home."

The next day, after swimming, we all raced back to the bunk to change for our big softball game against Bunk 13.

"Mail Call!" Sam yelled as I tied my sneakers. I ran out to the porch in time to see Sam yank out the first letter from his pouch.

"David Stevenson! Today's your lucky day. Miss Mildred found this letter in the bottom of a drawer," Sam said, waving a crumpled envelope in the air. "She can't imagine how it got there. She mumbled something about elves. Anyway, she says she'll keep looking for more."

I practically ripped the letter from his hand. I checked the name on the front just to make sure it was really mine. Then I tore it open.

Dear David,
We're not coming up for Visiting Day. Your sister misses you. See you in August.
Mom and Dad
P.S. Don't write back.

Huh? That's it? I turned the paper over, then back again. I gazed around suspiciously. This had to be a joke from one of the guys. But they all had their heads buried in their letters. No one even glanced in my direction.

I sat down and read my letter again.

We're not coming up for Visiting Day.

How could that be? They promised. They *always* came up for Visiting Day. Always.

Your sister misses you.

No way. My older sister Carly danced around the house like a lunatic the day I left for camp. She said it was the happiest day of her life.

And *P.S. Don't write back*. That was the weirdest part of all. Why would Mom write something like that? She said she loved getting letters from me.

A huge lump stuck in my throat. I wanted to cry. But I didn't. Not until the next day.

The next afternoon, another letter came for me. Excellent! This will explain everything. I started to read.

Dear David,

We're sending you to live with your Great-uncle John. He's coming to pick you up on the 27th. We think it's for the best.

Mom and Dad

P.S. Don't write back.

"What?" I choked.

The letter shook in my trembling hands. How can they send me to live with Great-uncle John? I mean, he's eighty-seven years old and lives in an old-age home!

I glanced up and stared into the trees across from my bunk. They started to spin around me. My hands grew numb. Then they turned to ice. My eyes filled with tears.

I leaped up and ran. All the way to the camp office. Up the steps. To the front door. It was locked.

I peered through the window screen. No one inside. But there — hanging on the wall. The phone! I had to get to that phone.

I twisted around to my left. Then to my right. No one in sight. Good. I gently raised the screen and crept over the windowsill into the office. Then I darted for the phone and dialed.

By the third ring, my palms dripped with sweat. Beads of perspiration clung to my forehead.

"C'mon! Pick up!" I shifted my weight from one foot to the other. "Come on already!"

Then, finally! On the fourth ring my mother answered!

"Mom!" I cried. "What's going on?"

" — not home right now. Please leave a message. And have a nice — "

Oh, no! I heard voices. Outside. Coming toward the office. No time to leave a message.

Think, Dave! Think! Get out of here quick!

Then I spied it. A window at the back of the office. I threw open the screen and dived out.

I charged back to the bunk. Panting wildly. I leaped up the porch steps. The door flew open.

And there stood Sam. A stone statue. Glaring at me.

"Stevenson! You're in big trouble."

"But, Sam — " I started to explain.

"No, Stevenson. You're late for the scavenger hunt. In the woods. Remember? Now you'll have to catch up with the other guys." He shuffled down the stairs and headed for the trees.

The scavenger hunt. Right. A hike through the woods. Then a campfire supper. Then the hunt. I had forgotten.

I tossed everything out of my drawers, searching for stuff for the scavenger hunt. My sweatshirt. Backpack. Flashlight.

How could my parents do this to me? I kept repeating over and over to myself as I searched the bunk frantically for my flashlight.

And then I saw it. Under my bed, *next* to the flashlight. The envelope. From the letter this afternoon.

I read the address again. David Stevenson, Camp Timber Lane Hills.

That's it! Why hadn't I noticed it before? My camp is Camp Timber *Lake* Hills!

Now it made sense. Camp Timber *Lane* Hills stood on the other side of the lake.

A mix-up. Simple as that. I breathed a small sigh of relief. Those letters weren't for me. They were for some other David Stevenson. At some other camp. And he probably had *my* letters!

I grabbed my flashlight and stuffed it into my backpack.

I knew what I had to do. While everyone searched for clues on the scavenger hunt, I would escape across the lake and find Camp Timber Lane — and the other David Stevenson.

* * *

As soon as the scavenger hunt began, I slipped away in the dark and headed for the dock.

The camp rowboats bobbed gently up and down on the moonlit water. I steadied one and climbed inside.

I leaned over and tugged on the rope that held the anchor. Heavy. Very heavy. I clutched the rope with two hands and heaved.

Uh-oh. Not as heavy as I thought.

The anchor flew out of the water — and crashed on to the boat floor.

The boat pitched from side to side. I crouched down and grasped the oarlocks tightly. And waited. Waited to be caught.

Silence.

I breathed a low, steadying sigh. Then I locked the oars in place and began to row.

As I cut through the water, the twinkling lights from camp grew smaller and smaller. I turned to glance at the opposite shore. Thick woods. Total blackness. Maybe this wasn't such a good idea.

But I had to get to the other camp. I wanted my mail.

I rowed faster. My arms ached. Tiny splashes around the oars thundered in my ears. My head throbbed.

Then, finally. A dock!

I dropped the anchor and stepped up. The

dock's rotted wood splintered and cracked under my sneakers.

Where is the path? I wondered, sweeping my flashlight over thick weeds.

I stumbled through the dark. Through the tall, scratchy grass that scraped against my legs.

Suddenly, the beam from my flashlight fell upon a big wooden sign. I stood directly in front of it to read the worn letters. CAMP TIMBER LANE HILLS.

I found it!

I gazed beyond the sign. I squinted in the darkness. Yes! Bunks.

But where were all the kids? And why didn't they have any lights in this camp?

Weird. Very weird.

I trampled through the grass to the first bunk. A skinny boy, about my age, hunched over the porch railing. He raised his head slowly. His hollowed eyes met mine.

"Uh, excuse me," I stammered. "Is there a David Stevenson in this camp?"

He lifted a bony arm and pointed to the blackened doorway behind him.

"Uh, thanks," I said. But I didn't budge. I wanted to go back. Back to my cheery, normal camp.

Just go in, I told myself. Just get your letters.

I inched past the boy and pushed open the

creaky door. My hand trembled as I searched the dark room with my flashlight. No one here.

I'm leaving, I decided. This place is too creepy. Way too creepy. But as I turned, I caught sight of something. No. Someone. Someone moving in the shadows.

"Who . . . who's there?" I choked out.

"What do you want?" a harsh voice replied.

"I'm, uh, looking for David Stevenson."

"Well, you found him," the voice snapped back.

I shone my light to the very back of the bunk. And there he stood. A scrawny kid with long brown hair and torn, dirty clothes.

"What do you want?" this David Stevenson demanded with an icy stare.

I couldn't answer. My heart thumped wildly.

"I said, what do you want?" he repeated.

I gulped loudly and began. "I have your mail."

His eyes narrowed angrily. "My what?"

I pulled the letters from my pocket and held them out. "Your mail. Letters from home," I explained. "And I'd like mine. If you have them."

"Who are you?" he demanded. He stepped closer to me.

"I'm David Stevenson, too," I replied. "You see, I go to Camp — "

"Leave!" he screamed, shaking his fists violently. "You can't let them see you here!"

Oh, wow! This kid is crazy!

"Listen," I pleaded. "Just give me my letters and I'll go."

"Go! Go! Go!" he shrieked.

I flew out the door and down the steps. The skinny kid had disappeared.

I staggered through the thick grass, darting around tree stumps and boulders.

Then I noticed a familiar smell. The smell of a campfire. I listened. Crackling. Loud snapping.

I crouched down behind a large rock. I spied the flickering light of the campfire. And kids, hundreds of kids, circling it. Arms wrapped around each other. Swaying back and forth. Moaning. Moaning.

What kind of camp is this? I wondered.

I swallowed hard. Something is really wrong here!

I jumped up, ready to bolt. But a long, skinny arm swooped down and grabbed my hand.

The kid from the porch! His eyes glowed an evil red as he tugged me toward the fire.

I struggled to break free. But I couldn't escape from the skinny kid's grip.

The swaying campers turned to face us. Moaning.

Their sunken eyes stared blankly into mine. Were they in some kind of weird trance?

They dropped their arms. And parted for us.

My face flushed in the heat of the leaping flames.

And then I knew what would come next. They were going to push me. Into the fire.

"Nooo!" I screamed.

With a hard tug, I broke free. And ran. Faster than I'd ever run before.

I leaped into the boat. I rowed swiftly across the lake. Then I charged up to my bunk.

Sam paced on the porch, back and forth. Back and forth.

"Sam! Sam!" I cried breathlessly.

"Stevenson! Where have you been? The whole camp is out searching for you! And your mother called. She said they had to go away — "

"Sam! Listen!" In one long breath, I told Sam about everything. The camp. The other David Stevenson. The sad, moaning campers. The skinny kid who tried to drag me into the fire.

Sam stared hard at me. "David, what are you talking about? We're the only camp on this lake."

"No! You're wrong, Sam. I saw it. The sign said Camp Timber Lane Hills!"

Sam rubbed his chin thoughtfully. "Well, there once was a camp across the lake," he said. "But it burned to the ground one summer thirty years ago."

"No!" I shrieked. "It's there. I'll show you!"

Sam ushered me up the bunk steps. "We're not going anywhere tonight. We'll straighten all this out in the morning."

"But — "

"In the morning!" Sam repeated sternly. "Now get inside and go to sleep!"

I staggered to my bed in a daze.

"I know what I saw," I mumbled as I climbed into bed.

I grabbed my flashlight and pulled the covers up over my head. I flicked on the light and flashed it on one of the envelopes that I had just received.

"See. I'm not crazy. It says right here. David Stevenson. Camp Timber Lane Hills."

Then I pointed the light along the top right corner of the envelope. And gasped.

The postmark.

It was dated July 10.

1964.

SOMETHING FISHY

"You mean I have to sit in this horrible, hot apartment ALL SUMMER! But, Mom — it's so boring here!"

We always go to the lake. Every single summer. And now she was telling me that we couldn't go.

"It's the money, Eric," Mom said. "It costs a lot to rent a house on the lake, and we don't have it this year."

This had been a terrible year for money. The year of the divorce. The year that everything had gone wrong.

Mom stood in the corner of my bedroom and stared at me. I guess she thought I was going to cry or something. But I didn't cry. I smiled and told her it was okay — even though it wasn't.

After she left, I sprawled on my bed. I closed my eyes and tried to picture the lake. The water was probably bluish-gray today. And clear.

I scrunched my eyes tightly and tried to imagine how it felt. Cold. Nice. I could almost feel the sandy bottom of the lake squish between my toes.

"Eric?" It was my sister, Sarah. Her voice brought me back to my own room.

"Can't you ever knock!" I shouted.

Sarah never knocks. She's nine. Three years younger than me. But she should still knock.

Sarah and I are different in lots of ways. I have brown hair and brown eyes. She has red hair and green eyes. I'm nice, and she isn't. I knock, and she doesn't.

"Well?" I sighed as I rolled off the bed and stomped across the room to my fish tank.

"We're not going to the lake," Sarah announced.

"I know that, Sarah," I groaned.

"But it's boiling here in the city. And we don't have air-conditioning, or anything."

"Don't remind me," I said. "Leave me alone. It's too hot to talk."

She shuffled her feet for a while, but then she left my room. Of course she forgot to close the door behind her.

I gazed into my fish tank and thought about the sweltering city heat. My T-shirt was already sticking to my back. And it was only June. What would it be like by August?

I sprinkled some food into the water and sat down. The fish raced toward it. First the big fish. Then the medium-sized fish.

The little fish almost killed each other fighting over the leftovers.

Well, at least the fish will be able to go swimming this summer, I thought. Lucky fish.

I woke up early the next day. It was brutally hot. It must have been 100 degrees in my room.

I glanced at the clock and groaned. Eight in the morning, and the heat was unbearable. I didn't even bother getting dressed. I just put on my shorts and shuffled out to the kitchen.

Mom was frying bacon and wiping her forehead on her sleeve. "I'll buy some fans today," she promised. She slid a plate of pancakes and bacon under my nose.

I took a few bites. I wasn't very hungry. It was too hot to eat.

I walked back into my room and gazed into the fish tank. The fish seemed fresh and happy. They were flicking through the water like silver and gold flashes of cool lightning.

I wondered what it would be like to be a fish. It must feel fantastic, swimming around like that in the cool water.

I followed the fish for a long time. Back and forth. Back and forth. Until my mother came in.

"Allowance day, Eric," she announced. "Maybe you can buy something cold this afternoon. Like an ice cream. Or buy another fish. One of those exotic fish that you love so much."

I didn't want to buy a fish. I wanted to BE a fish. In the lake.

I called my friend Benny, but there was no answer. And then I remembered. Benny went to Colorado with his parents. My friend Leo was on his way to camp. And Dweezle the Weazel was at his grandmother's for the summer.

Wow. What a boring summer.

I spent my allowance at the pet store. I bought a castle for my fish tank. It was pink, with all kinds of doors and windows.

The fish seemed to like it. They swam in and out of it as if it were their new home.

They liked it so much that the next week I bought them a tiny purple rowboat. And the week after that, I bought them a new friend — a plastic diving figure with a long, sharp spear in his hand. They seemed to like that, too.

I gazed at my fish whenever I wasn't at the playground behind school or watching TV or at my computer. I couldn't stop staring at them.

And then, late one night, something seriously strange happened.

My room felt like a furnace. I lay on my bed without moving. My shorts were sticking to the backs of my legs. My socks were clammy and gross.

I turned and glanced at the tank. I stood up. The glow from the fish tank drew me across my shadowy room.

I pulled my desk chair over to the fish tank and gazed at the fish. My gourami streaked through the castle and circled the boat. Again and again.

One of my platys disappeared under the boat. The bubbles from the filter kept swirling round and round and round. The bubbles faded in and out of focus. Gurgling, gurgling, gurgling.

I raised my left index finger and touched the cool water. I dipped my finger deeper into the tank and twirled it.

My finger seemed to have a mind of its own. It moved in a circle, then drew a perfect figure eight. It formed another, and then another. Five times clockwise. Two counterclockwise. Three to the side. Again, and again, and again.

In the hall, I heard the clock strike ten times. I drew one more figure eight through the water with my index finger.

And then, as I sat there with my eyes half closed, the weirdest thing happened.

As the clock struck ten, I suddenly felt wet. And cold.

I blinked several times, trying to understand. I spun around and kicked my feet.

And faced a fish. Eye to beady eye. It was right there, goggling me.

"Whoa!" I cried. "Did I fall in the fish tank?"

I plunged through the water and looked above me. The fish were staring down at me. And they were HUGE! Like whales. Even the smallest goldfish were gigantic.

"How did I get down here?" I gurgled. "What's

happened to me? I'm smaller than a goldfish! And I can breathe under water!"

I should have been scared. But this was too exciting!

I couldn't believe it! I dived to the bottom of the tank and did a somersault. Awesome!

I swam around for a long time. I did a dozen surface dives. I plunged down and touched the bottom. I stood on my head. Then I zoomed back up to the top and flicked some water at one of my goldfish.

The goldfish didn't seem happy. His jellylike eyes gazed at me menacingly. And then he began to move. Slowly. Straight toward me.

I raced to the purple rowboat and threw myself into it. The boat lurched and water poured in. But it didn't sink.

The goldfish took his time. Slowly, it began to circle the boat. Around, and around, and around, watching me menacingly.

Did it plan to attack?

I huddled in the bottom of the little boat all night. I wished the goldfish would stop circling me.

I lost all track of time. After a while, sunlight washed over the fish tank. Morning!

I heard a familiar voice from far away. "Eric? Eric?"

My sister! I was never so glad to hear her voice.

"Sarah!" I called. "I'm over here! I'm in the fish tank!"

Peering over the side of the boat, I could see her moving around my room. "Sarah! Over here!" I shouted, cupping my hands around my mouth. "Look in the fish tank! Over here!"

She didn't turn around. She couldn't hear me. I was about the size of an ant. How could I expect her to hear an ant's tiny cry?

Gazing through the glass side of the tank, I saw my sister step closer. "Yes!" I cried aloud. "Yes! She's coming over here!"

She bent down and stared at the fish.

"Here! Over here!" I cried. I jumped up and started waving both arms. I nearly tipped over the boat. "Sarah! Sarah!"

A big gourami floated in front of me, blocking me from view.

When the fish swam away, Sarah was gone.

Now what? I asked myself. I've had my swim. I've had my excitement for one summer. It's time to get out. It's time to get big again.

The enormous goldfish came rolling toward me again. "Look out!" I cried.

Too late. The big fish bumped up hard against the side of the boat. "Hey —!" I cried out as I felt the boat tip. I toppled into the water with a splash.

The fish slid past me. I could feel his scaly skin brush my side. Yuck!

I heard a disgusting sucking sound. I turned and saw the gaping round mouth pulling at the water. Pulling me toward the hungry fish.

I'm going to be fish food! I realized.

I tried to swim faster. But my side started to ache. The sucking sounds grew louder. The fish was pulling me into its mouth.

A desperate idea flashed into my mind. The deep-sea diver! I kicked my feet hard and dived down to the plastic figure.

I grabbed the spear away from the diver — and spun around to face my enemy.

The other fish all scattered to the sides of the tank.

The goldfish attacked, shooting through the water.

I dodged away. Kicked hard. Dived to the bottom of the tank.

I waited, watching it circle. I raised the spear.

I took aim — and sent the spear sailing toward it.

Missed.

That fish was too fast.

I saw its eyes flare with anger. It dived toward me. I pressed my back against the side of the tank. It whipped around and smacked me with its tail.

Stunned, my knees buckled, and I started to drop to the tank floor.

The spear floated down to the bottom. I grabbed it just as the fish attacked again.

The huge yellow body soared toward me. I drew back my arm — and drove the spear into the fish's underbelly.

What am I doing? I asked myself, watching it float onto its side. *I just killed one of my pets!*

But I couldn't worry about it. I mean, it had just tried to *eat* me!

The dead goldfish floated to the top. But I didn't have time to relax. The other fish were eyeing me now.

I grabbed the spear and held it ready. Was I going to have to fight them all, one by one?

Two neons darted close. They were my smallest fish. But now they were bigger than me! If they decided to attack together, I was doomed!

Then, from far away, I heard voices. The words were muffled by the water. But through the glass, I saw Mom and Sarah.

They were walking about my room. I guessed they wondered where I was.

I knew I couldn't call to them. Especially from the bottom of the tank! But how could I signal them? How could I get their attention?

My heart started to pound when I saw Sarah walk over to the fish tank. She stared down into the water. Then she poked a finger in and flicked the dead fish.

"Mom — there's a dead fish in here!" I heard her call.

I saw Mom step up beside Sarah and stare down

at the dead goldfish. Then I saw Mom pick up the white net I keep at the side of the tank.

The net! She's going to use it to lift out the dead fish, I realized.

I took a deep breath and leaped off the tank floor. I started swimming to the top as hard as I could.

I kicked and thrashed through the water. I had to get into that net. It was my only chance to escape.

Up, up, I swam. I reached the surface, gasping, every muscle aching. I grabbed the rim of the net with both hands — and pulled myself up and in.

Yes!

I tried to stand. Tried to wave to my mom. But the net wiggled in the water. It dipped low. I struggled to stay inside.

"Owww!" I cried out as something heavy landed on top of me.

Something heavy. And very smelly.

The dead goldfish.

I tried to shove it off me, but I wasn't strong enough. I couldn't breathe. It was *crushing* me!

And then I felt the water fall away. The net was lifted from the tank. The heavy fish bounced on top of me.

Mom was carrying the net out of the room. I tried to call out. But the dead fish smothered my face.

Where was she taking me?

Oh, no! I knew where! She was taking me to the burial place of all pet goldfish.

The bathroom!

"Please, Mom!" I cried, shoving the dead fish off me. "Please don't flush me! Please don't flush your only son, Mom!"

I climbed on top of the dead fish. But she still couldn't hear me.

"Please don't flush me! I'm in here, too, Mom! It's me! Please don't flush me!"

She tilted the net. I tried to grab the side. Missed.

And went sailing down.

Down, down.

I shut my eyes as I fell. I felt the air whip around me, drying my tiny body.

I waited for the splash.

But my feet hit the floor instead.

Startled, I opened my eyes. I stood face to face with Mom.

She was so stunned, she dropped the net. "Eric! Where did you come from?" she shrieked.

"Oh. Uh . . . I was in my room," I said, trying to sound casual.

But I didn't feel casual. I felt like leaping up and down and screaming, "I'm me again! I'm me!"

How did I get back to my old size? I thought about it a lot that day. I decided that getting dry was the answer. As soon as the air dried me off, I zoomed up to my old size.

And I'm going to stay this size, I promised myself.

I kept the promise for two days. Then the temperature outside soared to 102. I could barely breathe. I needed a swim — desperately.

I stared into the fish tank, remembering how cold and refreshing the water felt. Yes, I knew it was dangerous. I knew what a close call I'd had. I knew that going back in the tank was a crazy idea.

But it was also really exciting. *And* I was sweltering.

This time, I'll be more careful, I told myself. First I got a bag of little stones. I built a wall down the center of the tank. The fish could swim on one side of the wall. I'd swim on the other.

My own little swimming pool.

When I'm tired of swimming, I'll stand up on the rocks and let the air dry me. And I'll instantly return to my big size.

What could go wrong?

I slid my finger into the fish tank and traced a clockwise figure eight. I did it five times. Then I changed directions and traced five more figure eights.

The filter bubbles gurgled . . . gurgled . . . gurgled. . . .

And once again I was tiny, plunging into the water for a refreshing swim.

I had swum for only a minute or two when I heard voices at the top of the tank. Floating slowly, I glanced up. I was surprised to see Mom and Sarah.

"Where's Eric?" I heard Mom ask, her voice muffled by the water. "Where is he? I brought him such a nice surprise."

"Who knows?" I heard Sarah reply. "He keeps disappearing."

Mom leaned closer to the tank. She had a plastic bag in her hand. The bag held two fish. I stared up from the bottom of my private pool.

"Look, Sarah," I heard Mom exclaim. "Eric built a perfect little swimming pool for my present. He piled up rocks and moved the fish to one side. I'll bet he guessed what I was going to buy for him."

"What is it?" I heard Sarah ask. "What did you get him?"

Mom held the bag over the top of the tank. Then she dumped the two new fish into my private swimming pool.

"They are Siamese fighting fish," Mom told Sarah. "The meanest fish on earth! Look at them snap their teeth. Won't Eric be surprised?"

YOU GOTTA BELIEVE ME!

I know you won't believe me. Nobody else does. I told my parents. I told my teachers. I told the police. I told the newspapers. I've even written to the President of the United States. Hah. I might as well have told my pet turtle, Mable. (Which I did.)

I just saved the world from weird aliens from outer space.

Uh-oh. I can almost hear you thinking, "Weird aliens from outer space? This kid must be nuts!"

But I'm not. Really.

The whole thing started because of the flying saucers. And the flying saucers started because of the no-TV rule. I must be the only kid in the entire *world* whose parents won't have a TV in the house.

"TV rots your brain," my dad says.

"There're plenty of things to do. You don't have to sit in front of a box that tells you how to think," my mom insists.

My parents are old hippies from the sixties. They believe that stuff. So the only TV I get to watch is at Robbie's house, and at Melanie's house. They're my best friends. I try to catch the most popular shows so I don't sound like too much of a geek when everyone talks about them. But I don't watch much.

To make up for no TV, my parents bought me a telescope a few years ago. It was nice of them, I guess. They knew I liked reading science fiction about outer space and stuff.

When you don't have a TV, there's not much to do after homework. So I started watching the sky every night.

And I started seeing flying saucers.

Some were round, with red and green lights. Some were shaped like paper-towel rolls. Some were big. Some were small. It was truly amazing how crowded it was up there.

Most of them turned out to be weather satellites and stuff from Earth. But others were real. I swear they were. Sure, nobody else saw the flying saucers. But nobody else watched for them.

My mom and dad just laughed. "It must be an airplane, Stanley," Dad would tell me. "Or a bird, dear," Mom would add.

"He just wants attention," my older sister, Laura, said. *She* was the one sneaking out early to put on makeup. To get the attention of Herbie, the high school heartthrob.

"Stanley is a geek," offered my little brother, Dan. *He* was the one who made giant balls out of aluminum foil. And *I* was a geek? Hah!

All my teachers thought I was telling stories. And when I called the police, they treated me like a nut.

Then there were my so-called best friends.

"Stan," said Robbie, best friend number one, "you are a total weirdo."

Now, I can tell you that I'm not a weirdo. I'm a perfectly normal twelve-year-old guy. I'm in seventh grade at Piscopo Junior High. I'm five feet four inches tall. I have brown hair and blue eyes, and I wear wire-rimmed glasses. I'm good at math and science. And I play a mean game of hoops.

"He just has a good imagination," said Melanie, best friend number two.

Well, that's probably true. But I don't make things up. Not things that count.

"Look," I told Robbie and Melanie, "I can understand if my family doesn't believe me. I can understand if my teachers don't believe me. I can understand if the cops don't believe me. But you are different. We've been best friends since we were wearing diapers."

Melanie sighed. "Stanley. We *are* your best friends. And we've been your best friends for a long time. That's why we think you should give this outer space thing a rest. There isn't enough room up there for all the flying saucers you've seen!"

And that was that . . . until two days later. Wednesday, July 12. The night that would change my life forever.

It was eleven o'clock, and I couldn't sleep. I felt crummy. It was really hot in my bedroom. Sweat dripped down my neck.

I stared at the green digital numbers on the clock next to my bed. 11:01. 11:02. 11:03.

I couldn't sleep. I got up and trotted downstairs. I poured myself a glass of carrot juice (my parents' favorite drink). Then I stood at the back door. I stared out through the window. It was hazy and dark.

A crack of lightning flashed across the sky. Then came the thunder. *Ka-boom!* It made me jump. Then it started to pour.

At first, I thought I saw another lightning bolt. I squinted and stared hard. Something flashed — but it wasn't lightning.

I ran upstairs to my bedroom. My telescope sat in the window. I pointed it at the flashing light to take a better look. And what I saw made me sweat harder than ever.

A flying saucer!

Round, big, and bright. With lots of white lights around it. The lights kept flashing, which is why it looked a little like lightning. It floated above the ground over one of Mr. Tribble's cornfields.

I rubbed my eyes. Was I dreaming? I didn't think so.

I pinched myself on the arm just to be sure. It hurt.

The saucer suddenly lifted off and shot away.

Mr. Tribble had a bad reputation. He used to chase kids off his land with a pitchfork. He acted mean and strange, and his wife seemed just as weird. Nobody showed up anywhere near his farm if they could help it.

But I couldn't help it. I had to go over there. I had to see what had happened in that field.

I pulled on my jeans and a T-shirt. I picked up my sneakers.

Carefully, I tiptoed downstairs. I didn't want to wake anybody. I wanted to see what was going on for myself. I opened the front door and sneaked out.

It was still raining, but I hardly noticed. I ran all the way. Finally I reached Mr. Tribble's big red barn. I tiptoed over to the end. Then I peered around the corner.

The cornfield was empty. But when I glanced down, I noticed something weird. It looked as if someone had burned a circle in the ground.

I walked slowly over to the burned part. I reached down to touch it. Something had been here.

When I turned around, Mr. Tribble stood behind me.

His eyes were glittery and angry. And he carried a pitchfork.

"What are you doing in my cornfield?!" Mr. Tribble demanded.

"Mr. Tribble!" I gasped. "Am I glad to see you! A flying saucer landed in your cornfield. Look at those marks — "

"There wasn't anything here," Mr. Tribble said sharply.

"But you *had* to see it!" I cried. "It was here a minute ago. Then it flew away. . . ."

"No. Nothing here!" Mr. Tribble repeated.

He started walking toward me. His eyes glittered. He bared his teeth. The pitchfork glimmered in the dark.

I ran.

The next morning at breakfast, I told everyone my big news.

"And I think Mr. Tribble knows something," I finished. "What do you guys think we should do?"

"Pass the whole-grain toast," Laura said.

"Mrph," Dan said with his mouth full.

"Dan, don't talk with your mouth full," my mom warned.

"Look at this. The factory is closing," my dad groaned. "Another defeat for the workers. It says right here. . . ."

And that was that.

My friends were no better.

"Look, Stan," Robbie said. "This has happened before. It's just your imagination."

"Imagination my foot!" I yelled. "Come on over to the field and see for yourself!"

"There is no way I'm going over to Tribble's farm," Melanie shivered. "He is totally creepy."

"All right," I said angrily. "Suit yourself! I'll figure out what to do alone."

And I did. I came up with a brilliant plan. I decided to get my dad's camera and take pictures of the burned circle. Then they'd have to believe me.

Wouldn't they?

The next night, I wore my clothes to bed. I pulled the covers up to my chin so my parents couldn't tell.

I had Dad's camera under my pillow. I was ready. I just had to wait until everyone fell asleep.

I stared at the clock. 11:46. 11:47. I planned to leave at midnight.

I looked out the window. And then I looked again.

The spaceship slid down into Mr. Tribble's cornfield.

I grabbed the camera and quietly ran out of the house.

I crept past Mr. Tribble's house. I could see the light from his TV through the window. I breathed a sigh of relief. If he kept watching TV, maybe he wouldn't come looking for me.

When I reached the barn, my heart practically stopped beating.

The flying saucer stood there.

It was much bigger than I thought. It was about as big as half a football field!

It was bright and shiny. There were stairs going up into the center of it. And walking up and down the stairs were THEM.

The aliens! The things from outer space!

They were big, too — the size of Mr. Tribble's cows. But they didn't look anything like cows.

They didn't look like anything else I'd ever seen, except in nightmares. Their skin was a mucus-green color.

They had giant, mushed-in heads with big, glittery eyes. They had tentacles all over their heads where their hair should be. They walked on six legs. Two arms grew out of their backs. And instead of hands, they had giant claws.

A slimy green goo dripped from their bodies.

My mouth dropped open, and I started to shake. I wanted to get out of there . . . fast.

But I couldn't leave. I had to see what they were doing there.

A few aliens held strange-looking silver instruments. Every few minutes, they pointed them at the sky.

And then two aliens slithered right toward me.

Had they seen me?

No.

The aliens started to talk. Their voices sounded gloppy, as if they had bad colds. And to my surprise, they were definitely speaking English!

"We are almost at stage three," slobbered Alien Number One. "This signal will be the final one."

"It is the Earthlings' own fault," slobbered Alien Number Two. "Sending television waves out into space gave us the idea."

"Once we learned their language," Alien Number One said, "and we understood the importance of television to them, it was just a matter of time."

"It has been ten long years. The invisible messages we have been broadcasting through their TV programs have made them weak and stupid. Earthlings do not believe in flying saucers. They think we are science *fiction*." Alien Number Two snuffled. Maybe it was laughing.

"This last message will finish them," Alien Number One continued. "They will not be able to resist. They will be helpless before us. They will simply give up."

"When do we broadcast?" Alien Number Two asked.

"In exactly twenty Earth hours," Alien Number One answered. "We start at eight o'clock tomorrow. What the Earthlings call 'prime time.' "

I couldn't believe my ears.

All these years, TV really *had* been weakening the human race! Just as my parents said!

Maybe the no-TV rule had been a good idea after all.

The two aliens slithered away. Then I saw a big door open in the top of the spaceship.

All the aliens stopped what they were doing and turned around to watch. I heard a whirring sound. A big silver dish rose out of the ship.

It looked a lot like a TV satellite dish.

That's when I remembered the camera. I had to take some pictures. With my luck, they probably wouldn't come out. But I had to try.

My hands were shaking so hard, I almost couldn't work the buttons.

When I had taken about five pictures, it happened.

I felt a tickle in my nose. It grew and grew. I didn't want to make any noise. But I couldn't help myself.

I sneezed.

Five aliens turned around and stared at the spot where I hid. Before I could move, they darted toward me.

My heart pounded in my chest. I tried to yell. But all that came out was a croak.

I couldn't breathe. I tried to run. But my feet felt as if they were stuck to the ground.

One of the aliens carried a silver bag. The creature took out a kind of tube.

Another alien grabbed me. The first one jammed the tube into my side.

"Ow!" I cried. Then everything went black.

When I woke up, it was dark. I tried to get up, but I couldn't. Someone . . . some*thing* . . . had strapped me to a table.

I was on the spaceship.

I picked my head up and gazed around. The only light in the room came from a giant TV. It hung in the air about six feet in front of me.

"Just watch the television," a gloppy alien voice said in the darkness.

A rerun of *Space Trekkers* was on. I had heard of the show, but never seen it.

I closed my eyes. I didn't want to watch. But the alien voice said, "Open your eyes, human." Something in its tone told me I'd better listen. So I did.

And I watched.

For three hours.

I expected to feel strange. I expected to get hypnotized or something.

But nothing happened.

I guess you had to watch a lot of alien TV for their waves to work.

Suddenly, the TV went blank.

"How do you feel?" asked the alien voice.

"Fine," I replied in a flat voice. I tried to sound hypnotized.

"Good," said the voice. "Now, go home. You have not been here. When we come, you will be ready."

"I will be ready," I said again in my hypnotized voice.

The next thing I knew, I found myself outside the spaceship. I wanted to run, but I thought it wouldn't be a good idea. I had to pretend to be under the aliens' spell. So I just strolled away, slowly.

Inside the house, I raced upstairs to my parents' bedroom. My legs were weak. My chest burned. I could hardly breathe.

"Mom! Dad! There's a flying saucer!" I gasped. "They caught me. And they're sending a TV signal out that will make us all slaves! Tomorrow night at eight! We've got to do something!"

My dad sat up in bed. My mom opened her eyes.

"You had a bad dream, Stanley," Dad told me. "Go back to sleep."

"No, no! It was real!" I yelled. "You've gotta believe me. You've got to!"

"Stanley." Mom sat up, too. "It was just a dream. But I'm glad you're beginning to understand why we don't watch television."

"Go to bed, son," my dad said. "We'll talk about it in the morning."

"The entire world is in danger, and you don't believe me!" I wailed.

Then I remembered the pictures. "I have pictures!" I cried. "I took them tonight! They prove it!"

I reached around my neck for the camera.

It was gone.

The next day, Saturday, I called Melanie at eight o'clock in the morning. I think I woke her up. I didn't care. I told her everything.

"Uh, Stanley." Melanie sounded unhappy. "This is really getting too strange. Could you just stop it?"

"I can't stop it," I told her. "I'm telling the truth."

"Yeah, right," she muttered.

When I called Robbie, it was the same story.

"Sure it happened," Robbie said. "And I come from Jupiter!"

I decided to try the police.

"Hey!" Officer Banks cried when I walked up to the station. "It's the flying saucer kid. See another one, kid?"

A couple of the other officers laughed. I just stared at them. They wouldn't believe me, either.

I left the station. I looked around. It was a normal, sunny day. People walked around. No one knew that aliens were about to take over the world. No one seemed to care.

I cared.

And I had an idea.

The aliens had built something to send out their

weird waves. Maybe I could build something that would get in the way of them, so they wouldn't reach anyone's TV set.

Maybe I could build a mirror, to reflect the alien waves back at them. I raced over to Robbie's house.

"I need to borrow some money," I told him. "As much as you have."

"How come?" he asked.

"To save the world, of course!" I told him.

Robbie didn't believe me. But he did lend me the money.

So did Melanie. They're pretty good friends. I raced over to the supermarket. I grabbed a cart. And I filled it with every single roll of aluminum foil in the store.

When I got to the checkout, Mr. Barnes looked at me and blinked. "What do you want with all that foil, Stanley?" he asked.

"Science experiment for school," I lied.

The total came to $134.59. I didn't have enough money.

"My parents will come in tomorrow and pay you," I told him. *If the aliens don't win,* I added under my breath.

I dragged the foil home to my garage. I started building my giant mirror.

I ran out of foil when the mirror was about twice as big as my dining room table. Then I carried it to Mr. Tribble's farm. Luckily, silver foil doesn't weigh a whole lot.

I made sure no one saw me with my mirror. I hid it in the woods behind the barn. Then I crawled closer to see what was going on.

The alien ship sat there. The satellite dish appeared ready.

It looked awfully big. I didn't think my little foil screen would do the trick. But I was running out of time. It was already six-thirty. Then I had another brilliant idea.

I raced home. I crept into my brother Dan's room. And I stole his gigantic foil ball.

I never thought it would come in handy. I guess Dan isn't such a dweeb after all.

The foil from the ball made my screen a lot bigger. I still didn't know if it would work. But I had to try.

I managed to haul the screen up to a high branch of a big maple tree. From there, I could see the alien satellite dish.

I only hoped the aliens couldn't see me. But they didn't seem to be around. Maybe they were in their ship, getting ready.

I pointed my screen in the right direction.

Then I waited.

At exactly eight o'clock, a blue light came streaming from the alien dish.

I held my breath.

The light hit my reflector and bounced right back to the alien ship.

I waited. That's when the blue light went out.

I held my breath.

The alien dish pulled back into the ship. And then the ship took off, straight up into the air. The last I saw of it, it was soaring toward the stars.

I left the silver foil up in the tree. I don't know what happened to it. Mr. Tribble probably thought some kids were playing a joke on him.

And then I went home.

What was I supposed to do? Tell somebody? No way.

Maybe the flying saucer will come back. But I doubt it. My guess is, the aliens got a dose of their own medicine. They're probably flying through outer space right now, watching reruns of *I Love Lucy* and slobbering all over each other.

I saved the world from weird aliens from outer space. But no one will believe me.

I finally did tell Robbie and Melanie, a few days later. But they just asked for their money back.

Then I tried telling my parents, one last time.

"I totally agree," my mom said. "TV could definitely take over the world."

"Pass the tofu," my dad said.

"How do I look, Mom?" my sister Laura asked. "I'm going out with Herbie later."

"You stole my aluminum foil ball!" My brother Dan glared at me. "I just know it."

So that's the end of my story. Unless the aliens come back. And I can get some pictures to prove that the whole thing happened.

I spend a lot of time behind my telescope these days.

Hey. Over there. Did you see those flashing lights?

It's back! Look — the alien ship is back!

You believe me — *don't* you?

SUCKERS!

"Gross!" I shrieked.

Alex Pratt shook the wiggling jellyfish in my face. "What's the matter, Ashley? Scared of a little jellyfish?"

"She's a wimp! All summer people are wimps!" Jimmy Stern exclaimed. He's Alex's best friend.

Alex and Jimmy are fourteen years old. A year older than me. They think they're really cool because they live on Black Island all year round. And anybody who doesn't live here is a wimp.

And that includes my little brother, Jack, and my cousin Greg.

"Drop it on her head! Go on! Do it!" Jimmy urged, pushing his dark, greasy hair out of his eyes.

Alex snickered. He dangled the jellyfish over my head. Then he lowered it. Slowly.

"Leave her alone!" my cousin Greg yelled. He was hiding behind me. You know, I think they might be right about Greg. He is kind of wimpy.

Alex pushed me aside. Not hard to do. Alex stands at least a foot taller than me and is twice as wide!

"I smell gummies," Alex crowed. He moved in closer to Greg. He shoved him back hard. "Hand them over, Greggie."

"No way," Greg replied. "And quit shoving me. Please."

"Yeah," Jack echoed. "Quit shoving him. Or you'll be in big trouble. I take karate, you know."

"The Karate Kid," Jimmy sneered.

"And Gummy Boy," added Alex. "Get them!"

Alex and Jimmy jumped. They knocked Greg and Jack down into the sand. Then Alex sat on top of Greg.

"Look what I found!" Alex said, pulling out a big bag of gummies from Greg's pocket. He lifted the bag and emptied it into his mouth.

Then the two tough guys jumped up and ran.

"Alex and Jimmy are ruining our whole summer!" I wailed.

We walked along the beach. Greg plucked a piece of driftwood from the shore and hurled it into the ocean.

"I hate those creeps more than anything," he muttered. "I'm going to make them pay."

"Yeah," Jack cried with enthusiasm. "When I earn my black belt, I'll karate them. My teacher says I'm lightning!"

Greg rolled his eyes. "You have about ten belts

to go," he reminded Jack. Then he slid his hands into the front pocket of his shorts. His face lit up.

"Hey! They didn't get all my gummies!"

He fished a crumpled bag out of his right pocket. Then he dropped a few of the slimy candies into his mouth. Greg chomps a few dozen of them a day.

He passed the bag to Jack. "Want one?"

Jack chewed away in silence. Quiet for once.

"How about you, Ash?" He offered the bag to me.

"No way!" I replied. "Worm candy. Ugh. Totally gross."

"You're nuts," Greg replied. "These are awesome. They're the best." He raised the bag to his mouth and gobbled the rest of the worms down.

"Hey, Ash. Look." Greg grinned at me. Little bits of green, purple, and red gummy worms stuck to his teeth.

"Yuck! You are gross. Totally gross. Right, Jack?" I asked. "Right?"

Jack didn't answer. "What's that?" he said, pointing to a big trunk up ahead on the beach. At Bowen's Cove.

The three of us raced through the sand to the trunk. Jack reached it first.

The rusty old chest was as long as a coffin. Draped with barnacles and seaweed. And padlocked.

Jack hopped up and down. "It's a pirate's chest! Full of treasure. Gold and jewels!"

"It's not a pirate's chest," Greg replied. "It probably just fell off a boat and washed ashore. I bet it's full of fishing gear."

I wrinkled my nose. The chest smelled moldy and sour. "I bet it's full of rotten fish."

Jack danced around the chest. "Let's open it. Hurry!" He slammed the lock with the side of his left hand. It didn't budge.

"I'll open it!" Greg bragged. "Stand back." He lifted his foot. Then smashed it down hard on the lock. Nothing.

I scanned the beach. A few yards away I spotted a sturdy piece of driftwood. I hurried over and carried it back.

Then I shoved the wood into the tiny space between the lock and the lid. With two hands, I slowly pushed down on the wood.

Pop! The lock shot open.

"Way to go!" Jack cried.

Then the three of us started to lift the damp, heavy lid. Inch by inch.

"Whoa!" I cried as it banged wide open.

A big, green, quivering blob sprang out. And flew right at me! It latched on to my leg.

"Help! It's got me!" I shrieked. "Pull it off! Pull it off!"

I shook my leg wildly. But the thing held on. Cold and slimy. Clammy. And as smelly as a hundred dead fish.

It wrapped itself tightly around me. It covered my leg from my ankle to my knee.

"Help!" I yelled to Jack and Greg. But they stood frozen with fear.

I pushed frantically at the slimy blob. My fingers sank into the cold, green gunk. "Ohhh!" I let out a moan as I felt underneath the skin.

The thing had suckers!

Suckers that twitched and tugged at my skin. And the more I struggled, the tighter they grasped my leg.

THWOCK!

It moved! It dragged itself up my leg by its suckers. Leaving a burning, itchy trail.

"Get it off!" I moaned.

Greg and Jack awoke from their trance. They grabbed for the blob. They yanked at it. But the suckers dug deeper into my leg.

THWOCK. THWOCK.

The blob inched up my thigh. Squeezing harder.

Greg pounded the blob with a stick. "Off, slimeball!" he yelled. "Off!"

"Greg! Stop!" I cried. "You're smashing my leg."

THWOCK. The blob yanked a moist sucker off my thigh. And wiggled it in the air. Almost as if it were sniffing. Then it nosed the sucker into Greg's T-shirt pocket.

"Whoaaa," Greg cried and jumped back.

The sucker emerged with a gummy worm. Schlop! It sucked the candy into its slimy body!

"It — it ate a gummy worm!" Greg stammered. "Did you see that?"

"But it doesn't have a mouth," Jack shuddered. "It doesn't even have a head."

Now the blob quivered up my stomach. The suckers jerked at my skin. Would it slurp *me* down, too?

"Stop talking! Do something!" I screamed.

Greg grabbed a bunch of gummy worms from his pocket. He dangled them in front of the blob.

THWOCK. THWOCK. The creature flew off me and heaved itself at the gummy worms. Then it slurped them down.

"Yes! You did it!" I cried.

"But now it's on me!" Greg moaned. "And I'm out of gummies!"

I stared in horror. The blob clung to Greg's arm. Writhing. Pulsating.

Jack gaped at the creature. "I think it's growing!"

Jack was right. The creature strangled Greg's arm and oozed across his chest.

"More candy!" Greg choked. "In my bedroom. Hurry! It's squeezing me."

Jack and I raced to the front door of our beach cottage. We turned the doorknob.

Locked.

Nobody home.

Jack flung the doormat aside and found the key hidden there for us. He opened the door, and we sprinted up to Greg's bedroom.

"Check his dresser," I ordered. I yanked open Greg's closet door. I pawed through his sweatshirts and jeans.

Not a single gummy.

"I can't find any in the dresser," Jack cried.

"Check under the bed," I said. "Check *everywhere*."

I dug through the bottom of the closet. Sneakers. Dirty socks. Finally I spied the familiar bags. Dozens of them.

"I found gummies!" I cried in triumph.

I snatched up a bag. Empty! Then another. And another. All empty.

"What are we going to do?" Jack wailed.

"We'll go to the store. Come on — hurry! Let's find our bikes!"

We pedaled furiously to Simpson's General Store.

We dropped our bikes outside the store and dashed inside. Packages of gummy worms were piled up on the counter.

I snatched about twenty bags. All I could carry. Jack did the same.

"That will be — " Mr. Simpson started.

Oh, no! *Money!* I didn't have any money!

"Mr. Simpson. Please. I don't have any money.

And I need these gummy worms," I explained frantically. "It's a matter of life and death. They're for Greg."

"Greg? He's my best customer. Always buying gummy worms. Okay. Go ahead. I'll charge it to your parents' bill."

"Thanks, Mr. Simpson!" I called. We rushed out of the store.

Jack and I tossed the bags of candy into my bike basket.

"There's the shortcut to Bowen's Cove," Jack cried. He pointed to a dusty road off Main Street. "Let's take it!"

I hesitated. "Okay," I agreed. "But you'd better be right."

We raced to the road. Then skidded into the turn.

"Oh, no!" Jack cried. "My gear chain slipped. I have to fix it. Go ahead without me. Just stay on this road. Then turn at the cutoff. It's not far."

"Perfect," I mumbled, rolling my eyes. I zoomed down the deserted dirt road. I whizzed by the tall dune grass. So quiet. So still. No one in sight.

And no cutoff for the cove.

I braked to a complete stop. Turned my bike around. "I think I'm lost," I said out loud.

"You're found now."

The dune grass parted. Alex and Jimmy came lumbering out. They gripped my handlebars.

"Roadblock," Jimmy smirked. "No summer people allowed."

Alex peered inside my bike basket. "Yum. Gummy worms. Hey, Jimmy. Ashley wants to share her candy."

"No!" I shrieked. "I need those."

Alex and Jimmy began tearing into the gummy worm bags. I tried to yank my bike away, but Alex grabbed on to the handlebars again.

Then, Jack came pedaling up. Hair flying. Racing up the path. His tires throwing huge dirt clouds up in the air.

Alex and Jimmy turned to face him. I quickly moved my bike to the roadside.

"Clear the path, jerks!" Jack cried out.

"Uh-oh. Watch out, Jimmy. The Karate Kid is going to run us over." Jimmy laughed.

Jack kept coming. When he was nearly on top of them, he flung his legs out. And kicked them both into the dirt.

With a cheer, I jumped on my bike. We sped away.

"You'll be sorry!" I heard Alex call after us.

"Yeah. You guys are in big trouble!" Jimmy yelled.

We flew down the road. And there it was — the cutoff to Bowen's Cove! We reached the beach in minutes.

We scooped up the candy and sprinted down to Greg.

And gasped. The oily blob bulged and quaked. Much bigger. Bigger than Mom's beach umbrella.

And no sign of Greg.

Then I heard a faint cry. "Help me. Help me."

"Greg!" I screamed. "Where are you?"

THWOCK. THWOCK. The slimy blob quivered in the sand. And that's when I saw a sneaker. Greg's sneaker.

"He's *under* the blob!" I screamed to Jack.

"Can't breathe," Greg moaned.

"Hold on, Greg," I cried. I quickly ripped open a small bag of gummy worms. And placed six candies down in a thin line.

THWOCK. THWOCK. Schlop!

The slime monster slid forward and slurped the gummies up eagerly.

"More! Open more bags!" I told Jack.

He tore through the bags. And I flung huge handfuls onto the sand.

THWOCK. The blob plucked a slimy sucker off Greg. It quivered excitedly. *Let Greg go,* I thought. *Please let Greg go.*

I threw a mound of gummy worms on the sand.

RRRIP! The monster yanked its suckers off Greg. It rolled forward and slurped down the candy.

I spun around to Jack. "Lots more gummies. Fast! Try to lead the creature back into the chest."

Greg stumbled as he tried to stand on his wobbly legs. Then he and Jack tore open bags and bags of candy. I placed a thick trail of gummies in the sand. A river of gummy worms. Leading to the chest.

THWOCK. THWOCK. Schlop. Schlop. The creature followed our trail. Slurping down candy.

A foot from the chest.

"The chest! Throw some gummies into the chest!" I commanded.

Jack and Greg pitched the candy in.

THWOCK. The blob lurched forward. Inches from the chest.

"Throw the bags right in! There's no time to open them!" I shouted.

The blob wriggled its way up the chest wall. But it had grown too big. Too big to heave itself up.

"We have to push it in!" I cried.

Jack drew back. "*You* push it in!" he shouted. "I'm not touching that blob. What if it grabs me?"

"Not me!" Greg protested. "That thing nearly strangled me."

"But it's our only chance!" I wailed. "We have to boost it back in."

They didn't move.

I threw myself against the creature and shoved. But my hands kept slipping. "It's too slimy," I moaned. "I need your help. Please!"

Jack and Greg stepped forward. Then we all pushed. And pushed. And pushed.

Sweat ran down my forehead. The boys' faces turned a bright red.

Slowly we hoisted the monster into the chest. One oily bulge at a time.

Then we slammed the lid down and jumped on top.

"Hey! Look!" Jack pointed down to the front of the chest. A bag of gummy worms hung out.

"Gummies!" Greg cried gleefully. "Awesome! Exactly what I need right now." He leaned over to lift the lid.

"Are you crazy?" I shrieked. "That thing in the chest almost squeezed you to death. Don't lift that lid!"

"Uh-oh," Jack warned.

We glanced up to see Alex and Jimmy angrily charging toward us.

"Jack! Just the guy we're looking for," Alex called. "I think we owe you something."

We scrambled off the chest and headed full speed for the dunes.

I turned back and saw Alex and Jimmy stop in front of the trunk. "Look! Gummy worms!" Alex cried, pointing to the bag poking through the lid. "Excellent!"

"There's plenty more inside!" I called.

Then Jack, Greg, and I watched as Alex and Jimmy eagerly pulled up the lid.

DR. HORROR'S HOUSE OF VIDEO

"Help! Help!" Screams echoed through the crowded streets. Something huge and menacing and green rose above the steel-gray city.

A giant monster. A plant monster.

The plant had grasping leaves. Leaves that reached out like hands to grab frightened people below. The people twisted and screamed as the plant lifted them in its leafy grip. Up, up, up to certain death.

I yawned. *Bor*-ing!

I'd seen *The Plant That Squeezed St. Louis* three times already. I rewound the videotape. As far as horror movies go, this one just didn't hold up.

And I should know. I'm Ben Adams — I've seen them all. Movies with mummies, movies with werewolves, movies with creatures from other planets. I'm kind of an expert.

In fact, my best friend, Jeff, and I plan to make horror movies when we're older. Right now, we're twelve. Too young to be taken seriously. But we've already made some home horror movies with my dad's camcorder.

I usually play the victim. It helps that I have red hair that stands on end and very pale skin. I'm great at acting scared. But what good does that do me now? With Jeff at camp and me on vacation?

That's where I am. On vacation for the summer with my parents. My mom and dad rented a house near the mountains for the whole month of August. There's nothing to do here. Nowhere to go. And worst of all, no kids my age.

Mom and Dad say, "Go out! Have fun!" But where? I'd rather stay inside, watching horror movies.

And I have. For two whole weeks now, I've been watching videos I brought from home.

"Ben!" my mom called from the other room. "You've been stuck in front of that TV all afternoon." She walked in, then yanked open the blinds.

I blinked in the sudden light. "It's time you got some fresh air. It's not healthy for a growing boy to sit inside all day. I'm going into town for gardening supplies. Why don't you come with me?"

Dad works in the city during the week and is here on weekends. But Mom is a teacher, so she has the summer off. And what does she do? She works in the garden.

"Ben," Mom said in a voice that meant business. "Do you want to come to town?" It wasn't an invitation. It was an order.

"But, Mom," I argued, holding the monster video box so she could only see the plant. "I'm watching this educational movie about nature."

Mom rolled her eyes. "That's a horror movie, and I know it. You're wasting your summer, Ben, watching that stuff. Now let's get going."

In town, Mom headed straight for the garden supply store. I gazed up and down the street. I'd never been in this part of town.

Something caught my eye. A video store! "I'll meet you up the block," I called to Mom.

Hurrying away, I tried to control my excitement. I could get a fresh batch of videos! And best of all, the store was called Dr. Horror's House of Video. It must be all horror movies.

How lucky can a guy get?

I stopped outside the store. The frayed awning drooped in front. A layer of dust covered the window. I wiped the dirty pane and peered inside.

The inside looked as old and dusty as the outside. Videos were piled everywhere.

Fine with me, I thought. Who knows what I'll find under all that mess?

The door creaked open — and I hadn't even touched it. This just got better and better! Quickly, I slipped inside.

"Can I help you?" someone asked in a low, whispery voice. I whirled around. An elderly man with flowing white hair stood behind me. He had white bushy eyebrows and a face creased with a thousand tiny lines.

"My name is Dr. Horror," he said in that whispery voice. He leaned heavily on a cane, then waved it at all the shelves. "Welcome to my store."

Dr. Horror smiled, and I saw that he was missing most of his teeth. "Do you like horror movies?" he asked.

"Are you kidding?" I replied. "I think I've seen every horror movie ever made."

"I bet you haven't seen any of these," Dr. Horror said, chuckling. "I make my own in the old garage behind the store."

I grinned. "Really?" Just wait until I tell Jeff about this, I thought. He'll be totally jealous. Even if he is having a great time at camp, I'll bet he hasn't met anyone like Dr. Horror!

"Go on. Look around," Dr. Horror told me. "I'm sure you'll find something to frighten you."

This was so cool! I hurried to check out the videos. *Ten Tales from the Mummy Files. Monsters at Midnight. A Boy and His Werewolf.*

"These are terrific!" I said, lifting a vampire video. The vampire on the front had deathly white skin. A drop of ruby-red blood ran down his pale chin.

But it was his expression that really grabbed me. His eyes bored into mine — as if he were gazing into my soul.

Which video should I get? I couldn't decide. They all looked so good!

Then I saw a movie playing on one of the video monitors, off in a corner. On screen, a huge monster — half man, half lizard — stepped out from a slimy swamp. He was searching for something to eat.

Squish, squish, squish went his webbed feet as he spotted a boy in the distance. Lizardman advanced.

I watched, spellbound.

The monster crept closer and closer to the boy. I moved closer, too. The boy's face twisted in fear.

I could feel the boy's fright. I sensed his horror — right in my gut.

Creak! A noise from behind me. I started to turn. But then Lizardman clutched the boy's shoulder. And I felt something grab *my* shoulder.

Something cool and smooth. I looked down. A green hand gripped me. Hard!

"Lizardman!" I screamed.

"Excuse me?" said Mom. She let go of my shoulder and took off a green glove. "I just wanted to show you my new gardening gloves."

She shook her head and stepped in front of the set. "These horror movies make you so jumpy,

Ben. I don't think you should be watching them. Let's go home."

I peered around Mom, trying to see the screen.

"Now!" Mom insisted, and she dragged me out the door.

The next morning I woke up early. I wanted to get to the video store. I had to see how *Lizardman* ended. But I couldn't say that to Mom. She wouldn't understand.

"I'm going for a bike ride," I told her.

Mom's mouth dropped open in surprise. "You're going *outside*?"

Before she could ask any questions, I wheeled my bike down the driveway and hopped on. Fifteen minutes later, I stood in front of the video store.

A CLOSED sign hung on the door. The store was dark.

I hopped from one foot to the other. When would it open? When would I find out about Lizardman?

I peered through the dusty window, hoping to spot Dr. Horror inside.

No such luck. But I did see a flickering light in the corner. A movie played on one of the sets. I squinted at the screen. Lizardman!

"Dr. Horror!" I called, knocking. "Are you in there?" I jiggled the doorknob.

The door swung open with a creak. "Dr. Horror?" I called in.

No answer.

The only sounds I heard were the voices in the horror movie. And the only light came from the TV.

I'll sneak in, I decided. I'll watch the movie, then sneak back out. No one will even know.

I edged forward, staring at the TV. . . .

An hour later, the movie ended. Lizardman gobbled the boy in a few quick bites. Then he had the other townspeople for dessert.

Cool! Definitely one of the best horror movies I'd seen all summer!

The VCR switched off. The room suddenly fell dark. Time to leave.

I made my way to the door and pulled at the knob. Nothing happened. I tried pushing. The door wouldn't budge.

"Oh, no," I groaned. "I'm locked inside."

Now what? I thought, squinting in the darkness. To my right, I spotted a sliver of light. Another door? A back exit? I crept toward it.

Yes! A door! Behind it, I heard noises. Thumps, and muffled shouts. What was going on?

I leaned against the door, pushing with all my might. The door swung open easily. Startled, I stumbled and fell.

I landed hard on my side. My eyes opened wide. A big webbed foot stood an inch away. Make that two big webbed feet.

"Huh?" I let out a cry and jumped up.

Lizardman in all his green glory towered over me like . . . like . . . a monster!

A living, breathing monster, flicking his long sharp tongue. His hot breath hit me like a blast from a furnace.

Bright lights beat down on me. Blinding me. I turned to run. Lizardman stretched a long sinewy arm to stop me. He had me in his grip! A grip as strong as an iron band.

I let out a frightened squeal and squinted into the bright light. Was anyone else here?

I heard sounds. Feet pounding.

Hands grasped me. But they didn't pull me from Lizardman. The hands held me in place. Hairy hands. Pale white hands. Hands wrapped with cloth.

Werewolves! Vampires! Mummies!

"Wait a minute!" a familiar voice shouted. I squinted into the light. Dragging his cane, Dr. Horror shuffled over. "Hello again," he said.

"H-h-h-i," I stammered.

Dr. Horror's eyes gleamed. I twisted hard. But I couldn't break the monsters' hold.

"I see you found the door to the garage," said Dr. Horror. He waved his cane around. "What do you think?"

For the first time, I took it all in. The monsters. The lights. The cameras.

I gazed around the huge room. The monsters

all looked familiar. The deathly white vampire. The mummy. And, of course, Lizardman. The horror movie monsters!

This garage was their film studio! How could I have forgotten?

I grinned at Lizardman. "Love your work," I said.

Lizardman nodded and released his grip.

"And these costumes!" I went on. "They're the coolest!"

Dr. Horror smiled. "Yes, you're a horror fan. Right?"

"The biggest!"

"Good, good, good." Dr. Horror rubbed his hands together. "How would you like to be in *Return of Lizardman*?"

"Excuse m-me?" I stammered.

"We're filming the *Lizardman* sequel, and we need a new victim."

Me in a real horror movie? I couldn't believe it!

"Do you have acting experience?" Dr. Horror asked.

"Some," I said, thinking of our home movies.

Dr. Horror tilted my head and examined my profile. "Well, you seem like a natural. It's a small role. You don't even have lines." He thrust a bunch of papers at me. "Here's the script."

I leafed through the scenes. Lizardman emerging from the swamp . . . destroying a school . . .

one boy escaping. "Is that me?" I asked Dr. Horror.

"Yes. Any other questions? We're ready to start now."

Now? I wanted to call Jeff at camp. Tell Mom and Dad. Maybe phone a few more friends. I wanted to play this for all it was worth.

"Can I make some phone calls first?" I asked.

Dr. Horror checked his watch. "You have time for just one. I suggest you call your parents. We like to have their permission before filming. We can take care of your contract later."

The phone rang ten times before Mom answered. Of course she had been outside gardening.

"I'm not sure," she said when I explained about the movie.

"But, Mom!" I shouted. "This could be my big break. Please, please, please! It's so important to me!" I took a deep breath.

"Just be home in time for dinner," Mom said, finally giving in.

I hung up the phone, then turned back to Dr. Horror. "It's all set."

Small alien-creature actors wheeled a swampy backdrop behind me. Everyone bustled around, getting things ready. A four-armed actor plopped a tree right next to me. The vampire and mummy stood behind the cameras. The werewolf set the lights. "There!" he said. A murky glow bathed the room.

Dr. Horror motioned for me to stand against the tree. "We'll tie you up," he whispered, strapping me to the trunk. "For your big scene with Lizardman."

"Oh, right," I said, remembering the part in the script. All I had to do was act frightened. Simple enough.

Dr. Horror shuffled over to his director's chair. "Now," he said. "You lost your way in the swamp, and fell asleep. When you woke up, you were tied to this tree. You know Lizardman is coming back. But when?"

He turned to the vampire actor running the camera. "Roll 'em," he said. "Okay . . . action!"

Lizardman crept through the swamp. I tried to look scared. But I was too excited. Too happy.

"Cut!" shouted Dr. Horror, shaking his head. "More feeling!"

I tried again. I opened my eyes wide.

Lizardman glided closer. His tail swept from side to side. His eyes darted back and forth. He really seemed hungry. What an actor!

Lizardman flicked out his tongue to catch a fly. Great effect!

And the makeup! As Lizardman slid nearer, I saw just how monsterlike he looked — even up close. Green skin, red bloodshot eyes. Long, slimy tongue.

"Hey, wait," I called out.

"What?" snapped Dr. Horror impatiently.

"Don't I need makeup, too?"

Lizardman stood inches away. "I know I'm supposed to be an ordinary boy. But these other actors look terrific!"

I reached up to touch Lizardman's face. "Is this a mask?" Ugh. The skin felt bumpy and cold. It had to be a mask.

"Hey, can I see it?" I tugged at the mask. It didn't budge. "It's stuck," I announced. The other actors crowded around. How nice, I thought. They want to help.

The vampire actor stretched his mouth into a teeth-baring grin. His sharp teeth glinted in the light. Coming closer, he pulled my arms back around the tree. Then he tied them with another rope.

I didn't remember this from the script. "Hey!" I shouted. "What's going on?"

Nobody answered.

Instead, the mummy unwound the wrapping from his face.

I gasped when I saw its decayed flesh hanging from its bony frame. And its eyes — glowing red eyes.

The werewolf shimmered for a moment, growling deep in his throat. He raised his paws, and deadly nails popped out. Two sharp fangs burst from either side of his mouth. His nose quivered with excitement.

This couldn't be trick photography. What was it?

I started to tremble as I answered my own question. These weren't actors from a horror movie! They were *monsters* — real monsters.

"Let me go!" I cried, struggling to get free. The heavy ropes cut into my hands.

I had to escape! I had to! But the ropes held me tight.

I was trapped!

His eyes glowing excitedly, Lizardman breathed in my face. His hot breath hit me full force. A smell like the bottom of a swamp. My stomach turned.

Lizardman's teeth scraped my face. His scaly hand gripped my neck. His tail sliced through the air.

"Dr. Horror!" I shrieked. "Save me! Please — *do* something!"

"Whoa! Stop, monsters!" Dr. Horror called out. "Stop at once!"

The monsters stepped back. Lizardman froze in place.

Oh, thank goodness! I thought. I'm okay. It was all my imagination.

I let out a relieved sigh. How could I get so carried away?

Dr. Horror reached out — to untie me, I thought.

But I was wrong.

He reached up to my head. And he fixed my hair!

"Okay, monsters. Now we're ready for the big eating scene," he said. "Roll 'em!"

THE CAT'S TALE

"Come on down, Marla," my little brother, Scott, called. "We're telling ghost stories!"

"No thanks," I shouted back. Then I covered my ears so I wouldn't hear the next blast of thunder. Thunderstorms weren't so loud when my family lived in the city. Here in the country, the lightning flashed so close — and the thunder boomed so hard — it shook the house.

Last year when I turned twelve, my folks decided it would be safer for my brother and me to grow up in the country. So we moved from New York City up here to River Falls.

Scott loves living in an old house with a big yard. But not me. I hate it. I miss Central Park. I miss taxis. And most of all, I miss my friends.

I listened to the tree branches brush against my window. I suddenly pictured ghosts trying to claw their way through my window and into my room.

I'm not a *chicken* or anything. I'm not even

really afraid of the thunder and lightning. I just like it better when there isn't any.

I gasped as the room went black. Now the only light in my room came from the lightning. With every flash, the trees left frightening shadows on my wall.

Downstairs I could hear my parents and Scott still telling ghost stories — in the dark! I wanted no part of *that.*

I couldn't stand the sound of the branches scratching against the glass. I opened the window. Then I felt my way around the room in the darkness. I touched my desk. My chair. My headboard.

"Oh!" I cried out as something big, wet, and hairy flew through the open window. It slammed into my chest — and I fell to the floor.

Long, sharp nails scratched at my arms and neck.

High-pitched screeches rang in my ears.

I stared into two glowing green eyes. Then I started to scream.

Mom and Dad bolted into the room. "Marla, what's the matter?" Dad cried. He held a candle in one hand and Scott's Little League bat in the other.

"A hairy monster!" I shrieked. "It flew into the room! And-and — "

"Is this the monster?" Mom asked sweetly. She held up her candle so I could see. In her arms she carried a small, wet, shaking black cat.

"It's just a cat, honey," Mom said softly. "She must have climbed up the tree and jumped in here to get out of the storm." She examined the cat. "A stray. No tags around her neck."

"Meow!" A loud roar from behind me. I spun around. "Stop it, Scott!" I cried. He laughed. "Meow! Meow!" He thought it was a riot.

I ignored him and reached for the cat. My mother placed her in my arms. "You're nice and safe here," I said to the cat. I turned to my parents. "Can I keep her?"

Mom and Dad glanced at each other. "Marla, a cat is a big responsibility," my Dad began.

My face fell. "Please, Dad," I pleaded. "She needs me. She's all alone. And I need *her*. I have no friends around here."

"Well, we'll talk about it in the morning," my mother said. "She can stay tonight, anyway. Come on, Scott, it's bedtime."

I petted the black cat. The storm had stopped. The air was filled with a fresh mist. "I think I'll call you Misty," I said. "And don't worry. You'll be able to stay here — for life! I'll make sure of it."

Misty spent the night curled up at the foot of my bed. And the next morning, she did the weirdest thing. She followed me into the shower!

Misty purred happily as the hot water pounded on her fur.

I'd always heard that cats hate baths and

showers. They keep themselves clean by licking themselves.

Not Misty. Misty was special.

When we went down to breakfast, we both had wet hair. "I see you two have washed up," my father said.

I smiled. Misty also showed her pointy white teeth in a grin.

We all laughed when Misty tried to eat my eggs. "You must be hungry, you poor thing," my mother said.

She gave Misty a saucer of milk and some tuna. "I've spoiled you now," Mom told Misty. "You'll never go for cat food after that." I knew then that Mom would let me keep Misty.

"Kids, I have a great surprise!" Mom said excitedly. "I've joined the swim club. You two can bike over there today and take a swim. There will be lots of kids your age there."

Scott jumped out of his seat. "All right! A pool! Right here! And we don't have to take a taxi to a stinking old gym. I love it out here!"

I frowned at my brother. He was so easy to please. All it took was a few ghost stories and a swimming pool. I still missed New York.

But since I was stuck here, meeting some other kids didn't seem like such a bad idea. Besides, I love to swim. And the heat wave was starting to get to me. I ran upstairs to put on my swimsuit.

"Hurry up, Marla!" Scott called from the front door. If you're not here in one minute, I'm going without you."

"See you later, Misty," I said, waving. Misty leaped up on my desk and meowed. She sounded so sad, like a baby who had lost her mother. She cried and cried. I cuddled the cat in my arms and tried to calm her.

"I know how you feel. I don't like being alone in a new house, either," I said, petting her black fur. Then I called downstairs. "Hey, Scott, you go on. I think Misty and I are going to hang out here today."

At dinnertime, Scott told us about the great kids he met at the pool. I felt a little jealous. All I did was read a book while Misty napped.

But when I gazed down at Misty, snuggled in my lap, eating pieces of my frankfurter, I knew I had done the right thing. Misty needed me.

That night I dreamed about my old neighborhood. My friends and I were rowing a boat in the park. We were having a picnic lunch, and laughing. Then, suddenly, a stranger grabbed me from behind and covered my mouth. I tried to lift my head, but couldn't! I couldn't breathe!

I woke up. I *still* couldn't breathe!

Misty! The cat was sitting on me. Covering my nose and mouth.

I tugged at her with all my strength. But I couldn't budge her.

I started to feel dizzy and weak. The room spun around me.

I struggled to get air into my lungs.

I grabbed at Misty's fur. But the cat pressed even harder against my face.

Beads of sweat dripped from my forehead. My skin turned cold and clammy.

Finally, I curled my hands around Misty's neck. I ripped her off my face and held her far from my body.

Then I gasped in breath after breath. Holding the cat tightly, I carried her downstairs to the family room. My parents were watching a video.

"Mom! Dad!" I cried. "Misty tried to kill me!"

"What?"

"She tried to kill me. She plopped on to my face. She wouldn't get off! She — she tried to suffocate me!"

My mother took Misty from me and petted her back. "Marla, Misty was probably just cold. You know you like to turn the air-conditioning up too high. She was trying to get warm."

Maybe what Mom said made sense. I don't know. But that's when I started getting afraid of that cat.

The next day, when Misty started crying again, I ignored her. I locked the front door on my way out, hopped on my bike, and took off for the swim club.

The club seemed to be a really fun place. And there were lots of kids my age.

Scott ripped off his shirt and did a belly flop into the deep end. I took my time climbing the ladder to the high diving board.

I was about to dive in. I stared down at the water. And stared again.

For some reason, I suddenly didn't feel like diving. I began to edge back down the board. I didn't want to go in that water.

"Hey, Marla. What's your problem?" Scott called from the pool.

I cupped my hands and started to answer Scott. But I suddenly realized I wasn't the only one on the diving board.

Something brushed up against me and scratched my leg.

"Ow!" I screamed out in pain and surprise.

I lost my balance. I tumbled into the water below.

Cold, blue water poured into my mouth and nose. I thrashed my arms and legs in a panic.

I couldn't swim.

I struggled to reach the surface. But everything went black.

A crowd of people huddled around me. I could hear them congratulating the lifeguard who had jumped in and saved my life.

The lifeguard helped me to a lounge chair. He wrapped my cut leg in a towel. "Stay here," he said. “I’ll call your parents and get you some bandages for that cut.”

The blood seeped through the white towel. Ow! That was some cut! Who could have scratched me so badly?

Scott raced over to me. I thought he wanted to make sure I was okay.

Instead, he dumped Misty into my lap.

“Mom told you to leave this dumb cat at home,” he said. “She followed you all the way up onto the high dive!”

Mom and Dad showed up a few minutes later and drove me home.

“Marla, to celebrate the fact that you’re all right, I’ve made your favorite meal — spaghetti and meatballs!” Mom said.

I felt queasy. I really craved something else. “Uh, Mom?” I asked. “Do you have any of that tuna casserole left? And how about a big glass of milk?”

That shocked my parents. “Are you sure you’re okay?” Mom asked. “It’s not like you to give up your favorite dinner — especially for leftovers!”

I had a very restless night. I kept hearing whispers. Soft, breathless whispers.

Then the whispers became a creepy chant.

“Nine lives, nine lives. I will have thy body before I’ve lived my nine. Thy life is mine, and mine is thine.”

My eyes darted around the room. No one there. No one — except Misty.

Was I going nuts?

After that, I couldn't sleep at all. I sat straight up in my bed and stared at Misty as she slept.

Had she really spoken?

The next day at the swim club, I stayed as far as I could from the water. Instead, I joined a volleyball game on the back lawn.

I'm not a great volleyball player. But I managed to spike the ball hard enough to earn my team the winning point.

After the game, Sarah and Melissa, two girls from my team, asked me to go to the snack bar for ice cream.

"You're a pretty good player," Sarah said. She twirled her ponytail around her finger. "We've got a volleyball team at school. You should join. What grade are you going into?"

"Sixth," I replied shyly.

"Oh, I thought you were older. We're in junior high," Melissa said.

"A mouse!" Sarah cried. She jumped up onto a wooden picnic table.

I saw the little gray creature scurry by. Melissa leaped up next to Sarah.

I didn't join them. I crouched down on the ground and pounced on it.

"Gotcha!" I cried.

I picked up the wriggling mouse by the tail and held it up.

Melissa and Sarah stared at me in horror.

"Yuck!" Sarah cried. "That's so gross! Get that thing away from me!"

"Eew!" Melissa turned her head away from me. "Marla — *why* did you do that?"

The mouse thrashed about in my hand. I tossed it into the nearby bushes.

Why did I do that? I asked myself.

I hate mice!

Any other day, I'd have been up there on the table with Melissa and Sarah. Instead, I acted really stupid in front of two junior high girls.

I acted like a real jerk. I acted absolutely . . . catlike!

Thy life is mine, and mine is thine.

It was all becoming clear to me. Now I knew why I was afraid of water. Why I had a sudden craving for tuna casserole. Why I found it so easy to pounce on a mouse.

Misty had just about taken over my mind. And, little by little, she was taking over my body.

I'll have thy body before I've lived my nine.

Misty didn't want to share a body with me. She wanted my body all to herself!

I needed a plan. I had to fight back. I had to get rid of Misty before she got rid of me!

I raced home and grabbed Misty by the collar. "We're going for a little ride," I said, trying not to frighten her. Then I placed Misty in the basket in the front of my bike and pedaled off to the local animal shelter in town.

"Don't worry, Miss," the man at the shelter said. "We're sure to find a nice home for a pretty cat like this."

I watched as he tied a name tag around Misty's neck and placed her in a large cage with other cats. Then I biked home.

For the first time in days, I felt relaxed. Happy.

What a relief! I had done it. I had gotten rid of Misty and saved my life!

I parked my bike on the side of our garage. I glanced toward the house and gasped. A black cat with deep green eyes stood on the porch.

No! I told myself. It can't be Misty. It just can't! I locked Misty up in a shelter a mile away. My legs trembled as I walked over to the porch. I lifted the tag on the cat's neck and read it.

Misty! It *was* Misty.

But how did she get home? How?

I feared going to sleep that night. What would Misty do to me? I lay there staring into the darkness.

Then I heard that same, horrifying, breathless voice, whispering ever-so-softly in my ear.

"Nine lives, nine lives. I will have thy body before I've lived my nine. Thy life is mine, and mine is thine."

That was enough to keep me awake for a long, long time!

Just before dawn, I shoved Misty into her cat carrier and sneaked out of the house. The carrier had a heavy lock. It could be opened only from the outside with a key.

No way Misty could escape this time! I told myself.

I strapped the carrier to my handlebars and rode through the gray morning to the bus station. The time had come for Misty to take a trip across the country!

We reached the station about half an hour before the bus was scheduled to leave. I watched the morning sun come up over the little town.

Suddenly I felt so thirsty. I set the cat carrier down on the sidewalk and hurried to the soda machine.

I had just dropped two quarters into the machine when I heard the deafening *screeeech.*

The screech of brakes.

A shrill cry.

I spun around in time to see the big red truck squeal to a stop. The driver leaped out of the cab. His face was bright red. "Was that your cat?" he called to me.

I ran over to him, my heart pounding.

"I didn't see her until it was too late," the truck driver told me. "I'm so sorry. Really. Why did you let her walk in the street?"

I opened my mouth to reply, but no words came out.

How had Misty escaped from the carrier? How

had she broken the lock and climbed out of the case?

I didn't really care. Misty was dead. Dead and gone.

I wasn't exactly sorry.

That night, I slept soundly, peacefully, for the first time in days. I pulled the covers up high and snuggled my head into my soft pillow. I'm sure I had a smile on my face as I drifted to sleep.

The smile faded when I heard the whispers.

I sat up with a shiver. And listened to the soft chant of the words:

"Eight lives, eight lives left. I will have thy body before I've lived my nine. Thy life is mine, and mine is thine."

SHELL SHOCKER

"Oh, no, you don't!" Tara Bennett yelled to her eight-year-old brother, Tommy. "That's my shell! Mine!"

Tara jumped up from the beach blanket and ran to the shore. She saw the waves wash over Tommy's toes as he rinsed the sand off the shell.

"Give it to me," Tara demanded, wrenching the gleaming white object from her brother's hands. "It's for my shell collection!" she sneered. "The biggest and best shell collection in the world!"

"No fair, Tara. I saw it first."

"No fair!" Tara mimicked. She narrowed her blue eyes. "You're a baby."

Tara held the seashell up to the light and admired its smooth curves and pointed spiral. It sparkled like a jewel in the afternoon sun.

"It's the most perfect shell in the world!" she announced. "Everybody is going to be jealous when they see it."

She closed her eyes. And pictured herself back at school. Winning the seventh-grade science fair with her new shell. All the kids in my class will be green with envy, Tara thought happily.

"Can I hold it?" Tommy asked softly.

"No way!" Tara snapped. "You can't even look at it without my permission!"

Clutching the shell tightly, she turned and marched across the beach. Far away from her annoying little brother. Then she flopped down on the sand to examine her newest treasure.

"It's beautiful," she gasped, turning the shell back and forth in her hands. "And it's mine. Not Tommy's. Mine!"

Whenever Tommy found a seashell, he pressed it to his ear. He said he could hear the roar of the ocean inside.

Tommy is such a jerk, Tara thought. She turned the shell over and over in her hand. Everyone knows you can't really hear the ocean inside a shell. Just the same, Tara held the white shell up to her ear.

"Oh, gross!" Tara cried.

A clump of wet seaweed slid down her cheek.

She wiped the green slime away. Then she placed the shell against her ear again.

And listened.

"Help me!" a tiny voice called from inside.

Tara screamed and dropped the shell.

"Who — who said that?" she stammered, gazing down at the shell. Then she jerked her head up. Expecting to see Tommy laughing at her.

But no one stood there.

Tara sat alone.

She jumped up and backed away from the shell. She stared suspiciously down at it. "Was it you?" she whispered. "Did you talk?"

Don't be silly, Tara, she told herself. Shells can't talk.

Creeping forward, she kicked the shell gently with her toe. It rolled across the sand, then stopped.

"Help me!"

The voice cried louder this time.

Tara screamed again. She began to shiver under the rays of the hot summer sun. She wrapped her arms tightly around herself. Then took a deep, steadying breath.

"Who's in there?" she demanded.

"I'm trapped," the tiny voice wailed. *"Help me!"*

Tara gasped. "I can't believe it!" she cried out. "The shell is talking. To me!"

Tara's head reeled. Beads of sweat dripped from her long blond hair.

"Of course I'm talking to you. I need your help!" the tiny voice pleaded. *"I'm a prisoner! Please. Pick me up."*

Tara didn't know what to do. She inched closer

to the shell. She leaned over and peeked inside. It appeared to be empty.

I have to find out where that voice is coming from, Tara thought. I just have to. Tara carefully lifted the shell from the sand.

"How can I help you?" Tara asked. Her voice trembled.

"Take me to the cave. To help me escape. Please. Trust me," the voice begged.

"Trust you?" Tara asked breathlessly. "I can't even *see* you!"

"Come to the cave. To help me escape. Then you'll understand. Then you'll see me!"

Tara hesitated. A talking shell, she thought. What an opportunity!

She grasped the shell in her hands and smirked. "Why should I help you escape?" she asked. "You're the world's first talking shell! I can make a fortune with you! I'll be rich and famous! People will pay a lot of money to hear a seashell talk!"

Tara's mind raced with all the possibilities. Maybe she would star in her own TV show! Tara and Her Amazing Talking Shell!

"But, Tara, I will talk to you only. When you're alone. So no one will believe you," the voice replied. *"But listen to me! There's something inside the cave that will* really *make you rich and famous."*

"What is it?" Tara demanded, shaking the shell. "Tell me!"

"It's the biggest seashell in the world," the voice told her.

The biggest shell in the world?

Tara pretended not to care. "Oh, really?" she muttered. "The biggest shell in the world? Where is this cave?"

"I'll show you," the voice answered. *"Just walk along the shoreline. To the north end of the beach. I'll show you where it is. I promise."*

Tara bubbled with excitement. I'll be the most famous shell collector in the world, she thought. I'll be Tara, the Shell Queen!

"Okay," she agreed. "I'll do it! I'll take you to the cave!"

"Yesss!" the voice hissed.

Tara took a small step across the sand. "What about my mom and dad?" she asked. "I should tell them where I'm going."

She gazed across the crowded beach. She spotted her mother and father sprawled out under their neon-pink beach umbrella. Mom turned the pages of a book. Dad slept.

"Don't worry. They won't even notice you're gone," the voice urged. *"Let's go."*

Tara turned toward the north end of the beach. The sun cast an eerie glow over the towering sand dunes. The ocean waves hammered the shore.

"Maybe I'll bring Mom with me. There's no lifeguard over there," she muttered.

A loud screech echoed inside the shell.

"Help me!" the voice screamed out. *"Help me — now!"*

"Okay, okay," Tara snapped. "I'll help you. But remember your promise! The biggest shell in the world belongs to me."

Clasping the seashell in her hands, Tara stomped across the beach. The hard, wet sand hurt the bottom of her feet, but she was determined to find the cave . . . and the biggest shell in the world!

Tara walked and walked. "Aren't we there yet?" she whined.

"Keep going," the voice replied.

"But it's getting late!" she moaned.

Tara gazed out over the water. The sun floated on the edge of the sea like a big red beach ball.

"I'm kind of scared," Tara mumbled. "I'm all alone out here."

She turned and searched for her mom and dad and Tommy. She thought she spotted them alongside their pink umbrella on the edge of the beach. Three tiny specks in the sand.

"I want to go back," Tara whimpered. "We've wandered too far."

"But we're so close," the voice said softly. *"We can't turn back now. Look to your right. By the rocks."*

Tara scanned the beach.

There! The opening of the cave! Practically in front of her!

"Finally," Tara gasped.

She dashed to the cave's dark entrance. And listened. From deep inside the cavern she heard a frightening earsplitting screech!

"What's that?" Tara whispered.

"It's only the wind," the tiny voice explained. *"Let's go in."*

"But . . . but I'm a little afraid," Tara admitted. "It's so dark in there!"

"Don't worry," the voice replied. *"I can guide you through the cave. Just do exactly as I say. Walk straight ahead . . . and don't touch the walls."*

Tara took a deep breath and stepped forward. The darkness swallowed her up. She stumbled blindly ahead.

The cave floor dipped and pitched. Tara reached a hand out in front of her. She groped at the curtain of dark. She staggered on.

A rock. A huge rock stood in her path. Her foot slammed into it.

"Oh, no!" she screamed as she stumbled. Her arms flew up from her sides. Up to the walls of the cave.

Tara shrieked.

The walls. They moved. They squirmed.

With thousands and thousands of black hairy spiders!

The spiders crawled over Tara's neck. Through her hair. Up her arms.

Tara leaped away from the wall. She swatted frantically at the spiders. Their hairy legs tangled her hair. Pinched her skin.

"I'm getting *out* of here!" she shrieked, frantically batting them off.

"But you can't go now!" the tiny voice in the shell pleaded. *"You've got to help me! We're so close now. Don't you want to own the biggest shell in the world? Don't you want to be rich and famous?"*

Tara hesitated. Her skin still prickled from the spiders.

"Wait until you see it," the voice crooned. *"It's the biggest, most beautiful shell you could ever imagine!"*

Tara closed her eyes.

Yes, she thought. The most beautiful shell. MY shell!

"This had better be worth it," she grumbled.

"Oh, it is," the tiny voice replied. *"Just wait. You'll see."*

Tara sighed. She crept deeper into the cave. Slowly. Very slowly.

"Keep walking," the voice in the shell whispered. *"We're almost there. Almost there."*

Tara staggered ahead. Barely breathing. No turning back now, she thought to herself. She had to find this huge shell! She had to have it!

CRUNCH! CRUNCH! CRUNCH!

Something cracked beneath Tara's feet.

"What's that?" she asked nervously. "What am I walking on?"

"Nothing to worry about," the voice in the shell answered. *"Keep walking. But watch your step!"*

Tara took another step and felt something shatter under her toes. "What is it?" she demanded. "It hurts my feet! I want to know!"

Tara spun around and slipped.

"Look out!" cried the voice. *"Don't fall!"*

Too late! Tara tumbled down. Into a huge pile of large white stones. Sharp stones. She cried out as the rough edges cut into her skin.

What are these? She peered closer.

Tara shrieked. And shrieked again.

Her horrified cries echoed through the large cave.

These weren't stones. They were bones. A carpet of bones!

"Nooo!" Tara wailed. She scrambled to her feet. "You can keep your big shell! I'm going home!"

"Wait! Wait! Don't go!" the tiny voice begged. *"There's nothing to fear!"*

Tara stopped. "Nothing to fear?" she yelled. "Look at all the bones in here!"

"They're only fish bones," the voice insisted. *"The tide carries dead fish into the cave."*

Tara gazed at the huge pile of bones on the floor. "Fish bones? They look awfully big to be fish bones."

"They're very big fish," the voice explained. *"But not as big as the biggest shell."*

"Really?" Tara said. Her heart raced with excitement.

She lifted the little shell up to her eyes and shook it hard. "Tell me where it is!" she demanded. "Tell me now, or you'll be a prisoner for the rest of your life. Where is the biggest shell in the world?"

"It's close," the voice told her. *"It's right around the corner. You can almost reach out and touch it. Turn the corner, Tara."*

Tara gasped.

The biggest shell in the world, she thought. It's almost mine!

Tara rounded the corner. She stopped. Listened.

POUND. POUND. POUND.

From the darkest depths of the cave. The beating of a giant monster heart!

"Wh-what's that sound?" Tara gasped.

"It's the pounding of the waves," the voice replied. *"Hurry up now. If you want to see the shell before the tide comes in."*

Tara trembled. She carefully stepped toward the back of the cave. The pounding grew louder. Clutching the shell nervously, Tara inched forward.

A shaft of light filtered down through the cave-top. Tara followed the ray. Down. Down. Down.

And there it sat.

The biggest shell in the world.

Tara's eyes popped open wide with wonder.

The huge shell filled the whole cavern. Its pointed spiral nearly touched the top of the cave. It glistened white and pink. So big. So beautiful.

It stole Tara's breath away.

It was a perfectly formed shell — like the little one in her hand, but a thousand times larger!

"The biggest, most beautiful shell in the whole wide world," Tara whispered in awe.

"See? I told you," the little voice crooned.

Tara rushed forward, hugging the gigantic shell in her arms. It was so big. Her arms didn't even stretch halfway around it! She stroked its smooth pink curves and gazed up at its tall, twisting spiral.

I have found the biggest and best shell of all! Tara thought. "I'll be famous!" she crowed. "I'll be rich! I'll be the greatest shell collector in the whole universe! And everyone will be so jealous!"

"There's something I forgot to tell you," the little voice said. *"This is truly the biggest shell in the world. And inside it lives — the* biggest hermit crab *in the world!"*

With that, the huge shell rose up. Tilted back. And out crawled a monstrous hermit crab!

The biggest, ugliest sea creature Tara had ever seen.

Its bulging red eyes bounced on the ends of two long stems. Its huge green mouth slammed open and shut with a hideous slurp.

Its enormous, cruel claws were the scariest part of all.

They waved frantically in the air. And snapped hard over Tara's head!

Tara shrieked. And tried to run.

Too late.

The monster crab snatched Tara up in its giant claws!

"Help me!" Tara screamed. "Somebody! Help me!"

The tiny voice in the shell burst out laughing. *"Help me! Help me!"* it mocked.

The huge claws of the monster crab pinched Tara's waist. Its pounding heart thundered in her ears. Slimy drool dripped from its hungry jaws.

Tara dropped the small shell to the ground. It rolled across the cave. And stopped.

A tiny hermit crab popped out.

"Look, Mommy, look!" the tiny voice screeched. *"I caught another one!"*

Tara screamed, and the giant claws snapped shut around her.

POISON IVY

Camp Wilbur.

What kind of a name for a camp is *Wilbur?*

I still can't believe my parents sent me here.

"Matt," they said, "you'll love it."

Well, I've got news for them. I don't love it. I don't even *like* it.

I've never been to sleepaway camp before. I'm a city kid. Why would I want to sleep away?

I like hanging out with my friends all summer. Rollerblading up and down the sidewalks. Hanging out at the playground. Going to the movies.

I like the city. How am I supposed to get used to all this fresh air?

Oh, well. I have four weeks to get used to it. Here I am in a tiny cabin. Not even any screens on the window.

I've got three bunkmates. Vinny and Mike aren't bad. They're twelve, like me.

Brad is the problem. He arrived on the first day

with *three* trunks. All filled with perfectly ironed clothes. Name tags sewn on every item.

Brad has blond hair pulled back in a ponytail down to his collar. He has blue eyes and about a thousand teeth when he smiles. He's real preppy-looking.

As soon as he walked into the cabin, Vinny and I held our noses and cried out, "What's that smell?"

"Yuck!" Mike sniffed several times and made a sour face. He turned to Brad. "What did you step in?"

"It's probably my aftershave," Brad replied calmly. He began carefully unpacking his trunks.

"Huh? Do you shave?" I asked him.

He shook his head. "No. I just like aftershave."

"Smells like sour milk," Vinny whispered. I don't think Brad heard him.

"It keeps my face fresh," Brad said, rubbing his smooth cheeks. "It comes in a spray can. Great stuff. You can borrow some if you like."

I groaned and hurried out the door. How was I going to stand living with a skunk for a whole month?

The cabins are on a low hill that overlooks the baseball field. I jogged down the hill, taking deep breaths, trying to forget that incredible odor.

Some guys from other cabins were starting a softball game. I asked if I could play, too.

The rules at Camp Wilbur are really loose. The place isn't organized at all. The rule is pretty much "Do whatever you want. Just don't get into trouble."

"You can play left field, Matt," a kid named David told me. He waved me to the outfield.

"Anybody got a glove?" I called, trotting over the grass.

"You won't need it. No one here can hit that far!" David joked. At least I *think* he was joking.

"Matt — watch out for that poison ivy," a kid named Jonathan called.

"Huh?" I glanced around. "What poison ivy?"

It wasn't hard to find. I spotted a large patch of the stuff at the edge of the outfield. It was starting to grow over the path that led to the main lodge and the dining hall.

Three leaves. A plant with three leaves. That's how you identify poison ivy. Even a city kid like me knows that.

I gazed at the square patch for a second. Then I stepped away from it and turned to home plate.

Just in time to see the first batter send a high fly ball sailing out to left field. Leaping around the poison ivy patch, I raised my hands and got under it.

"I've got it!" I called.

I didn't have it. The ball sailed over my head.

By the time I chased it down, the batter had

run the bases and was sitting in the grass drinking a Coke.

I told you I hate camp.

That night I was awakened by a loud scratching sound. I sat up in my bed and listened.

Scratch. Scratch. Strettttch.

The mosquitos are doing push-ups, I decided.

I settled back on my pillow.

But the sound repeated. Scratching. Stretching. A dry rustling from outside.

It wouldn't let me get back to sleep. I climbed out of bed and crossed the cabin to the window. My three bunkmates didn't stir.

I peered out at the purple night. The trees were tall black shadows against the clouded sky. Nothing moved. The leaves didn't rustle.

Something else was making the sound.

Scraaatch. Scraaaatch. Strettttch.

I was wide awake now. I decided to check it out. Silently, I pulled on my high-tops and crept out into the night.

I glanced up and down the hill. Totally dark. Not even any lights on in the counselors' cabins at the top.

No moon. No stars. No breeze.

I turned and followed the sound down the hill. It grew louder as I approached the baseball field.

Scraaatch. Scraaaatch. Strettttch.

I pictured giant snakes — as long as trains — stretching across the grass.

What could be making that weird sound?

I stepped on to the outfield. The grass was wet from the heavy dew. My sneakers slipped and slid.

What am I doing out here? I asked myself. Has all this fresh air warped my brain?

And then the clouds slowly pulled away from the moon. And as pale white light washed over the ground, I saw the creature.

Its head bobbed on its slender shoulders. Its hands shook on either side of its skinny body.

It rose up. Up.

"Ohhh!" I let out a low moan as I realized I was staring at a plant.

Or rather, a whole bunch of plants — rising up together!

I swallowed hard and started backing up.

The poison ivy patch! It was alive! Alive!

The three leaves formed a head and two hands. They bobbed as the plant stretched on its vine. Stretched over the baseball outfield.

Scraaatch. Scraaaatch. Strettttch.

I couldn't believe it. It was horrifying.

Long tendrils reached out toward me, curling through the darkness. I turned and ran.

I slipped and fell in the dewy grass. But I scrambled to my feet and ran even faster.

I burst into the bunk. The screen door slammed behind me.

"Hey — !" Vinny cried out sleepily.

"Poison ivy!" I screamed. "Run! Run!"

"Huh?" Vinny sat up, rubbing his eyes.

"What's up?" Mike jumped down from his bunk. "Matt — what is it?"

Brad groaned. "Give me a break. It's still night!"

"Run!" I cried. "Poison ivy! It's coming! It's coming up the hill!"

They laughed.

Do you believe it? They laughed at me.

I guess it sounded kind of stupid. And I guess I was exaggerating just a little. It was so dark out there. I probably imagined the whole thing.

Vinny and Mike accused me of having a nightmare. Brad just groaned, rolled over, and went back to sleep.

It took me a while to calm down. But then I fell back to sleep, too. And dreamed about long green snakes.

The next morning, the poison ivy patch had crept over the entire baseball diamond. It covered the outfield and the bases. And it had spread over the path that led to the main lodge.

"Hey — watch out!"

Some guys playfully shoved each other into the poison ivy patch as we made our way to breakfast. Some kids showed off by rolling around in it. They picked up clumps and tossed them at each other.

They claimed it couldn't be poison ivy since it grew so fast.

They were wrong.

By that afternoon, about half the kids in camp had horrible red rashes all over. They scratched and moaned and groaned. The camp nurse ran out of lotion by dinnertime!

That afternoon, the poison ivy had spread over the soccer field and the archery ground. And it had climbed halfway up the hill to the cabins.

Luckily, no one in my cabin had touched the stuff. We sat at dinner at our table in the corner and watched the other kids scratch and complain and carry on.

The sun was sinking down behind the trees when we came out of the dining hall. We saw Larry and Craig, two of the counselors, carrying weed whackers and weed poison.

"See you later, guys!" Craig called. "We're going to knock out that poison ivy patch if it takes us all night!"

Craig and Larry slapped each other a high five. I watched them make their way into the evening mist, heading toward the poison ivy.

We never saw them again.

Late that night, all four of us in the cabin were awakened by the frightening scratching, stretching sounds. We hurried to the window and peered out.

A thick fog had lowered over the hill. We couldn't see a thing.

I shivered. The scratching sounds were really close. I wondered if I looked as scared as Vinny, Mike, and Brad.

We went back to bed. But I don't think any of us could fall asleep.

The next morning, I wearily pulled myself out of bed. I slipped into the T-shirt and shorts I had worn the day before. Still yawning, I crossed the cabin to the door.

Started to push it open.

Pushed harder. Harder.

The door was stuck.

"Hey — what's up?" Vinny called, yawning.

I told him the problem. "I can't get out the door."

"Then climb out the window," he suggested.

Good idea. I turned to the window.

"Oh, no!" I shrieked. I *wondered* why it was such a dark morning!

The window was completely covered over. Covered by a thick curtain of POISON IVY!

"It — it climbed up here!" I stammered, pointing.

My three friends were on their feet now. We were all wide awake. Staring at the heavy curtain of leaves that blocked out all light.

"The poison ivy must have grown over the door, too!" Vinny cried.

As we stared in horror, the ivy started poking into the cracks of the cabin. Long tendrils uncoiled and reached in for us.

"Help! Somebody — help!" Brad shrieked.

"Come on!" I cried. "Let's all try the door!"

Vinny, Mike, and I ran to the door and started to shove. We lowered our shoulders to the door and pushed with all our might.

Brad hung back, clinging to a wall, trembling in fright. I turned and saw the ivy tendrils reaching, reaching into the cabin.

We pushed again. A desperate shove.

Yes! The door budged. Just an inch. We could see the thick poison ivy that had grown over the entire cabin.

"Don't touch it!" Mike cried.

"Brad — come help us!" I called to him. "Hurry. We moved it a little. But we need your help."

"Hurry! We've got to get *out* of here!" Vinny urged.

His eyes on the uncoiling tendrils, Brad obediently joined us at the door.

"Everyone push on the count of three!" I cried. "One . . . two . . ."

Brad stepped to the front and lowered his shoulder to the door.

And to our surprise, the poison ivy appeared to creep back.

We pushed the door open another inch. Then another inch.

"Shove hard!" I cried. "It's retreating or something!"

"We need only a few more inches. Then we can slip through!" Mike shouted.

Brad leaned forward.

The plant backed up.

Brad leaned further.

The plant moved back.

"Why is it doing that?" Brad asked, turning to us.

"I think I know!" I cried excitedly. "It's your aftershave! The plant can't stand your aftershave!"

"That's impossible!" Brad cried. "*Everyone* likes my aftershave!"

"Get the can," I cried. "Let's try to spray the poison ivy!"

Vinny quickly ran to the shelf over Brad's bed. He grabbed the can of aftershave and brought it to the door. Then he raised the can, aimed it at the thick poison ivy — and sprayed.

The can went, *Phhhht.* Nothing came out.

"It's empty!" I shrieked. "We're doomed!"

"No! I have twelve more cans!" Brad cried. "But I don't want to waste them!"

Ignoring Brad's protests, we pulled the twelve cans from his trunk. I ran to the door. I raised the can. I sprayed.

The ivy slid back.

I sprayed again. The ivy slid back some more.

"It works!" I cried. "The horrible smell of the aftershave makes it retreat! Come on, guys — let's get it!"

The three of us edged out the door, spraying the thick plant as we moved.

"Don't use it all up!" Brad called. But his cry was nearly drowned out by the loud *whissssssh* of the spray cans.

Back, back, we pushed the poison ivy. It had covered the whole camp. All the cabins. All of the fields. It had even covered the dining hall.

We had our work cut out for us. But we knew we could do it.

We held our noses and sprayed. Pushing the poison ivy back. Watching it retreat with every smelly whiff.

Finally, after hours of spraying, we backed the plant into the lake. Its tendrils rose up as if surrendering. And then the whole plant sank beneath the water with a loud *whooooosh*.

"YAAAAAY!" A cheer rang out through the camp as everyone shouted out thanks and congratulations. The counselors carried my three friends and me around on their shoulders. And we danced and laughed and celebrated.

But not for long.

I was the first to spot the black funnel cloud in the sky.

"A t-tornado!" I stammered.

The black cloud whirled and spun toward us.

But it *can't* be a tornado, I realized. The black cloud was making a buzzing sound. A droning buzz.

Closer. Closer. The buzz grew louder as the dark cloud lowered over the camp.

"Uh-oh!" I heard Brad exclaim over the droning roar.

"Uh-oh?" I demanded. "What do you mean *uh-oh?*"

"I forgot one bad thing about my aftershave," Brad replied.

"One bad thing? What is it?" I asked.

"It attracts mosquitoes," he said.

THE SPIRIT OF THE HARVEST MOON

Before last weekend, I'd never heard of the Pine Mountain Lodge. Neither had my parents. But then a brochure came in the mail. It advertised the lodge as "Wood Lake's 100-Year-Old Best-Kept Secret."

That's all my parents needed to hear. They have a thing about visiting out-of-the-way places. And the older the better.

"Oh, Jenny," Mom said to me, "doesn't it sound perfect? We'll go in September, over the long holiday weekend."

So here we were. At Pine Mountain Lodge. The only guests here.

"The whole place to ourselves!" Dad exclaimed as he carried in our luggage from the car.

"We'll be like part of the family," Mom said, signing the register. She gave Mr. Bass, the owner of the lodge, her cheeriest smile.

Mr. Bass grunted. He looked like Frankenstein without the green skin.

His son, Tyler, who is twelve like me, helped Dad carry our fishing poles. I nearly choked when I saw Tyler. He reminded me of a goldfish. He has light orange hair, bulging blue-gray eyes, and skin pulled so thin that you could see his veins right through it.

So far, I had only glimpsed the back of Mrs. Bass. She sat like a sack of laundry, in front of the TV.

The only normal-looking one here was Bravo, the Basses' golden retriever. He nuzzled his warm nose in my hand. "You're a good boy. Aren't you?" I said, reaching down to pet him.

"Don't get too many guests here after August," Mr. Bass said gruffly. He handed Dad the room key. "Too cold."

Dad grinned. "That's how we like it."

"Absolutely," Mom said. "We love the mountain air."

Mr. Bass led us down a long, narrow hallway to our rooms. One dirty lightbulb hanging from the ceiling cast a creepy yellow glow on the walls.

"Well, here it is," Mr. Bass said as we approached the end of the hall. He opened the door to two connecting rooms. The first room had knotty pine paneling, a rickety bed piled high with scratchy woolen blankets, and a worn braided rug on the floor.

Across the room, next to a beat-up old dresser, I saw a small, smudged window. On the other side of the dresser stood a green door that led outside.

Everything in the room smelled like my dirty gym socks.

I walked through the first room to the second room and peeked inside. It looked exactly the same as the first.

I wandered over to the green door, jerked it open, and poked my head out. It was growing dark out. So I couldn't really see much — just a porch, and, beyond it, trees. Lots and lots of trees.

"Time to close up now," Mr. Bass barked. I jumped. I hadn't seen him there.

I ducked out of his way, and he tugged the porch door shut. Then he locked it. Next, he pulled a set of heavy wooden shutters across the front of my window and latched them securely on the top and bottom.

"What are you doing?" I asked.

"Locking up," he said.

"Excuse me, Mr. Bass," I replied in my most polite voice. "I like to sleep with the window open."

Mr. Bass stared hard at me. "Too cold at night to do that," he said flatly. "Don't want to catch a chill, do you?"

"I guess not," I answered. I glanced into Mom and Dad's room. Their window was shuttered, too.

After Mr. Bass left, I unpacked my clothes. He was right. It was freezing up here. I climbed into bed wearing two pairs of socks, sweatpants, and a T-shirt with a sweatshirt over it.

I pulled the blanket up to my chin and studied the room once again. No TV. Just like Mom and Dad to find the one place on the planet without TV!

I spent the next hour or so reading. Then called good night through the connecting door.

"Sleep tight, Jenny," Mom called back. "See you in the morning!"

I guess I was pretty tired because I fell asleep right away. But I kept waking up. I couldn't find a really comfortable position. As I fluffed up my pillow for the tenth time that night, I heard a voice call out my name.

No. Can't be. It's the middle of the night. I plopped my head down on the pillow and closed my eyes.

"Jen-ny."

There! Again! I did hear it! Was it Mom or Dad? It didn't sound like either one of them. Too low and gruff.

I sat up and shivered in the dark. A strong wind rattled the shutters.

"Jen-ny."

"Is that you, Dad?" I quivered. No answer. I knew it wasn't my dad. The voice wasn't coming from his room. It came from outside. From the porch.

"Jen-ny," it cried again. "It's cold out here."

My heart hammered away. What should I do? I crept out of bed to the green door. I leaned my ear against it. "Who's there?" I croaked.

No answer.

I flew back to bed and yanked the covers up to my ears. And waited.

"Jenny! Jenny!" My eyes jerked open. Sunlight peeked through the shutters. I must have fallen asleep.

"Time to get up!" Mom chirped in the doorway. "Did you sleep well?"

"Uh, I was cold," I mumbled. "How did you sleep?"

"Like a rock," Mom sang out happily. "I love this crisp mountain air."

Did I really hear a voice last night? It must have been a dream. Just a weird dream.

After breakfast, Mom and Dad decided to hike up to Devil's Peak.

"Aren't you coming along?" Dad asked as he and Mom buttoned up their identical red-and-black-checkered jackets. Then they tugged on matching red-and-black caps with furry red ear-flaps. Boy, did they look dumb.

"Mr. Bass says the view up there is spectacular," Mom explained. "Come on, honey. Put your jacket on."

I hate hiking. "Um. Can I hang out with Tyler? And, uh, explore the woods around here?"

"Well, okay," Mom replied. "But don't go too far. We won't be gone long."

Tyler and I played a few games of horseshoes. Then he gave me a tour of the lodge while Bravo tagged along. The tour took two minutes. There was the lodge and then there was the woods. Period.

By now, things were getting pretty boring. Tyler didn't talk much. We sat cross-legged on the porch, staring at each other.

"So, Tyler," I began. "Do you have any friends around here?"

He stared at me with those bulging eyes. "Not really," he answered. "But I don't mind. I like playing alone."

"Oh," I said. I kind of expected him to answer that way. Then I thought about the strange voice from last night.

"Does anybody live near here?" I asked.

"No," he replied. "The next house is a mile away."

"Are you sure there's no one else around here?" I asked. "Because last night I thought I heard someone out here on the porch."

Tyler's body stiffened. "What do you mean?"

I told him about the creepy voice calling my name. "But I'm sure I dreamed the whole thing," I ended.

"Well, you didn't," Tyler said.

"What do you mean?" I gasped.

Tyler moved in close. "There's something I should tell you," he whispered. "I'm only telling you this for your own good. Okay?"

I nodded.

"This lodge is haunted. That voice you heard was the spirit, calling to you."

"The sp-spirit?" I stammered. "What kind of spirit?" I reached out for Bravo and hugged him close to me.

Tyler's eyes narrowed. "A long, long time ago, a tourist hiked up Devil's Peak and never came down."

I gulped loudly.

"They say," Tyler continued, "that his spirit turned into a wandering mist. And the mist takes over a different body every year."

"Really?" I croaked.

"Uh-huh," Tyler said. "A different body every year. At the end of each summer, during the harvest moon, it finds a new body. A warm body. That's why we lock the doors and shutters at night. To keep the spirit from coming inside."

I swallowed hard. I knew we shouldn't have come here. I *knew* it.

"What exactly happens if the spirit comes inside?"

Tyler lowered his voice. "If you let it inside, it will jump out of the body it's in and enter yours.

Then *you* will be forced to live on Earth for a year as a wandering mist."

"That's ridiculous," I blurted. "You're making this up. You're just trying to scare me."

"Jen-ny!" I nearly jumped out of my skin. I turned to see Mom and Dad waving from the end of the trail. I was never so happy to see my parents. Even in those dumb jackets.

I ran to them, practically knocking them down. "Mom! Dad!"

"Hi, Jen." Dad smiled. His cheeks glowed rosy red from the crisp mountain air. "Did you have fun?"

"Uh, sure," I answered. "I'm glad you're back, though." And I meant it, too.

That night, I didn't look forward to bedtime. But I kept telling myself that Tyler was just trying to scare me. Nothing would happen. Tyler was just a creep. Who had no friends. And I could see why.

After Mr. Bass came by to close the shutters, I crawled into bed. I tried really hard to fall asleep. I couldn't.

I was so wide awake, I heard Dad snoring through the door. I hummed along with his snores. And began to drift off. . . .

"Jen-ny! It's cold outside."

My eyes popped wide open. I instantly began

to shake all over. The voice. It was real. Not a dream.

"Jenny!" it called louder. *"It's cold outside."*

I flew out of bed. "Mom! Dad!" I screamed. I shoved open the door to their room and jumped into bed with them.

Mom bolted straight up. "Jenny! What's wrong?" she cried.

My heart pounded in my chest. "A ghost is after me," I sobbed. Then I told them Tyler's story.

"Oh, honey," Mom said. "Tyler's just playing a mean joke on you. Dad will talk to him in the morning."

"But I heard the voice, Mom. I know I did." I sobbed even harder.

"Calm down, Jen," Dad said softly. "It's only your imagination."

"It is not," I wailed. "I'm not kidding about this. I'm really not."

"We know, dear," Mom replied.

But they didn't know. They had no idea.

The next morning, I shuffled into the dining room. Tired and confused. I sat with my parents, even though I could tell Tyler wanted me to sit with him. But I wasn't going to let that creep near me.

Bravo curled up underneath my chair. As I ate my scrambled eggs, I fed him little scraps of bacon. He took my mind off Tyler.

But I couldn't help stealing a glance at the window. I saw that Tyler hardly ate a thing. In fact, he never seemed to eat much at all. No wonder he was so thin and pale.

Tyler shoved his chair away from his table and headed for ours. Bravo whimpered and nudged my knee. My stomach churned.

Tyler grinned at me. "Want to play some more horseshoes, Jenny?"

My heart began to thud. "No," I said, my eyes glued to my plate. Suddenly I knew. Tyler was pale. Tyler never ate. Tyler's own dog feared him. *Tyler was the spirit!*

"Please, Jenny?" Tyler begged.

"I'm busy," I told him. Then I gave Mom and Dad a look that said don't butt in.

I hung around with Mom and Dad all day. I even hiked up a nature trail with them. I'd do anything to avoid Tyler.

At dinner that night, I hardly touched my food. On the way back to our rooms, Dad gazed outside. "Look, Jenny! The harvest moon!"

A chill shot through my entire body. Hadn't Tyler said that the spirit finds a new body during the harvest moon?

"What's wrong, honey?" Mom asked. "You look upset."

"I want to go home right now!" I wailed. "If we stay here, the wandering spirit is going to take over my body."

"Jenny," Mom cooed, "you know better than to believe a silly ghost story."

"But there is a ghost!" I cried. "Why won't you believe me?"

Mom just shook her head from side to side. But she walked into my room with me and sat on the bed for a long time.

Then, just before Mr. Bass came to lock the shutters, Mom peered out the window to check the porch. "Jenny! Look!" she said. "Bravo's out there. He'll protect you."

Knowing Bravo sat out there did make me feel a little better. And even though I'm too old to be tucked in, I let Mom tuck me in that night.

"Sleep tight," she said, kissing me good night. "If you need us, Dad and I will be in the lounge playing bridge with the Basses."

"Bridge!" I shouted. "You aren't going to be next door?"

"Jenny," Mom said firmly. "Stop this. You're acting like a baby." Then she left.

I lay very still for a long time. The wind howled through the woods. It blew hard against the porch door. A tree branch scraped against my window. I covered myself with three blankets, but I still shivered underneath them.

I was all alone.

I waited.

Waited for the spirit to call my name.

No voice. Nothing but the sound of the howling wind and the rattling shutters.

BANG! Someone knocked hard on the door. "Jenny. It's cold and windy out here. Let me in. It's me, Tyler!"

I clutched the blankets close to me. He was here. Here to steal my body. "Go away!" I shouted. "You're evil!"

"Please! Let me inside! I lost my key! Jenny, please! Don't leave me out here. It's so cold. Please!"

"No!" I screamed. "Never. Never!" The wind shook the shutters hard now. Tyler kept banging. Tears ran down my face. My whole body trembled. "Go away!" I yelled.

Then I heard Bravo barking. Good boy, Bravo! He must have heard my cries. His paws clattered up the porch steps. He snarled angrily at Tyler.

"Stop it!" Tyler shouted at the dog. "Leave me alone!" I heard Tyler stumble down the stairs.

And then — silence. Bravo had chased Tyler away. The horror had passed.

I was safe.

I let out a long, relieved sigh.

Soft whimpering cut through the quiet. Bravo!

I rushed to the green door, opened it, and Bravo trudged in.

Bravo gazed up at me gratefully. His sad brown eyes stared up to meet mine. "Thanks, Jenny," he said. "It's cold outside."

Even More TALES TO GIVE YOU

Goosebumps®

THE CHALK CLOSET

I wiped the sweat from my forehead. It was only seven-thirty in the morning. But the thermometer had already hit 95 degrees. And the air conditioner on the bus was broken.

This was not going to be a good day.

"Hey, kid," the bus driver yelled. "End of the line!"

End of the line was right, I thought. I jumped off the bus and checked out the school.

Millwood Junior High. It was a wreck.

The school stood four stories high. Its red brick — blackened with years and years of city soot — was chipped and crumbling. All the windows on the second floor were boarded over with plywood. And the roof sagged.

"Better get used to it, Travis," I told myself. I dragged myself up the steps. "You're going to be here all summer."

No matter what my mom says, I didn't exactly *try* to mess up sixth grade. Like lots of major disasters, it just happened. I tried to study. But stuff kept getting in the way.

Like when my cat, Lillie, had her kittens.

Or when my brother got a new computer game.

Or when something was on TV.

So . . . I messed up. And now, here I was in summer school. And looking at the school, I could see it was the pits.

I opened the rusty door and stepped inside. The main hallway was dark. I could barely see. The air was dry and smelled really stale. I started to cough.

I took a drink from the water fountain beside me. The water was warm and cloudy. And it tasted old.

I glanced up and down the hall. The place seemed deserted — no kids, no teachers.

No one.

I made my way down the hall and found a door marked PRINCIPAL. I jiggled the knob. Locked.

I checked out the classrooms. Empty. Except for the squeak of my sneakers, the place was totally dead.

What was going on? Was I here on the wrong day? Or was it the wrong school?

Then a voice broke the silence: "Travis Johnson?"

I nearly jumped out of my skin. I spun around and faced the tallest, palest man I'd ever seen.

"Y-yes?" I stammered.

"You're late, Travis," he said. His lips were unbelievably thin, and they hardly moved when he spoke.

Just great, I thought. My first day in summer school and I'm already in trouble. Way to go, Travis.

I followed the tall man to the classroom at the end of the hall. Of course, it was the only room I hadn't checked out. It was filled with kids. Many of them I'd never seen before.

Dooley Atwater and Janice Humphries were there. They came from my regular school. Janice was shy but okay. Dooley was the biggest goof in my whole school. He knew a million ways to get out of homework.

"The last row, Travis," the teacher said. "Be quick about it." Then he picked up a piece of chalk from the chalk tray and wrote MR. GRIMSLEY on the board.

Mr. Grimsley folded his arms across his chest and scanned the room. From the sour look on his face, I could tell he wasn't too thrilled about what he saw.

"Let me warn you, boys and girls," Mr. Grimsley announced. "I have very little patience with students who don't care to study. Got that, Dooley?"

"Me?" Dooley asked. "Why me?"

"I know about you, Dooley," Mr. Grimsley said, thumbing through a stack of cards. "I know about every single one of you. You're bright kids. But you're all lazy. Hear this warning. You won't get away with anything in my class."

Dooley smirked.

Mr. Grimsley glared at him. Then he continued, "You must do your homework every night — or be prepared to go to the chalk closet."

"The chalk closet?" one of the girls asked nervously. "What's that?"

"If you don't turn in your homework tomorrow morning, you'll find out, Amanda," Mr. Grimsley said.

"No teacher gives homework the first night!" Dooley protested. "You've got to be kidding!"

"I do not kid," Mr. Grimsley declared. "Now let's get down to work."

The first night for homework, we had to write five reasons we'd want to be a Pilgrim. As soon as I reached home, I sat down at the kitchen table and wrote down three:

1. Get to travel a lot.
2. Eat dinner with some really cool Indians.
3. Don't have to recycle.

Then my brother, Chris, came in. "Want to go to the Ice Cream Igloo?" he asked. "They have a new flavor — peanut butter marshmallow mint."

I didn't have a choice. I had to go — right?

After dinner there was a *Lethal Weapon* movie on TV. No way I could miss that.

So, when I arrived at school the next morning,

I still had only three reasons why someone would want to be a Pilgrim.

But it was three more reasons than Dooley had.

"Your homework, Dooley," Mr. Grimsley demanded.

"You have to give me a break," Dooley replied, "just this once, Mr. Grimsley."

"I have to?" Mr. Grimsley asked, arching his eyebrows.

"It kind of looks that way," Dooley began. "You see, a car alarm went off right outside my window. And it was so loud, I couldn't think. And by the time someone turned it off — "

"It was way past your bedtime?" Mr. Grimsley asked.

"Well, not exactly," Dooley admitted.

"But you did your homework anyway — and then when you woke up, the cat had eaten it. Is that what happened, Dooley?"

"Well, something like that," Dooley said, smiling a little.

"Sorry, Dooley. I don't give breaks," Mr. Grimsley declared. "It's time to go to the chalk closet." Then he stepped into the hall.

Dooley started to follow. But when he reached the doorway, he stopped. "I forgot my textbook," he said, turning back.

Mr. Grimsley grinned. A creepy grin. "The chalk closet isn't study hall, Dooley."

"So what is it?"

Mr. Grimsley didn't answer.

Dooley shrugged. Then he followed the teacher down the corridor. I heard their footsteps fade as they walked up the stairs to the second floor.

Mr. Grimsley returned in a couple of minutes — without Dooley. At recess, Dooley didn't show up. Or at lunch. Or the next day. Or any day after that.

I didn't miss him, and I didn't feel sorry for him either. I figured he was kicked out of school. And he had it coming to him.

But at the end of the week, the same thing happened to Marty Blank. Marty sat next to me. I didn't know him too well, but he seemed okay.

Grimsley handed back the homework he had graded the night before. I heard Marty groan when he received his. There was a big red *F* at the top.

"You didn't study, did you, Marty?" Mr. Grimsley asked.

Marty shook his head. "I couldn't," he said. "I had Little League."

"Little League was more important than your schoolwork?" Mr. Grimsley demanded coldly.

"It was the big game," Marty explained. "The team was counting on me."

"The chalk closet, Marty," Mr. Grimsley replied.

"But I did my homework, Mr. Grimsley," Marty

protested. "I'm not like Dooley. It's not like I didn't try!"

Mr. Grimsley picked up Marty's homework. "*F*," he stated. "I guess you didn't try hard enough — did you, Marty? Let me show you to the chalk closet."

Marty's mouth dropped open. It looked as if he were about to say something. But he didn't. He just followed Mr. Grimsley down the hall.

Four days later, Marty still hadn't shown up at school.

"Maybe Grimsley kicked him out of school," I told Janice. "Or maybe Marty convinced his parents to let him quit," I suggested. "For all we know, Marty could be having a great time at the lake."

"For all we know," Janice said, "Marty could still be in the chalk closet."

Janice and I gazed up at the second floor.

"That's probably where Mr. Grimsley took them," she said. "Those boarded-up windows give me the creeps."

We stared up at the windows in silence. "Travis, what do you think is in the chalk closet?"

"Chalk."

"Very funny, Travis. You might not be scared, but I am. I'm really scared. I got *D*'s on my last three assignments. What if I'm next?"

What if *I'm* next? I thought with a shiver.

* * *

The next morning, Janice's hands shook when Grimsley handed back our assignments.

"B-but I worked really hard on it," she stammered. "I really did."

I didn't need to see her grade. I knew from Janice's voice that she had failed.

Grimsley didn't say a word. He just walked to the door. And waited.

Janice stood up.

Grimsley waited.

She slowly made her way to the door. Then they both disappeared down the hall.

Mr. Grimsley returned in a minute or so, and the class went on as usual. Right before the bell rang, Mr. Grimsley made an announcement. "We're going to have a math test tomorrow. And I expect everyone to get an *A*."

An *A*? I'd never gotten an *A* on a math test — ever.

The bell rang and I dashed outside to wait for Janice. I thought about the test while I waited.

And waited. And waited.

Janice never showed up.

I ran all the way home and grabbed the phone. I dialed Janice's number. The phone rang and rang. No answer.

I looked up Marty's telephone number in the phone book and called him. A recorded message announced that the Blanks' number had been disconnected.

That night I tried to study. I never tried harder at anything in my whole life. But I was just too frightened to concentrate. What if Grimsley sends me to the chalk closet? I asked myself over and over again.

When I finished the test the next day, I knew I had blown it. I'd be lucky if I passed. But I'd have to wait till Monday — two whole days — to find out.

The weekend dragged. I couldn't think about anything except that stupid math test. And the chalk closet.

Monday morning finally arrived. My feet felt like lead as I walked up the steps to school. This was not going to be a good day.

I took my seat and stared straight ahead at Mr. Grimsley. He sat at his desk. The pile of test papers was neatly stacked in front of him.

He cleared his throat. "I'm going to return your test papers now," he said. "Most of you did very well."

He didn't look at me when he said that, I thought. But what did that mean? Was it good? Or bad? I didn't know.

"Bennett, Amanda," he began. "*A*."

Oh, no! He's calling out the grades, too!

"Drake, Josh — *A*. Evers, Brian — *A*. Franklin, Marnie — *A*."

Wow! I couldn't believe it. Everyone was getting *A*'s.

I broke out into a cold sweat. I wiped my sweaty palms on my pants. Hey, don't worry, I told myself. Everyone's getting *A*'s. I probably got one, too.

Grimsley continued calling out names and grades. I was next.

My temples pounded as I watched him stare down at my paper.

"Johnson, Travis — *D*."

The whole class gasped.

"You know, I — I can do better than that, Mr. Grimsley," I stuttered. "Let me take a makeup test. Okay? You'll see."

"No makeup tests in my class," the teacher replied sternly.

"Please, Mr. Grimsley!" I cried. "Don't take me to the chalk closet! Please!"

"Come, Travis," Mr. Grimsley said. "You don't want to upset the other students, do you?"

I glanced around the room at the other kids. A few of them stared at me. Their eyes filled with horror. But the others had their heads buried in their textbooks. They pretended that they didn't even know what was going on!

"Don't you care?" I screamed at them.

No one answered.

Mr. Grimsley stood at the door.

"Come, Travis."

My knees shook so hard I could barely walk.

I followed Mr. Grimsley into the hall.

The front door was at the end of the hall. Mr. Grimsley's legs were longer, but I was younger. Could I outrun him?

"Don't even think about it," he said, without turning back. "It's locked."

I followed Mr. Grimsley up the stairs. It was almost pitch-black on the second floor. The only light came from a naked bulb dangling from the ceiling.

I trailed behind Mr. Grimsley. Past Room 269. Then 270. Then 271.

When we came to 272, he stopped and turned toward me. "Good-bye, Travis," he said.

I took a step back. I couldn't speak. I was terrified.

Mr. Grimsley twisted the doorknob. Then he gave the door a little push. It creaked open.

I peeked in over his shoulder. My heart pounded. What would I see in there?

I couldn't see anything. It was totally dark.

Mr. Grimsley gripped my shoulder and shoved me forward.

I stumbled inside.

The door slammed shut behind me!

I was locked inside — inside the chalk closet!

I squinted. Waited for my eyes to adjust to the darkness.

And then I saw them.

Dooley. Marty. Janice.

And behind them, shadows of other kids I'd never seen before. Transparent figures. Ghosts.

I squinted harder. They were all doing something. They were all holding their hands up in the air.

Why? I wondered. Why are they doing that?

That's when I heard it.

That's when I knew the chalk closet was the worst place on earth to be.

My hands flew up in the air, too.

Up to my ears. To cover them.

To drown out the screeching.

The horrible screeching sound of chalk on a chalkboard — the sound that I'd have to listen to forever.

HOME SWEET HOME

"Sharon!" my little sister screamed. "Sha-RON!"

It always makes Alice nuts when I fool around with her dollhouse. That's why I keep doing it. I just can't resist.

It's bad enough to be twelve and still sharing a room with my little sister. But that dollhouse takes up way too much space.

Alice is always playing with it. She has a family of dolls that are the exact right size for the tiny furniture. They even have names — Shawna and Bill, the mom and dad dolls, and Timmy and Toni, the kids. They all have plastic hair.

"SHARON!"

I strolled down the hall to our room. Alice knelt in front of the dollhouse, putting everything back the way it had been.

"You called?" I asked.

She glared at me over her shoulder. "You changed the furniture all around again."

"So?"

"And you stuck Shawna upside down in the sink."

"Give me a break, Alice. Shawna is a doll. And in case you hadn't noticed, that's a fake sink. It's not like it's going to mess up her hair or anything."

"You are so mean!"

I made a face. "Get a life. Normal nine-year-olds don't spend all their time playing with stupid dollhouses."

"It isn't stupid!" she shouted.

"Is so!"

She stuck out her bottom lip and pouted. I felt bad. Well, a little, anyway. "Look, I'm sorry, okay?" I muttered.

I flopped down on my bed. Alice didn't say anything for a while. Then she set the roof back on the dollhouse and stood up.

"Sharon?"

"Yeah?"

"Want to ride over to a garage sale with me?"

"Don't you have any friends?" I asked.

"None of them can go. Besides, it's on East Bay Street, and none of us are allowed to go that far by ourselves. Please?" she begged.

I don't know why I agreed to go. I really don't. Maybe because I felt guilty for messing up her dollhouse. Whatever. A few minutes later, we hopped on our bikes and headed out.

* * *

We turned onto East Bay Street. Alice stopped in front of a big, old house set way back from the road. I spotted the name on the mailbox. "Hey, this is Mrs. Forster's place!" I cried.

"Uh-huh."

I glanced up at the house. A curtain twitched, and I had the feeling that somebody had peeked out at us. "Mrs. Forster is really strange," I told Alice. "At least, that's what I've heard. Some kids told me she has weird powers. They said she can change herself into animals."

"No way!" exclaimed Alice.

"I saw her one time," I insisted. "She's totally scary. She's got big, black eyes that glare right through you. Her hair is as black as her eyes, with a streak of white right down the middle that looks like a lightning bolt."

Alice stuck her tongue out at me. "What's the matter, Sharon? Scared?"

That got me. "Of course I'm not scared."

"So come on." She started pedaling up the long gravel driveway. I followed slowly. I didn't want to be there. Mrs. Forster *did* scare me. But no way was I going to look lame in front of my little sister.

Alice stopped in front of the garage. Two long tables had been set up to hold the stuff Mrs. Forster wanted to sell. But nobody else was there, not even to take the money.

"How come no one is around?" I asked.

Alice shrugged. "Maybe she's gone to lunch or something."

I turned to stare at the house. The windows seemed to stare back like black, rectangular eyes. "I guess we'd better go."

"Not yet." Alice pointed toward the nearest table. "There's a sign. It says 'Leave payment on the table.' "

"Too weird," I muttered.

"Well, I'm going to look," Alice replied. She dove in. I mean, this stuff was heaven for Alice. And I knew exactly what she was looking for.

"You don't really think Mrs. Forster is going to have dollhouse furniture, do you?" I teased.

"Even if she doesn't, maybe she's selling some lace or something I can use to make curtains. She's got some really old stuff here, and . . . hey!" Alice cried. "Look!"

She picked up a tiny object from the table and held it up. "It's a little doll lamp."

"Let's see." I ran my finger along the shade. It felt cool and grainy, like a frog's skin. A shiver went up my spine. "Yuck!" I exclaimed.

"It's perfect for my living room," Alice protested. "And she only wants two bucks for it — exactly what I brought."

She set the money on the table and tucked the lamp into her pocket. "Aren't you going to buy anything?"

No way. I didn't want anything that creepy woman owned. But I didn't want Alice to know how frightened I was. So I started poking through the pile of stuff on the far table. A big china bowl caught my eye. I thought it was kind of pretty, so I picked it up.

"Be careful with that," Alice warned.

A huge, hairy spider crawled over the rim of the bowl. It scuttled over my hand. I screamed and flung the bowl away from me. It shattered into a thousand pieces across the concrete.

"Sharon! Look what you did!" Alice gasped.

"I hate spiders!" I cried. "Hate them, hate them, hate them!"

I gazed up at the house. A woman stood at one of the upstairs windows, staring down at me. I could see the stripe of pale hair glinting in the sunlight. Mrs. Forster!

I panicked. I totally panicked. "Let's get out of here!" I cried.

We grabbed our bikes and rode like crazy down the drive. I glanced over my shoulder. Mrs. Forster remained at the window, glaring at me with her round, black eyes.

We didn't stop until we reached home. Alice ran upstairs with the lamp. I guess she forgot all about Mrs. Forster once she returned to her weird little dollhouse world.

But *I* didn't. That night, I dreamed about the old woman. In the dream, she knew me. She talked to me. "You broke my bowl," she whispered in a harsh, raspy voice. "And you didn't pay for it. But you will pay, Sharon. I promise. Now you are my problem. And I always take care of my problems."

She leaned over me. Her hair fell down and tickled my face. I opened my eyes.

And found myself staring at the biggest, ugliest spider I'd ever seen. It dangled from the ceiling on a long white strand. As it swiveled to stare down at me, I saw a white stripe down its back.

It tickled my face with its hairy front legs.

"Mom!" I screamed. "Dad! Help!"

A few seconds later, Mom and Dad came running in. I scrambled out of the bed and flung myself at them.

"It's a spider!" I shrieked. "A big, hairy spider right on my pillow!"

Mom clicked the light on. No spider. No spider anywhere in the room.

Only Alice, sitting up in her bed, her mouth open wide in surprise.

Dad checked under the covers and all around the bed. I kept watching for it to scuttle across the carpet.

But no. No sign of it. "It was right there," I insisted. "It talked to me."

Alice giggled. "Wow, are you messed up, Sharon. A talking spider?"

I forced a laugh, too. It *was* really silly — wasn't it?

The next day, I rode my bike over to a friend's house. I stayed longer than I had meant to. When I realized how late it was, I jumped on my bike and raced home.

By the time I reached our neighborhood, trees cast long shadows across the ground. One more block, and I'd be home. I checked for traffic, then started across the road.

"Huh?" I cried out as a car roared out of nowhere. I froze. Stared into bright headlights.

Then I swerved so hard my bike nearly flipped over. Tires squealed. I could feel a breeze as the car sped past me.

My legs started to shake, so I got off my bike and sat down on the curb. Wow! A close one! I couldn't understand where that car had come from. I'd looked both ways, after all.

A faint scrabbling sound floated up from the storm sewer beside me. I peered into the dark opening. I couldn't see anything at first.

Then something moved in the darkness. Something small and quick. My heart began to pound.

A big hairy spider clambered out of the sewer onto the curb. It had a pale stripe down its back.

I leaped up and ran down the block and into my house. It took me a while to get my breath back.

This didn't make any sense. Where were all the spiders coming from?

I didn't know the answer. But I did know one thing: I hadn't been dreaming last night. I kept picturing that pale stripe down the spider's back.

I shuddered. I suddenly felt so afraid. I didn't even go back out to get my bike.

After dinner, I headed upstairs to do my homework. Alice had dragged the dollhouse out into the middle of the room. Tiny chairs and tables, beds and bathtubs littered the floor.

"Hey," I protested. "You're trashing my side of the room. I can't even get to my desk to do my homework."

"So do it on your bed," Alice shot back.

I started to my bed — and heard a *crunch*.

"Oh!" I gazed down and saw that I had stepped on one of the dolls. Shawna. Her hand had broken off.

Alice instantly burst into tears. "Look what you did!" she wailed.

"It was an accident!" I cried. "I didn't mean to!"

"You did. You hate my dollhouse. And you hate Shawna. That's why you always stick her head in the sink. And that's why you stepped on her!" Sobbing, she grabbed the broken doll and ran out of the room.

With a sigh, I flopped down onto my bed. "Stupid dollhouse!"

I glanced up. My breath stopped. "No!"

The spider.

The spider with the white stripe.

It clung to the ceiling with its thick, hairy legs. If it let go, it would land on my face.

I shrieked and rolled off the bed.

When I glanced up, the spider was gone.

For the next couple of days, Alice wouldn't even talk to me. She walked past me as if I were invisible.

Just before dinner on Friday, I caught up with her in the hall. "Alice, listen," I pleaded. "I'm sorry about Shawna. I didn't mean to step on her. I really didn't."

She stared at me for a moment. "It's okay. Dad fixed her hand."

I felt better. But I just couldn't keep from teasing her. "I promise I won't put Shawna's head in the sink again," I offered.

"You won't?"

"Nope. I'll work on Bill for a change."

She stuck her tongue out at me. Then she spun around and headed for the dining room. Probably to tell.

I started after her. But then I heard the sound of glass tinkling above me, and gazed up at the chandelier. Its glass prisms quivered, sending rainbows shooting around the room. It happened every time a breeze blew in from the front window.

Except the window was closed.

The tinkling of glass grew louder. The prisms shook wildly. Before I could move out from under it, the chandelier broke away from the ceiling.

I dove to the wall.

The chandelier crashed to the floor beside me.

I shrieked and stared down at it.

Stared. Stared down at the spider.

"You — you tried to kill me!" I shouted at it. "I know who you are. I know what you're trying to do!"

I spun away. I had to get out of there. Away from the vicious old woman in her spider body.

I took three steps — and felt something drop heavily into my hair.

My eyes moved to the hall mirror. I saw it. I saw the spider in my hair.

I felt its hot breath on the back of my neck.

Felt its hairy legs slide through my hair, over my scalp.

"Noooooo!" With a cry of horror, I pulled at it with both hands. But it clung tightly to my hair. Clung so tight. So tight.

I screamed again. Couldn't anyone hear me?

I ran into my room. "Alice — help me! Help!"

She wasn't there.

And then I felt the spider legs — the points, the sharp points — digging into my scalp. Digging into my head.

Into my brain!

"Nooooooooo!"

Over my scream, I heard dry laughter. "You are a *tiny* problem," the spider rasped. So close to my ear.

The pain shot through my head. Through my whole body.

"You are a tiny, tiny problem."

Was the spider growing bigger? I felt its hot, spongy body press against my back.

Was it bigger now? No. It wasn't bigger.

I was smaller.

I was shrinking. Shrinking fast. Standing in the shadow of the hideous spider that still clung to me. Still drilled its forearms into my scalp.

"I have my revenge," the old woman's spider voice rasped in my ear. "You are a tiny problem now."

"Noooo!" With another cry of horror, I broke free. Broke free and ran into the dollhouse. Hid inside the dollhouse.

I was as tiny as a doll. I could hide there. I could be safe.

My life now? It isn't as bad as it sounds.

Alice has fixed up the dollhouse really nice. I'm comfortable inside it. My room is really great. She even put in a little color TV!

I feel very safe and protected.

I just have one big problem.

Alice.

Here she comes now.

"Hey — put me down! I mean it, Alice! Put me down!"

Why does she think it's so funny to stick my head in the sink?

DON'T WAKE MUMMY

The day the deliverymen brought a mummy case to our house, I tried not to act scared. I knew my older sister, Kim, would tease me forever if she knew how I felt.

"Oooh! A coffin," Kim said. "Are you scared, Jeff?"

Kim thinks that just because she is thirteen and I'm only eleven that I'm some kind of scaredy-cat. She's always jumping out at me and trying to spook me. That's Kim's only hobby. Teasing me and telling me I'm a wimp.

Dad is the curator of the town museum. So I've seen a lot of mummy cases — at the museum. This was the first one delivered to our house.

It was all a big mistake. But Mom had the men carry it into the basement. She warned us not to go near it.

After the men left, Kim and I stood at the top of the stairs, looking down into the basement.

"I've heard about these mummies," Kim said,

narrowing her eyes. "They wake at night and search for prey."

"I don't believe you," I said.

"No, really," she insisted. "Mummies are jealous of living people. So they creep around after dark and steal the life from people."

"Well, that mummy isn't stealing anyone's life. That box is chained up tight."

"You know, Jeff, the worst thing about you is that you're such a wimp," Kim declared.

"I am not," I protested.

"If you're not a coward, then why don't you go down there and check out the mummy?" she demanded.

"No way!" I told her. "Are you crazy? You heard what Mom said."

"Why don't you go down there and touch the box? Touch it one time. I bet you're too scared to even do that," she said.

"Fine," I said. "I'll do it." I regretted it even before the words finished coming out of my mouth.

The light switch was broken in the basement. It was so dark down there, it even smelled dark, like clay. I walked down the stairs slowly.

The box sat in the middle of the room. Everything else was covered in a layer of dust. But that box was spotless. The lid was so glossy it seemed to glow.

Step by step, I drew closer to the coffin. The only sound I could hear was the beating of my heart.

The air felt cold and moist. I rubbed my chilly, sticky palms together, working up my courage.

You can do it, I told myself. There's nothing to be afraid of.

I reached out my hand to touch the shiny black box — and the lid moved!

The chains clanked.

My heartbeat stopped for a moment.

I couldn't help it — I screamed.

Then I turned and hurtled up the stairs without looking back.

The basement door was shut! Kim had closed it behind me!

I threw my body against it and burst into the kitchen.

Kim sat at the dinner table, laughing at me.

"The mummy is alive!" I shouted. "The chains rattled! The lid moved!"

She roared with laugher. "You're such a jerk."

She strode over to the basement door, threw it open, and peered down at the box. "There's nothing to see," she announced.

She was right. The lid was closed. The chains were in place.

My imagination had tricked me again.

Or had it?

* * *

I had a hard time getting to sleep that night. No matter how I twisted my body, I couldn't get comfortable.

Why couldn't I get to sleep? I looked around my room. Everything was in its place. My books stood up straight on the bookshelf. My computer sat on my desk, casting a shadow over a pile of notebooks. I had thrown my clothes on the floor and they were clumped together near the closet door.

Go to sleep, I told myself. Everything is fine.

But then I heard a *THUMP*.

I sat up in bed. It sounded like someone dropped the phone book on the floor.

I waited. I listened.

THUMP.

Again.

What could it be?

THUMP.

There was a rhythm to the sounds. One after another. . . . Sort of like . . .

FOOTSTEPS!

Each heavy sound was a footstep!

THUMP.

And the steps were coming closer.

Then I heard an eerie clanking. I strained to hear it better.

THUMP. *CLANK*.

My heart raced.

It was a chain.

THUMP. CLANK.

I gasped. The mummy! Searching for a victim. Searching for me.

I screamed, for the second time that day. I heard someone running.

My door swung open.

The mummy! It had long tangled robes and wild frizzy hair. I screamed again and dove under the covers.

"Shhhh," a soft voice said. "Honey, everything's fine. I'm here now."

"Huh?" Mom. Wearing her terry-cloth robe.

She sat down on the edge of the bed and rubbed my neck. "Did you have a nightmare?" she asked me.

"No!" I exclaimed. "The mummy is out. I heard it coming for me, coming up the stairs."

"You had a bad dream, that's all." Mom bent over and kissed me on the top of the head. She smelled like cinnamon and soap.

I listened to her footsteps padding off down the hall.

The soft sound her slippers made on the floor was nothing like the heavy steps I had heard before.

I wanted to believe her, but I knew what I had heard. The mummy was out. It would be coming for me again.

* * *

The next day, I biked to the library to try to find out how to protect myself from mummies. Would you believe that the only books they had on mummies were scary novels and art history books? Not one practical how-to book?

As I pushed my bike home through town I noticed a new shop on Main Street. The sign read SAM BONE'S MYSTICAL MERCHANDISE. In the window a tapestry was laid out, with all sorts of crystals spread on it.

Through the glass I could see a guy, sitting up on a counter, leafing through a big book. He had long, bushy hair and a beard. Maybe he could help me. No one else was taking me seriously. What did I have to lose?

I locked my bike up on a No Parking sign. Then I pushed open the door to Sam Bone's Mystical Merchandise. A tiny set of chimes hanging on the door rang out.

"Good afternoon, sir," the man said, hopping off the counter and closing his book. "How may I be of service?"

"Are you Sam Bone?" I asked him.

"The one and only," he said, doing a corny little bow.

"I'm looking for some information on mummies," I said hesitantly.

"Is this for some kind of school project?" he asked me. "Or are you planning a trip to Egypt perhaps?"

"No, you see, my dad is the curator at the Museum of Natural History here in town. We had a mummy delivered to our house by mistake. . . ." The whole story poured out of me.

When I finished, Sam Bone began pacing up and down the crowded aisles of the store. Every so often he would grab a book off the shelf and rip through it, searching for something. Or he would rummage through a box full of oils or candles or crystals.

"Of course!" he shouted suddenly. "I've got it!"

He disappeared into a back room for a moment. When he returned he was grinning from ear to ear.

He held a closed fist in front of my face and then opened his fingers one by one. In his palm lay a small purple sack, with pictures of gold eyes sewn all over it.

Sam opened the neck of the pouch and poured a tiny bit of blue powder into his hand.

"Mummy dust!" he exclaimed. "This is an ancient mix of minerals. It is said that the Egyptians would scatter this dust around the entrances to tombs to keep the spirits from crossing into the world of the living. One puff of this dust and a mummy loses its power."

Then he blew the dust right in my face. I coughed. The dust smelled bitter and old.

"I'll take it!" I shouted. "How much does it cost?"

Would you believe mummy dust costs twenty bucks?

"Aren't you scared to be in the kitchen, Jeff?" Kim teased me during dinner. "After all, the basement door is right there."

She gestured over her shoulder. "Doesn't it bother you that down in that box there's a dead body all wrapped up." She rose from her chair and started staggering around the kitchen like a mummy. "He's waiting for the night to fall so that he can sneak up to your room and — "

"Shut up!" I cried. What is her *problem*, anyway?

"That's enough!" Dad groaned. "Kim, you're not funny. Stop scaring Jeff."

While our parents were doing the dishes, I scooped out the ice cream. Kim leaned over the table and whispered, "If you think you're so cool, wait until tonight."

"What are you talking about?" I demanded.

"You know," she teased. "The mummy. I heard it last night, too, you know. And I also heard you screaming like a baby."

So I didn't imagine the sounds! Kim had heard them, too.

"I'm not worried," I replied. "I'm protected. I'm not scared at all."

"Yeah right," Kim said. "We'll see about that."

* * *

After everyone had gone to bed, I lay awake. It was chilly in my room. A storm picked up outside. The glass in the windows began to shudder as a sharp wind started up.

I clutched my pillow. Waiting. Waiting.

I gripped the pouch of mummy dust in my right hand. The feel of the small sack in my palm reassured me.

Rain drummed at the window. The room filled with white light. Thunder crashed outside.

Then I heard it.

THUMP.

From the room below me. From the kitchen.

The sound terrified me.

THUMP. *CLANK*.

I heard a low wailing moan. Was it the wind — or the mummy?

THUMP.

The mummy was coming for me.

But I wasn't going to wait for it.

I jumped from my bed and threw open my bedroom door. I couldn't stop shaking, but I made myself step out into the upstairs hall.

CRASH! Lightning lit up the hallway for a second. No mummy in sight.

THUMP. *CLANK*.

I grabbed the banister and jumped down the stairs, two at a time. My feet felt all prickly as they hit the polished wooden floor of the front hall.

I turned the corner toward the kitchen.

THUMP.

Something blocked my way.

The mummy!

Too scared to scream. My throat jammed up.

There it stood, in the shadows of the hall. The mummy hunched over, its face wrapped in strips of cloth. Its skinny arms hung limply at its sides. The arms were weighed down by hands that were huge — gnarled claws, wrapped in layers and layers of cloth.

The chains from the case were draped over its shoulders. They clanked as the mummy lurched up to me. Through the gauze over its head, I saw the mummy's evil grin.

Quick! I tore my eyes away from the ancient monster. I fumbled with the powder. Struggled to get the pouch open.

It was tied in a knot! My fingers shook too hard to open it.

The mummy moaned a low, ugly moan and reached its arms out to me. Huge, hideous claws. Reaching. Reaching.

Finally the knot gave way. I turned over the pouch to empty the dust into my palm.

Grunting, the mummy swung both arms at me.

I lifted my hands to guard my face.

The rotting cloth brushed against my skin. I stumbled back.

I hit the floor hard. My teeth clashed together.

The dust! I dropped it! The pouch fell to the floor, spilling the dust all over.

I scrambled to scratch up a handful.

The mummy growled. Lightning flashed. The ancient mummy flickered in the jagged, white light. Again I saw its evil, leering grin.

"WHO'S THERE?" boomed my mother's voice from the top of the stairs.

The mummy stepped away from me. The hall light flashed on.

To my shock, the mummy turned around and ran!

I couldn't believe it! Mom had saved me!

The mummy staggered to the basement door. It disappeared into the basement.

I slammed the door behind it. Then I grabbed a chair and tried to wedge it under the handle the way they do in the movies.

Mom rushed into the kitchen, tying the sash to her robe. Dad stumbled in behind her, fumbling with his glasses.

"What on earth is going on down here, Jeff?" she demanded.

"Mom, the mummy . . . it's alive. . . ." I gasped. "It was coming to get me, I swear! It's trapped in the basement right now."

"This has gone far enough," said my mother. "Larry, for once and for all, tell your son that mummies are dead and don't stumble around at night."

"Well, actually, there's something I didn't tell you," my Dad replied, rubbing his chin. "You see, there's a rumor that this mummy really is alive. I thought it was a joke."

"Huh?" Mom and I both cried.

Dad explained. "This mummy was given to us by another museum. They didn't want it anymore because the night guards said the mummy rose after dark to wander the halls. But the curator promised there would be no problem — as long as nobody took the chains off the box. The mummy can't come alive, unless someone takes the chains off."

"Jeff, did you take the chains off the box?" Mom demanded anxiously.

"No, no. I didn't!" I exclaimed. "Of course not!"

Dad jumped up as if stung by a hornet. "We've got to lock that thing in!" he cried. He searched the drawers till he found a heavy padlock. Then he locked the basement door with a loud snap.

"I'm so sorry," Dad said, hugging Mom. "I can't believe I put my family in danger. I never thought that the rumor might be true."

"I'm sorry I didn't believe you, Jeff," Mom said, turning to me. They tucked me in upstairs. With the mummy safely locked up, I quickly fell asleep.

Wow! It's really dark down here. Dad should fix the light.

I can hardly see my way down these stairs.

This basement is creepy.

I can't wait until Jeff and my folks go to bed so I can get out of here and go upstairs to sleep.

Oh, man! I almost got caught. But it was worth it — just to see the look on my brother's face when I reached out to grab him. He almost fainted, the little wimp.

Kim, you are so mean! But he asks for it! He really does.

Okay. Sounds as if they're gone. I'll sneak back upstairs. . . .

The door is stuck. Really hard. It won't open.

They must have locked it.

"Mom! Dad! Hello, can you hear me? It's me — Kim. I'm locked in the basement!"

No. The wind is too loud. The storm is making too much noise.

I can't believe this.

"DAD! MOM! JEFF! SOMEBODY!"

They can't hear me. This is awful.

I'm stuck down here for the night.

Well, I guess these old sheets will keep me warm. I can even wrap the gauze back around my face the way I had it before.

Of course this chain is completely useless.

Maybe it wasn't such a good idea to take the chain off the mummy case. But mummies have to have chains. Everybody knows that!

Good. Some lightning from outside. I can see where to sleep. Is that our old couch over there?

Whoa. Wait a minute! The lid to the coffin — it's off!

I didn't move the lid when I took the chains.

How did that happen?

Who opened the mummy case?

THUMP.

THUMP.

THUMP.

I'M TELLING!

It stood alone in the middle of the woods.

The most horrifying creature Adam had ever seen.

He crept toward it. Slowly. Silently. Through the bushes. Closer and closer to the hideous thing nestled in the clearing.

"I'm not afraid of you," Adam said under his breath. "I'm going to destroy you."

He ducked down in the tall grass and studied his enemy. He was only a few feet away from it now.

It was a gargoyle. And its huge, scaly wings rose over him. If the creature flew at him, he knew he could never outrun it.

I don't know if I'm brave or crazy, Adam thought. He crawled forward for a closer look. That's when he noticed the creature's claws. Long, sharp claws that could probably rip him in half.

"I'm not afraid of you," he whispered again. But

I am afraid of those fangs, he thought, peering nervously at the gargoyle's long, pointy teeth.

All the better to eat you with! Adam remembered the line from an old fairy tale.

Adam gazed up at the monster and took a deep breath. The creature sat silent and still. Good — it hasn't noticed me, he thought. Instead, it stared coldly at some twittering sparrows that had gathered at its feet.

It's now or never, Adam thought. He leaped to his feet and charged the monster.

"Eat this!" he screamed, lifting his weapon and squeezing the trigger.

Nothing happened.

The monster remained still.

Only the sparrows were surprised by his attack. They flew into the air with a soft flutter of wings.

"I don't believe it!" Adam cried. "I'm out of water!" He stared down at his empty water gun. Then he glanced back at the monster — a statue made of stone.

"You're lucky," Adam muttered. "If my gun was filled, you'd be dead now."

The monster didn't flinch. It was only a statue after all, stuck in the middle of a dried-up, old fountain.

Adam liked to come out to the woods and pretend to hunt. His best friend, Nick, said that pretending was for babies. "When you're in sixth grade, you've got to be cool," Nick told him. So

Adam came out to the woods by himself to play — when Nick wasn't around.

"If only I had more water . . ." Adam grumbled, shaking the water pistol.

To his surprise, the statue moved. Its mouth opened wide — and something green gushed out.

Adam jumped back.

Green liquid spurted from the statue's mouth.

Adam gaped at the gargoyle. "I don't believe this!" he cried. "It's amazing!"

Adam stared at the statue as the stream grew more powerful. The thick, green liquid splashed against the dry stones of the fountain.

"This is really weird," Adam said out loud. "Where is the stuff coming from?"

I guess I can refill my gun now, he thought. He pulled the plastic cap off one of the gun barrels and leaned into the fountain.

Then he stopped.

He felt as if the gargoyle were watching him.

He peered up at the monster. Its stone eyes remained frozen in a cold stare.

Get a grip, Adam, he told himself. It's only a statue. Nick would laugh his head off if he saw you now.

Adam reached up toward the gargoyle's mouth and held the plastic gun under the stream of liquid. His hand trembled as the gun's tank slowly filled.

"This stuff smells really gross! And it's kind

of gooey," he said, replacing the cap on the tank.

He turned to face the gargoyle. "Okay!" he yelled. "I've got you now."

Adam squeezed the trigger. Nothing happened.

He held the gun up to the light. He shook it some more. Maybe it's clogged, he thought. He turned and aimed at a large tree next to the fountain. He pumped the trigger, again and again. The gun suddenly jerked in his hands, and a green stream of liquid splashed the huge tree.

"Yessss!" Adam cheered.

The tree began to crackle.

Adam stared in shock as the brown branches faded to gray. The leaves crumbled. And fell heavily off the crackling tree.

A leaf dropped onto Adam's head.

"Ow!" he cried, rubbing his scalp.

The leaf was as hard as a rock.

Adam gaped at the tree. Was it true? Was it *possible*?

Yes. It had turned to stone!

Adam gazed down in amazement at the water gun in his hand. "Wh-what's going on?" he stuttered.

"I'm telling! I'm telling!"

Adam jumped at the sound of the high-pitched voice. A short, brown-haired girl with pigtails and freckles stepped out of the bushes. She pulled a red wagon behind her.

Adam groaned. It was Missy, his seven-year-old sister. The *second* most horrible creature in the world!

"What are you doing here, Missy?"

"Looking for *you*," she snapped. "Mom says you have to finish your art project. I told her she should take away your water gun. Or else you'll never finish it."

"You little brat," Adam muttered. "Why don't you mind your own business?"

"Why don't *you* do your schoolwork?" Missy shot back. "Do you want to stay in the sixth grade forever?"

"Go home, Missy," Adam said, fighting back the urge to tackle her.

"*I* always do *my* homework," Missy bragged. "*I* get straight *A*'s."

"Good for you," Adam growled. "Now leave me alone."

"What about your art project?" Missy demanded. "The contest is tonight."

Adam sighed. He gazed at the gargoyle in the fountain. Then at the stone tree. The crumbled leaves. He glared at his little sister.

"I'm busy," he said, clutching his water gun. "Art classes are for losers like you. I have more important things to do."

"I'm telling Mommy," Missy squealed. "You're in big trouble, Adam!" She stuck out her tongue. Then she started to sing. "I'm telling. I'm telling. I'm telling!"

Adam clamped his hands over his ears. "Shut up!" he yelled.

"I'm telling! I'm telling! I'm telling!" Missy sang louder.

Adam felt his face grow hot. Before he knew what he was doing, he raised the squirt gun and pointed it at Missy.

He didn't mean to squeeze the trigger. But he did.

Green slimy liquid squirted from the gun, splashing Missy's face.

Missy shrieked.

Then her small, round face turned chalky gray. Her lips froze in an open-mouthed scream. Adam stared in horror as the grayish-white color spread down her small arms and legs.

Then Missy's entire body stiffened. And a powdery dust swirled around her.

Adam's eyes bulged as he watched Missy turn to stone.

"Missy! No!" he shrieked. "What have I done?" he howled. "Don't worry, Missy. I'm going to hide you in the basement — until I can figure out what to do."

With a grunt, Adam hoisted his stone sister off the ground. She weighed a ton! He nearly broke his back lifting her into her wagon.

As he struggled to pull the wagon away, he heard gurgling. And hissing.

From the fountain? Yes.

Adam snapped his head around. Green slime dribbled down one of the gargoyle's fangs.

Adam shivered. His heart began to pound. He grabbed the wagon handle. Pulled as hard as he could. He didn't look back. He tugged the wagon until he reached the end of the woods.

All he had to do was pass by the school and turn the corner. His house stood on the corner of the next block.

He turned to Missy. "We're almost home," he said. "As if she can hear me!" he mumbled, rolling his eyes. He shook his head. My sister — a stone statue. How can this be happening?

Missy bounced heavily in the wagon. Adam glanced back nervously. He didn't know what would happen if she broke — and he didn't *want* to find out! He had to move fast. He didn't want anyone to see Missy like this.

"Adam! Adam!"

Adam recognized the voice. It belonged to the last person in the world he wanted to see. Mrs. Parker. His art teacher.

Mrs. Parker waved her arms in the air as she ran up the sidewalk after him. "Adam!" she cried out. "You finished your art project. I'm so proud of you!"

The tall, red-haired art teacher peered down at Missy's statue and clapped her hands together.

Adam gulped. "Well, Mrs. Parker . . . it's . . . not . . . um, really . . ."

"It's wonderful, Adam!" Mrs. Parker declared. "I had no idea you were such a talented sculptor. You've captured Missy in stone. It looks so much like her! It's a masterpiece!"

"But . . . but . . ." Adam fumbled for words.

"Hurry, Adam! Take your sculpture into the school. The art contest has already begun. Maybe you'll win first prize!"

Adam sighed. He stared at his stone sister. He wondered if she could hear. He wondered if she could *think.*

"Sorry about this, Missy," he whispered. "Nothing I can do now." He pulled the wagon into the school.

Adam won first prize. The judges placed a blue ribbon on Missy's stone shoulder. Mrs. Parker congratulated him.

His friend Nick came up and slapped him on the back. "Cool project," he said. "Really cool. It looks just like your bratty little sister! Want to come over and play video games?"

"Um. I can't," Adam stammered. "I — uh — have to get home and baby-sit Missy."

"Okay, see you," Nick said. He took one more look at Adam's statue. "Really amazing. How did you do that?"

Adam brought the wagon into the auditorium.

He crouched down to lift Missy up. And almost dropped her when he heard the voice. Missy's voice.

"Help . . . me . . . Adam."

Adam gasped.

"Did you say something, Adam?" Mrs. Parker asked.

"No," Adam replied. He grabbed the wagon handle, tugged hard, and raced out of the school.

Adam started toward his house when he spotted his parents in the front yard. Admiring their vegetable garden.

"Oh, no!" he moaned. "We can't go back to the house," he told Missy. "Not yet."

He didn't know where to go. So he hauled Missy back into the woods. "We'll hide near the fountain until I can sneak you into the house," he told her.

The sky was darkening as evening approached. The wind howled through the trees. A shiver ran down Adam's spine.

He pulled the wagon into the clearing.

And screamed. "Nooooooo!"

The gargoyle was gone.

"Where is it?" Adam cried. "Where — ?"

Adam didn't finish. A shadow slid over him. He glanced up in time to see the huge wings.

The gargoyle was flying!

No time to duck. No time to run.

In a gust of sour air, the ugly creature swooped

down. Its heavy wings pounded Adam's head.

"Get away from me!" he shrieked, throwing his arms up. "Get away!"

The giant creature swooped down again. Its eyes glowed a deadly red. Adam couldn't get away. The gargoyle dug its sharp claws into his shirt, shredding the sleeve.

"Noooo!" Adam uttered a terrified wail.

The gargoyle soared up again and began to circle. Prepared to dive again, its eyes flaming angrily.

Green ooze seeped from its gaping mouth. The liquid hit Adam's cheek with a sickening splat. His face sizzled.

Adam wiped the ooze away. He felt dizzy. Faint.

The gargoyle soared down at him. Adam dodged the monster.

As the gargoyle plunged toward him again, Adam spotted the water gun on the ground.

"Yes!" He grabbed it. Waited for the creature to swoop in closer . . . closer . . . closer.

When he could feel its sour, cold breath on his face, Adam pulled the trigger.

A blast of the slimy liquid splashed over the monster's glowing eyes.

The creature opened its mouth in a hideous howl. Then it dropped to the ground with a heavy thud.

And became a stone statue again.

Green liquid trickled from its leering mouth and dripped down its fangs.

"Yes!" Adam cried happily. "I did it! I did it!"

"Help . . . me . . . Adam."

"Missy!" Adam had forgotten all about her.

What am I going to do? he asked himself in a panic.

An idea flashed into his terrified thoughts. He reached for his water gun. It had some green liquid in the tank.

Adam shrugged. It was worth a try.

He aimed at the Missy statue. He held his breath and squeezed the trigger.

Nothing happened at first. Then, slowly, the gray stone cracked and crumbled. Layers of dust flaked from Missy's face. Her arms. Her legs.

"Adam, you jerk!" her voice rang out angrily from the rubble. "How could you do that to me?"

Adam grinned and hugged Missy. "You're alive!" he cried. He happily brushed the dust off her clothes.

"No thanks to you, stupid!" she snapped.

Adam ignored her angry words. He was so happy to see her. So happy! He threw his arm around her shoulders and led her through the woods.

"I can't believe you put me in the art contest," she complained, shoving his arm away. "They put that stupid blue ribbon on me. I felt like a total jerk!"

Adam sighed.

"Wait until I tell Mom. You'll be in big trouble! I'm telling her everything. I'm telling! I'm telling!"

Adam stopped walking. "Please, Missy — " he started.

"I'm telling! I'm telling! I'm telling!" she chanted nastily.

Adam sighed again. "I don't think so," he said softly.

Then he aimed the water pistol at her and pulled the trigger.

THE HAUNTED HOUSE GAME

I opened the closet door and reached up to the top shelf. It was dark up there. I couldn't really see anything, so I groped around until my fingers found what I was searching for.

"Aha. Here it is!" I said, carrying the box over to the table. "We're going to play Haunted House."

"Oh, Jonathan," Nadine moaned. "Not that dumb game again!"

"Come on," I replied, opening up the box. "It's fun. It's really scary."

"Yeah, that game is dumb," Noah echoed.

"Can't we play Parcheesi?" Annie complained.

"This is better," I said. "There aren't any ghosts in Parcheesi."

"But we've played it a hundred times before," Nadine mumbled.

"It's always different," I insisted. "Come on. Let's play Haunted House."

I unfolded the game board and lined up the

playing pieces. *BOOM!* A booming thunderclap shook the house.

We all turned to stare out the big picture window. The rain beat against it — hard. A bolt of lightning sliced through the sky. Then — *BOOM!* More thunder.

There are three things I really hate. The first one is thunder. The second — lightning. And the third — baby-sitting my seven-year-old brother and sister, Noah and Annie. Tonight I was a three-time loser.

At least Nadine is here, I thought. I stared at her across our long, oak dining-room table. Nadine is my best friend. We're in the same sixth-grade class. Whenever our parents go out together, Nadine gets to sleep over.

I dropped the dice in the little cup that came with the game. As I swirled them around, another burst of thunder startled us.

The house rumbled. Every window shook. And we have a lot of windows. Thirty-nine to be exact. I know. Because I counted them the last time I baby-sat the twins — when we played the Let's Count the Windows game.

"I wish Mom and Dad would get home," I said as I swirled the dice some more.

"Jonathan is afraid of thunder," Annie chirped.

"And lightning." Noah grinned.

"I am not," I protested, feeling my face turn hot. "Let's start," I said.

"What are the rules again?" Noah asked.

"The object of the game," I explained, "is to go around the board, through the haunted house — and try to find the hidden ghost."

"Oh, yeah. Now I remember," Noah said.

"And don't forget," I said in my best scary voice. "Be very careful. Don't land on SCARED TO DEATH!"

I shook the dice up and down in the little cup. Then from side to side. Then up and down again.

"Come on, Jonathan," Nadine said. "Roll the dice."

I tilted the cup and the dice spilled out. "Seven," I announced. "Lucky seven!"

"One-two-three-four-five-six-seven," I counted. I moved my green marker seven spaces.

And landed on YOU HEAR CREAKING FOOTSTEPS ON THE STAIRS.

I placed my marker down on the square.

Creeeak.

"Did you hear that?" I whispered.

Nadine and the twins nodded.

Creaking footsteps on the stairs. The stairs that led to our bedrooms.

"Maybe it's the cat," Annie whispered.

"Yeah, maybe it's the cat," Noah echoed.

"We don't have a cat," I replied.

We sat hunched around the table. Listening. Everything remained quiet. Everything except my heart pounding in my chest.

"Hey! I know what it was," Nadine said, straightening in her chair. "I bet the hall window is open upstairs. It was just the wind blowing through the window."

"That's it," I said, not totally convinced. It definitely sounded like a creak to me.

I studied everyone's faces around the table. No one appeared worried. "Okay, Annie. It's your turn. Spin," I said.

"You don't spin, Jonathan. You roll," Annie declared.

"Go ahead, Annie," Noah whined. "Take your turn."

"All right," Annie replied. She slowly tilted the cup and the dice dribbled out. "Three!"

Annie moved her red marker three spaces. "Onnnne. Twoooo. Threeee."

And landed on WIND RATTLES THE WINDOWS.

She placed her marker on the square and — the wind outside started howling. Really loud.

Then all the windows in the house began to rattle. All thirty-nine of them. First with a tinkling sound. Then more forceful. Vibrating in their frames.

The gusts outside grew stronger. Meaner. They whipped the windowpanes. I thought the glass would shatter.

My hands began to tremble. I hid them under the table.

I glanced over at Nadine. She stared out the big picture window.

I shifted my gaze to the twins.

The twins!

They were gone!

"Annie! Noah!" I cried.

"Here." Two small voices called from under the table.

"Come on out," I urged. "Everything's okay." But I wasn't as sure about that as I sounded.

"I'm staying here," Annie answered. "This game is too creepy. Every time we land on something, it really happens."

"It's not the game," I said. "It's the wind. And it's not blowing anymore."

It was true. The howling had quieted to a soft whistle. The windows stopped rattling.

"Jonathan is right," Nadine backed me up. Then she peeked under the table. "It's your turn, Noah. Don't you want your turn?"

"Of course I want my turn," he replied. He popped up and landed in his chair. He tossed the dice into the cup.

Annie slowly surfaced and plopped into her seat. "Let's play fast," she begged.

Noah swirled the dice and rolled a 2. He pounded the board with his blue marker.

My eyes darted to the board to see where he would land.

I found the square.

Noah plopped his marker down on it.

It said YOU HEAR AN EERIE MOAN.

A quick bolt of lightning pierced the sky. And then we heard it.

A moan.

A low, sad moan. From somewhere — inside the house.

"There's a ghost in here!" Annie shrieked. "Hide!"

"Where?" I yelled.

"In the closet!" Annie cried, jumping up from her chair.

"How do you know it's in the closet?" I shouted.

"She means we should *hide* in the closet," Nadine said. "Will everyone please stop screaming."

We stopped. The room fell silent. No creaking. No rattling. No moaning.

"There's no one here but us," Nadine continued. "This house always makes weird noises when it rains."

I guessed Nadine was right. She seemed so sure of herself. But I didn't think the problem was house noises.

"Now," Nadine said, scooping up the dice. "It's my turn."

She rolled a 4. I watched her closely. I was afraid — afraid to see where she would land.

Nadine moved her marker four spaces. And plunked it down on THE LIGHTS GO OUT.

And we all screamed as the lights went out.

"Everybody, sit still!" I shrieked. "I'll find some candles."

I groped my way into the kitchen. Mom and Dad kept candles in here somewhere. But where?

I couldn't see my own hands in front of my face. How was I supposed to find those candles? I opened every drawer in the kitchen, fumbling for them.

"Can you hurry up?" Nadine called from the dining room.

"Sure, Nadine," I muttered. "No problem."

Aha! Found them! Right on the counter. In their holders. Where they always are. I lighted them and returned to the other room.

We gathered at the end of the table — around the candles. Annie and Noah's eyes flickered with fear.

I was afraid, too.

"I don't want to play this game anymore," Annie whimpered. "It's too scary!"

"Our house is haunted." Noah's voice quivered.

"It's not the house," Annie whispered. "It's the game. This game is haunted."

I grabbed the dice and jiggled them in the cup. I glanced around the table. Everyone's eyes were opened wide. Glued to the board.

Lightning flashed outside the window. The candles sputtered in the dark.

Should I roll the dice? I wondered, gazing at our shadows dancing on the walls.

Should we stop playing?

Get serious, Jonathan, I told myself. It's only a game.

I spilled out the dice. 5.

I moved my marker. Slowly.

I held my breath as it landed on YOU HEAR A SCREAM IN THE ATTIC.

We sat quietly. Listening.

And then we heard it.

From upstairs.

A terrifying scream!

"Wh-what was that?" I stammered.

"Uh. The storm," Nadine replied. "Just the storm. Your turn, Annie."

I knew Annie didn't want to play anymore. But she rolled the dice. And moved her marker six spaces.

"YOU HEAR A BONY HAND TAPPING ON THE WINDOW." I read the words in the space.

No one spoke.

The room remained silent.

No tapping.

"See?" I said, walking over to the window. "Everything's — "

BANG!

A hand! A pale, bony hand — flew up out of nowhere! It banged the window hard.

The twins shrieked. I leaped back.

The wind picked up, and an icy draft blew through the dining room. The candles flared.

Nadine wrapped her arms around herself. Annie shrank back in her chair.

I studied the game board. Then I wiped my clammy hands on my jeans as Noah picked up the dice. *Not a three! Not a three!* I chanted to myself as Noah prepared to throw.

The dice tumbled out of the cup. They rolled. And rolled.

And stopped on — 3!

SCARED TO DEATH!

A candle blew out. Blinding white lightning flashed through the room. We screamed. And screamed. It seemed as if we screamed for hours.

The windows shuddered and quaked. Footsteps creaked on the stairs. An eerie moan floated up from the basement and flooded the room.

And then we heard the terrifying tapping.

Tapping. Tapping. Tapping.

We couldn't see it in the dark. But we knew what it was. The bony hand. Tapping against the window.

And then we were screaming again. Screaming so loud, it drowned everything out. Screaming so hard the whole house seemed to disappear.

I screamed until I couldn't hear myself.

Screamed until I couldn't breathe.

And then I stopped screaming, and the silence felt good.

I ran to the front door. I had to get out of that house. I had to!

But I stopped to pick up the newspaper on the mat. A yellowed newspaper.

The candle glow washed over the bold headline:

4 KIDS DIE IN MYSTERY DEATH!

My eyes rolled over the first paragraph:

> Police were completely baffled when they found four kids dead in an old mansion last night. "It looked to me as if they were scared to death!" declared one police officer.

Scared to death. Scared to death.

I glanced at the date on the newspaper. March 14, 1942.

So *that's* when we died, I realized. We died over fifty years ago. And we've been haunting this old house ever since.

I couldn't stay at the door. Nadine and the twins were waiting at the table for me.

Rain beat hard against the windows. The lights flashed back on. I opened the closet door and reached up to the top shelf. It was dark up there. I couldn't really see anything, so I groped around until my fingers found what I was searching for.

"Aha. Here it is!" I said, carrying the box over to the table. "We're going to play Haunted House."

"Oh, Jonathan," Nadine moaned. "Not that dumb game again!"

"Come on," I replied, opening up the box. "It's fun. It's really scary."

"Yeah, that game is dumb," Noah echoed.

"Can't we play Parcheesi?" Annie complained.

"This is better," I said. "There aren't any ghosts in Parcheesi."

"But we've played it a hundred times before," Nadine mumbled.

"It's always different," I insisted. "Come on. Let's play Haunted House."

CHANGE FOR THE STRANGE

Jane Meyers, twelve-year-old track star. That's me. As I stepped up to the starting line, I could hear the crowd scream. The fans roared. They were waiting. Waiting to see my spectacular long jump.

"Jane? Jane? Earth to Jane."

"Huh?"

"Jane — stop daydreaming. It's time to go!" Lizzy called from across the practice field.

Lizzy Gardner is my best friend. I watched as she walked toward me, careful to keep away from the dirt patches. Lizzy hates to get her shoes dirty. Today she wore sparkly pink sneakers and a short pink skirt. A pink headband held her blond hair in place.

"Are you ready to go?" she yelled, cupping her hands around her mouth.

Lizzy doesn't understand anything about track or why I practice so much. She thinks I'd have more fun at her house, hanging out.

But I want to be a track star more than anything else. Unfortunately, I didn't make the school team. I heard one of the girls on the team say I wasn't good enough to carry their towels.

That was so cold. But I'm not giving up. Every afternoon after school, I practice out in the field. Some day I'm going to be an incredible jumper. No matter what it takes.

After I practice, I always hang out at Lizzy's house. First we watch *Animaniacs*. Then we put on the CD player and dance around to our favorite band, Fruit Bag.

Sure, it's fun. But lately I've been more into track than hanging out.

Lizzy has changed, too. She still wants me to come over and do the same things — only now she's added a new one. She likes to go through her closet, thinking up new outfits.

"Do these shoes go with my new skirt? Does this top match my eyes?"

We do that until Ivan the Terrible barges into her room. That's what we call Lizzy's little brother. Ivan has a dog. A really mean pit bull. He named it Lizzy — just to make his sister angry.

Lizzy the dog ate Lizzy the person's new yellow scrunchy last week. He swallowed it in one gulp.

Ivan also has a whole collection of mice, snakes, and other weird animals. He likes to chase us all over the house, dangling his disgusting creatures in our faces.

"Hello! Anybody home?" Lizzy tapped me on the shoulder. "I've been talking for five minutes. And you haven't heard a word I've said."

By now, I'd gathered my things together. "Sorry," I said as we headed off the practice field. "What's up?"

"Before we go to my house," Lizzy told me, "I want to go shopping. I found a great clothing store. It's called A Change for the Strange. Have you seen it? It's right around the corner."

I shook my head no.

A minute later, we stood in front of the store. A neon pink-and-orange awning stretched over its front door. A CHANGE FOR THE STRANGE ran across the top in glowing letters.

I walked through the door and gasped.

The place was so . . . strange. It didn't seem like a clothing store at all. All sorts of weird items crammed the aisles.

Rain slickers hung from moose antlers. Yellow umbrellas with duck-head handles bobbed in puddles of water.

Green capes with velvet flowers dangled from leafy trees. Fluffy bunny slippers peeked out of rabbit hutches. Shark's-tooth necklaces floated in a tiny wave pool.

Lizzy disappeared between the racks. I usually

follow her around stores like a little kid. But this time, I stood in one place, gawking.

A store clerk stepped up to me. "May I help you?" she asked.

Something *had* caught my eye — a bright red jacket. It had tiny cracks in the material and a yellow trim that ran around the middle.

"Can I see that jacket?" I asked.

The clerk reached up and unhooked the jacket from a tree branch. The jacket looked wet. Slick. But when I ran my hand down the front, it felt totally dry.

"It's a cool-looking pattern," I told her.

She smiled and pointed to the cracks. "Those are scales," she explained. "That jacket is snake-skin."

"Ugh!" I snatched my hand away.

The salesclerk slipped the jacket off the hanger. "Try it on," she urged. "I bet it will look great on you."

I slipped into it, then I turned toward the mirror. It looked great. I twirled around. A perfect fit!

"I'll take it!" I declared.

"You will?" Lizzy came over, surprised.

"Sure. It looks great with my eyes!" I joked.

Lizzy grinned. "I told you this store was great." She held out a pair of white bunny slippers. "I'm going to buy these."

I choked back a giggle. A snakeskin jacket was one thing. But bunny slippers? "Those will be great for when you get hopping mad!" I teased Lizzy.

"Ha-ha. Remind me to laugh later," Lizzy snapped.

We quickly paid for the clothes and rushed out of the store.

Out on the street, I zipped up the snakeskin jacket all the way to my neck. I hadn't taken it off since I tried it on — not for a second. I loved it!

I gazed at the bright snakeskin as we walked. It sparkled in the sunlight. It looked awesome — like something a model would wear.

When we reached Lizzy's house, we spotted Ivan crawling around the front yard. "Shh!" he whispered. "I'm on the lookout for caterpillars. I'm starting a new collection. So don't scare them away."

"No problem!" Lizzy shouted as loud as she could. Then she stamped her feet and waved her arms. "We'll be so quiet, you won't even know we're here!" she screamed.

I started to follow Lizzy into the house, then stopped. I felt kind of weird. Kind of weak. And dizzy.

"Are you okay?" Lizzy asked. "You look a little pale."

"I'm not sure," I answered. I took a few more

steps. Everything around me started to spin. I grabbed onto Lizzy so that I wouldn't fall.

"Maybe you're getting sick," Lizzy said. "Want me to walk you home?"

"No, that's okay," I replied weakly. "I can go by myself."

"Are you sure? You don't look good."

"I'll be fine," I told Lizzy. "I'll call you when I get home."

I started home, but I didn't get very far.

Suddenly I felt really hot. My skin felt as if it were burning up.

All I wanted to do was lie down, right there on Lizzy's lawn. Stretch out in the cool green grass.

But I forced myself to stand.

Then I flicked out my tongue.

It darted in and out. In and out.

I tried to stop. To hold it in. But I couldn't!

And each time it lashed out, it grew longer. Pointier.

I clamped my mouth shut. But my tongue shot back out. And I smelled something strange.

An animal.

A cat. Then I smelled a dog and a squirrel.

My mind raced with panic. I could never smell animals before. What was happening to me?

Then I sniffed something really tasty. A nice mousy smell coming from Lizzy's house. Ivan's pet mice! Mmm-mmm!

I clutched my head.

And then I screamed. "My head!"

I had no hair! No ears! My whole head was covered with dry, cracked skin.

I rubbed it frantically. I wanted to bring back my old head.

Then the world seemed to tilt. Everything swam out of focus, as if I were on a speeding merry-go-round. I couldn't hold myself up. I sank to the ground.

I closed my eyes. "I'll count to three," I said. "Then everything will be okay. I'll wake up and be back to normal."

Slowly I counted — one, two, three. I opened my eyes.

And I shrieked out in terror.

I wasn't Jane Meyers, track star. I wasn't even Jane Meyers, human being.

"I'm a snake!" I tried to shout. But a long *hisssss* was all that came out.

I felt sick to my stomach. I was a snake! A slithering, fork-tongued snake!

I need help, I thought desperately. I need Lizzy! She'll know what to do. I nosed aside a giant blade of grass and stared up at Lizzy's house.

How could I get inside?

I started to slither toward her front door — when her mother opened it! She stood in the open doorway, fumbling for something inside her bag.

This was it — my chance to get inside!

I slithered as fast as I could. Then a shadow fell over me.

Lizzy — the pit bull.

"Oh, no!" I tried to moan. But of course I hissed instead.

The dog lowered her head and growled. A low, menacing growl. Then she bared her teeth.

I tried to slither away.

Lizzy trailed me. Snarling. Drooling saliva on me.

I slipped under a bush. But she found me. She lowered her head to the ground. I could feel her hot breath on my skin.

With one bite, Lizzy was going to rip the skin off my back. She opened her mouth and —

"Lizzy! Go!" It was Mrs. Gardner. The dog jerked her head up and whimpered.

"Ivan! Come and get the dog. I don't want her in the garden! Ivan!"

No answer.

Mrs. Gardner grabbed Lizzy's collar and tugged the dog inside. I slid out of the bushes and followed right behind.

Mrs. Gardner put the dog in the basement while I slithered up the steps to the bedrooms.

"Lizzy!" I hissed to my friend. I glanced around the room. I spotted the TV. The CD player. The Fruit Bag poster on the wall. But no Lizzy.

And then the light snapped on.

There stood Lizzy in the doorway.

She was here! She would save me!

"Hey, Lizzy!" I cried, twisting my snake body into the air. "Help me! Help me!"

"Yaaaai!" Lizzy screamed. "A snake! Ivan, get in here!"

"No — it's me!" I wanted to shout. But of course I couldn't. What could I do?

Lizzy pressed against the wall as I wriggled over to the remote control on her night table.

I had an idea.

I pushed my head against the power button. The picture flickered on the screen.

So far so good.

I pressed another button until *The Animaniacs* came on. Now she'd understand!

"Ivan — !" Lizzy began. Then she stopped. A light came into her eyes. She did understand! She did! I writhed in happiness.

Lizzy stepped closer. She reached out. She was going to pick me up. To save me!

No! She grabbed hold of her tennis racquet and with a loud cry, swung it hard and whomped me across the room.

Splat! I hit her CD player. My tail struck a button. Fruit Bag began to play.

For a moment, I lay stunned on top of the player, while Lizzy shrieked for Ivan.

Then I got another idea. I began to dance.

"Lizzy!" I hissed. "It's me. It's Jane. I'm dancing the way we always do!"

Lizzy's eyes widened with fear. She cowered in the corner. "Ivan!" she yelled. "Get in here. Now!"

Ivan poked his head in the room. He grinned. "Got a problem?"

"One of your snakes is loose!" Lizzy shrieked. "Get . . . it . . . out . . . of . . . here. NOW!"

"Lizzy," I whimpered. I slinked off the CD player and slithered over to her feet. "You have to save me!"

Lizzy backed into the corner. I coiled around her leg. "Help me!" I hissed.

"Yaaiiii!" she screeched. She hopped on a chair, trying to shake me loose. "Please, Ivan. Take your snake. Take it!"

Ivan strolled over, taking his time. I threw a pleading look up at Lizzy. "Please!" I hissed.

Ivan crouched over me. He stared at me. "It's not my snake," he said. "I don't have any red ones."

Lizzy's voice screeched. "I don't care!" she shouted. "Just get it off of me!"

"All right. All right." Ivan said. He unwrapped me from Lizzy's leg and carried me to his bedroom.

Then he dumped me into his snake cage.

With two other snakes. Their fangs gleamed in

the light. Their hot snake breath washed over me.

I pressed myself against the cage. But they slinked closer and closer.

They know, I thought. They know I'm not a real snake like they are. And they're going to kill me!

They writhed forward — one on each side of me. Hissing. Hissing. They were going to surround me. And attack.

Their long tongues slid out. They darted forward with a sharp jerk and —

Ivan reached into the cage and pulled me out.

"You know, Lizzy," Ivan said, carrying me back into Lizzy's room. "There's something weird about this snake. It's got something on its stomach."

He flipped me over. Then he gasped. "Wow!" he said. "It looks like a zipper! A tiny zipper."

He shoved me into Lizzy's face.

"GET THAT THING OUT OF HERE!" she screeched.

"I mean it, Lizzy. Look! Let's try to unzip it." Ivan set me gently on the floor. He hesitated. Pulled back. Changed his mind again.

Then he took a deep breath, reached down, and tugged on the zipper.

RRRRRIPPPP!

I exploded into my full human body.

Ivan gasped. Lizzy screamed.

"Cool!" Ivan said, reaching over to touch me.

Lizzy kept screaming.

"Hey! How did you do that?" he asked.

My whole body shook as I told them the terrible story.

When I left to go home, Lizzy was still screaming.

A few days later, Lizzy and I sat out on the field. I had just finished practicing.

"That was awesome, Jane," Lizzy said. "That's the highest I've ever seen you jump."

I felt really proud. My jumping was totally excellent today. Yesterday too.

I hopped over to her.

She reached down and petted my soft white fur. "You're going to be the state high-jump champ," she said.

My pink nose twitched. "You're right," I said. "Did you bring any carrots?"

I had to admit it. Lizzy had been right back at that weird store. Those bunny slippers were *definitely* cool!

THE PERFECT SCHOOL

Going to boarding school was not my idea of a great time. It was not my idea at all.

Whose idea was it? My parents', of course.

I knew I was doomed the day the brochure for the Perfect Boarding School arrived in the mail. The slogan on the cover read: Why Settle for Anything Less Than Perfect?

"Perfect" is my parents' favorite word.

Unfortunately, they have me — Brian O'Connor — for a kid. And I'm far from perfect. I make my bed — sometimes. I take a shower — sometimes. I get my homework done — sometimes.

And I please my parents — never.

Before I knew what was happening, my mom and dad had signed me up for the two-week course. On the way to the train station, I begged. I promised to cut back on TV and video games. I promised I wouldn't tease the dog. I even swore I wouldn't eat three Snickers bars for lunch anymore.

But it was no use. They hustled me onto the train and told me to watch for the Perfect van when I got off at the Rockridge Station.

I found a seat across the aisle from a kid who appeared as unhappy as I felt. He was reading something I'd seen before. The brochure from Perfect.

"So what do you think of the place?" I asked.

"I think it stinks!" he snarled. He threw the brochure down on the train floor. "Perfect. Ha! How about a school to teach parents how to be perfect instead?"

"I'd send mine," I agreed. "I'm Brian. My parents are sending me to Perfect, too."

"I'm C.J. So why did your parents send you for training? What did you do?"

"It's more what I didn't do," I explained. "They're always telling me I didn't do this or I forgot to do that. Man, I wake up five minutes late, and the first thing I hear is that I didn't go to bed early enough, and that's why I can't wake up!"

We complained about our parents until the train man called out "Rockridge Station! Rockridge!"

I grabbed my duffel bag and followed C.J. to the door. "Here goes nothing," I muttered.

About half an hour later, the van pulled through the tall iron gates leading to the school. The driver parked near a row of kids standing behind a sign that said PERFECT GRADUATES.

These kids were *weird.* Their line was ruler straight. Each kid wore a gray uniform. Each kid stood straight up and faced forward. Each kid held a gray suitcase in his left hand.

They stood in silence waiting for their parents to pick them up.

Is that what my parents want me to turn out like? I asked myself. If it is, they can forget it right now.

The driver slid open the side door of the van. Another man stood next to him. "I am the director of the Perfect Boarding School," the new guy told us. "Line up in order of height. Tallest at the back. Shortest at the front. Leave your bags in the van. You won't be needing them here."

The director pointed to the first kid in line. "You are number one-twelve," he stated. He gave a number to each of us. I got 116.

"Your instructors will call you by number," the director explained. "You will call each other by number. You will call me and your teachers 'Guardian.' "

How am I going to make it through two weeks at this place? I thought. This guy is nuts!

A car pulled up in front of the other line. The director hurried over to present the parents with their perfect child — and get his envelope of money in return.

Were any of those kids like me when they got here? I wondered. What did the *Guardians* do to change them? What will they do to me? A shiver raced down my back.

Those kids were like robots. Robots!

Four more Guardians waited for us inside the door. One of them tapped me on the shoulder. "Follow me," he said in a low voice. He led me down a hallway and up a flight of stairs.

I caught sight of C.J. going into a room on the first floor. "See you later — " I started to call.

"No talking," the Guardian barked. At the top of the stairs, he turned left. A half-open door clicked shut as we passed it.

What are they trying to hide? I wondered. Why is every single door shut? Why don't they want us talking to each other?

The Guardian ushered me into the last room in the hall. "You will wear the clothing in the drawer. You will eat the meal on the tray. You will wait here until you are summoned," he ordered me. Then he shut the door.

I checked it — locked, of course.

I studied my new room. It didn't take long. There was a single bed with a small dresser on one side. A table with one chair on the other.

I wandered over to the dresser and opened the drawers. Only boring stuff. Gray uniforms, toothpaste, towels.

May as well check out the food, I decided. A

bowl of bumpy gray stuff sat on the table. I scooped up a little with my finger and licked it off. Tasted sort of like oatmeal.

Then I heard something. A rustling noise. From the heating vent near the floor.

The hairs on the back of my neck prickled. Is something down there?

I stretched out on the floor and pressed my ear against the vent. The rustling grew louder.

Not rustling, I realized. Whispering.

"Is someone down there?" I called softly.

The whispering grew louder. What were they saying?

"Can you hear me?" I asked.

"No talking," a Guardian called from down the hall.

The whispering stopped.

What was that? Did I hear voices from another room? Or was someone hiding down there between the walls?

No. That was impossible.

Right?

I was happy to find C.J. in my first training session. I wanted to ask him if he'd heard anyone whispering in the walls. "Hey, C.J.," I said softly.

"No talking," the Guardian in charge of our class ordered. "You will answer each question in the workbook on your desk."

How can he expect us to answer every question?

This thing is more than a hundred pages long. I flipped open the workbook.

Huh? I thought. These questions are strange: "What do you call your parents?" "What is your favorite food?" "What costumes have you worn for Halloween the last five years?"

Why did the Guardians want to know all this stuff? They already knew way too much about me.

So maybe I could confuse them a little. "I call my father Featherhead and my mother Jellyface," I wrote. "My favorite food is lumpy gray oatmeal. Every single Halloween, I've dressed up as a three-humped camel."

I tapped C.J. on the shoulder and held up my workbook so he could read my answers. C.J. snickered.

A strong hand grabbed my shoulder. Hard. "Number one-sixteen, you are a distraction to the others. You will be placed in the Special Training Course."

The Guardian marched me to the front of the room and hit a small buzzer underneath his desk. Another Guardian appeared at the classroom door.

"Take one-sixteen to the Pattern Room," the first Guardian ordered. "His training is being speeded up."

As the second Guardian herded me out the door, I glanced back at C.J. "Sorry," he whispered.

My mouth felt dry as I followed the Guardian

through the hallways. I tried to swallow, but I couldn't. I didn't know what the Special Training Course was — but I definitely didn't want to be in it.

The Guardian stopped in front of a wooden bench where a little girl sat swinging her feet. "Wait here," he ordered, then left.

As soon as the Guardian turned the corner, the girl leaned over to me. "Do you know what they're going to do?" she whispered. "I heard — "

A Guardian opened the door across the hall and called the girl inside. I slumped back against the wall. I was never going to find out what was going on in this creepy place.

I sighed and closed my eyes. Then I heard the whispering again. It was coming from the wall behind my head.

The whispers grew stronger. I pressed my ear against the wall. "Careful. Don't go in the Pattern Room," a voice cried.

My heartbeat thudded in my ears. "Why? What's in the room? Who are you?" I demanded.

"Don't go — "

The door to the Pattern Room opened. A Guardian ordered me inside.

I felt my legs trembling. I hoped the Guardian couldn't tell how scared I was. Slowly I stepped inside the room.

It looked like my doctor's office: a scale, an examining table, a counter with some cotton, bandages, and stuff.

"Step on the scale," the Guardian instructed. Maybe this won't be so bad, I thought.

The Guardian entered my height and weight into his handheld computer. Then he looped a tape measure around my head and recorded the information. He measured every part of my body, down to my toes. He even measured my tongue.

Why does he need all these measurements? I couldn't think of anything he could use them for. Did my special training take some special equipment that fit me exactly?

I remembered a movie my teacher showed in science class. Some scientists hooked wires up to a mouse and then dropped it into a maze. Every time it made a wrong turn, they gave the mouse a shock.

Maybe that's what the Guardians were going to do to me. Maybe they would give me a shock every time I did something my parents wouldn't like.

The Guardian picked up a color wheel from the counter. He held it up to my eyes, trying to find a color that exactly matched.

I felt more confused then ever. When the Guardian had recorded every detail about me, he sent me back to my room. Without a Guardian escort!

I had to find a way to escape. I paused at each

door and listened for voices. I didn't hear anything behind the fourth door. I opened it.

An empty office. With a phone. Yes!

I grabbed it and dialed my home number. The phone rang once. Please answer, Mom, I silently begged. Two rings. Three rings. Four rings.

I heard footsteps approaching the door. Answer. Answer.

Five rings.

"Hello?" my mom said breathlessly.

"Mom!" I whispered. "You have to get me out of this place! Something weird is going on here. I'm scared."

"Brian, you just got there yesterday. Give it a chance," Mom replied impatiently.

"But they — "

A cold hand pulled the phone away from me. I spun around. The director stood behind me.

"Hello, Mrs. O'Connor," he said. "This is the school Director. Your son Brian will be ready early. Truly special children often finish our program before the others. Yes. First thing tomorrow will be fine."

The director hung up the phone and marched me up to my room. "You have made your last error," he told me as he shut the door behind him.

What is that supposed to mean? I wondered. Are they still planning to give me the special training? Or are they sending me home — *un*perfect?

I flopped down on the bed. Every time I heard

footsteps in the hall, I thought a Guardian had arrived to take me for training.

I guess I finally dropped off to sleep. I had a dream about looking for my dog at the pound. All the dogs were whimpering.

When I woke up, the whimpering continued.

I jumped up and scrambled over to the vent. I peered down. Far below me, I saw dozens of glittering eyes.

"Save us!" a voice cried. "Save us — and yourself."

"Robots," another voice whispered. "The school makes a robot of you. They send home the robot in your place. A perfect robot. And then they make you live down here where no one can ever find you."

So *that's* why the Guardians asked those questions and took so many measurements! They were making a robot of me to send home to Mom and Dad!

My whole body trembled. I could barely breathe. "What do I do?" I demanded. "How can I — ?"

"Shhh. Someone's coming," another voice warned.

The eyes disappeared back into the darkness.

I had to get out of my room — now. I tore a piece of paper off the sheet lining one of the dresser drawers. Then I knocked lightly on the door. No answer. I knocked a little louder.

"Yes?" a Guardian called.

"I need to go to the bathroom," I said.

He opened the door. As I passed through, I shoved the paper into the lock.

The Guardian escorted me to the bathroom and then returned me to my room. He shut the door firmly behind him.

I waited a few minutes. Then I tried the door. It opened. The paper kept the door from locking!

I grabbed my spoon from the table and opened the door a crack. When the Guardian was looking in the opposite direction, I hurled the spoon down the hall as far as I could.

The Guardian heard the clattering sound and turned toward it. I slipped out of my room and ran down the hall the other way.

So far so good. I crept down the stairs.

"What are you doing down here?" someone demanded.

"N-nothing," I stuttered. Then my eyes adjusted to the dark hallway. "C.J., it's you!" I was so glad to see him! "We've got to get out of this school — now!" I told him.

His eyes bulged in surprise. "Huh?"

"There are kids trapped behind the walls. We have to save them — and us!" I exclaimed, tugging his hand.

"Follow me," C.J. answered. "I know where to go."

C.J. grabbed my arm and led me around the

corner and down a short hallway. He pressed on a wall panel — and it slid open.

"Quick. In here," he whispered. "It leads outside."

"Great!" I cried. I ducked my head and started into the narrow opening.

To my surprise, I saw only darkness. And heard whispering voices. Shuffling feet.

"Hey — !" I spun around to C.J. "This doesn't lead outside!" I protested. "This is where all the kids are hidden!"

"Sorry," C.J. replied in a cold, low voice. "This is where you will be hidden too, Brian. I work for the Guardians. My job was to guard you."

"No!" I shrieked. "No! Let me out! Let me out!"

But to my horror, the wall panel began to slide shut behind me.

"Thank you very much, Director," my mother said. "Brian looks perfect."

She admired my gray uniform, my perfectly brushed hair, my perfect smile. I stood straight as an arrow. I faced forward as a good robot should. I held the gray suitcase in my left hand, as all of the robots are programmed.

My mother shook hands with the Director. She handed him an envelope filled with money.

"He will be perfect now," the Director said. "We guarantee it."

That was two days ago. And I'm trying to be as perfect as I can be.

Because I don't want anyone to catch on.

It wasn't easy to pull C.J. into the dark chamber and escape before the wall closed up. And it wasn't easy to sneak into the robot room. To grab my robot and drag it up to my room. And then to sneak back into the robot room and pretend to be a robot.

Yes, I don't want anyone to catch on that the *real* Brian O'Connor came home. I don't want anyone to know that I escaped.

Some day soon I'm going back to that place and rescue those poor kids. But right now I'm being as perfect as I can be.

Okay, okay.

So I teased the dog this morning. And ate three Snickers bars for lunch. And spilled some grape juice on the white couch in the den.

But other than that, I've been perfect.

Really.

FOR THE BIRDS

"We're here!" Dad announced happily. "Happy vacation, everyone!"

Some vacation! I grumbled to myself.

My family piled out of the car. All five of us. I stretched my legs after the long ride. Then I gazed up at the lodge.

What a dump.

It looked like the log cabin on the maple syrup bottle. Except it was falling apart.

A log hung over the door with words carved into it: WELCOME TO BIRD HAVEN LODGE.

It should be called Bird *Brain* Lodge! I told myself, rolling my eyes. Only a birdbrain would come to a place like this!

Mom gave Dad's arm a squeeze. "Oh, Henry! It's so romantic!"

Romantic? Okay, maybe I'm only twelve. Maybe I don't think much about romantic stuff. But that wasn't exactly the word that came to my mind.

The word that came to my mind was *stupid*!

"Can't we go to a *real* hotel?" I pleaded for the thousandth time.

But Mom and Dad were too busy smooching to answer. They always acted this way on their wedding anniversary — which was today.

"Move it, Kim," ordered my fifteen-year-old brother, Ben. He had on his favorite T-shirt. It said: *So many birds, so little time!*

Do you believe it? A fifteen-year-old boy who's into bird-watching?

"Yeah, move it, Kim," echoed my other brother, Andy. He's thirteen. His hair hangs down over his eyes. I can never tell if he's looking at me. "We want to do some bird-watching before dark."

To me, if you've seen one bird, you've seen them all. But everybody else in my family is bird crazy! They spend all their time in the woods, staring through binoculars.

And if they spot a new bird to check off on their list, they go totally nuts.

It's sick. That's the only way to describe it.

And now here we are at Bird Haven Lodge. A whole week of bird-watching, bird talk — nothing but birds all the time.

Thrills and chills, huh?

Carrying my suitcase, I started up the gravel path to the lodge. Tall hedges lined the path on both sides. The hedges were trimmed into bird shapes. I passed what looked like a leafy pigeon. Then an eagle. I brushed by a bushy duck about ten feet tall.

"I'm going to hurl. Really," I complained.

My family pretended they didn't hear me. I guess they were sick of my complaints. But what was I supposed to do while they crawled through the trees gawking at birds?

"Check it out!" exclaimed Andy as we reached the lodge. "A pair of great horned owls!"

"No way," Ben scoffed. "Those are screech owls."

"Owls in the daytime?" I asked. "Where?"

"Right there, stupid," Ben said, pointing.

Then I saw them. They were standing guard on either side of the steps. Owls carved out of hedges.

Big deal — right?

"We're the Petersons," Dad told the big, jolly-looking man at the check-in desk.

"I've been expecting you," the man replied with a big smile. "I'm Mr. Dove."

"Mr. *Dove*?" I mumbled. "Give me a break!"

Mr. Dove's round, little bird eyes darted from Mom to Dad. "Mr. and Mrs. Peterson," he said, "you'll be in the Lovebird Suite."

Mr. Dove ran his fingers down the register. "Now . . . let . . . me . . . see. I have a double for the boys on the third floor in the Blue Jay Wing." Mr. Dove eyed me. "And for you — the Cuckoo's Nest."

"Cuckoo!" Ben and Andy hooted. "Cuckoo Kim!"

I shot Mr. Dove a dirty look. But he didn't seem to notice.

"Follow me," he said. "I'll show you to your rooms."

We followed him down the hall to the Lovebird Suite.

"These doors lead out to a terrace with an old-fashioned swing," Mr. Dove practically cooed. "Would you like to see it now?"

But Mom and Dad were too busy smooching to answer.

Uh-hmmm. Mr. Dove cleared his throat.

Mom giggled. "We can see the terrace later," she said. "Come on, Henry. Let's go see the kids' rooms."

We took the elevator up to the third floor. Ben and Andy dashed into their room, snatched binoculars from their backpacks, and ran outside to spot some birds.

"Now to Cuckoo's Nest," Mr. Dove announced.

"I'm the only one here who *isn't* cuckoo!" I muttered. I don't think anyone heard me.

Mom and Dad and I followed Mr. Dove again. We turned down a narrow hallway. We kept walking. And walking. We didn't see any other guests.

"Um, where *is* my room, anyway?" I asked.

"We're almost there," Mr. Dove sang out.

When we reached the far end of the hall, he stopped and opened a door.

"How unusual!" Mom exclaimed, stepping into the room.

Mom had *that* right. Cuckoo's Nest was small. Tiny, actually. And it was round. A round room.

"I don't know . . ." I began. "It's, um, so *far* from everybody."

"Don't be silly, Kim," Mom said. "It's a lovely little nest!"

I groaned. "Mom — can't you stop with the bird talk for one second? I'm sick of birds! Sick of them!"

I saw Mr. Dove staring at me, surprised by my sudden outburst.

Dad walked over to a window. "What a view!" he exclaimed. "Kim, you can see right into the famous Mockingbird Maze."

I joined Dad at the window. The maze looked like one out of my old *Pencil Fun and Games* book. Except that this maze was made out of twelve-foot-tall hedges. It went round and round and round. It seemed to have a hundred different dead ends.

I'd hate to get lost in there, I thought. "Hey!" I exclaimed. "There are Ben and Andy — inside the maze!"

Mr. Dove frowned. "You should save the maze

for tomorrow," he told Mom and Dad. "You'll need a full day to do it right."

"Why don't you go outside too, Kim?" Dad suggested. "Your mother and I have some unpacking to do."

Well, I went downstairs. But I didn't go outside. I don't really like to be outdoors at all. Too many birds.

I wandered around the lodge. I thought maybe I'd find someone else my age. Or a game room. Or a TV to watch.

But the place was empty.

Finally I sat down on a low couch in a room near the front desk. I guess it was some kind of rec room. I stared at the stone fireplace for a while. There were stuffed birds all around it on the wall. Pheasants and ducks and owls. Yuck!

I picked up an old magazine and settled back against the couch.

"Oww!" I cried out as a sharp pain shot up my back.

I jumped to my feet. A picture flashed into my mind. A huge, angry bird — a hawk or a falcon. It had dug its sharp beak into my back!

I spun around — and gazed down at a pair of hedge clippers.

"Huh?" I picked them up. Heavy, metal hedge clippers. I hadn't even seen them when I sat down on them.

I turned to see Mr. Dove enter the room. "You found them!" he cried. A smile crossed his round face. He hurried over to me. "Thank you! I've been searching all over for these!"

"I — I sat on them," I stammered. I handed them to him.

"I'm so grateful you found them." He beamed at me. "I owe you a big favor, Kim."

"No. Really — " I started.

"I owe you a favor," he insisted. His smile faded. "I guess you'd like revenge."

"Excuse me?" I thought I hadn't heard correctly.

"Revenge against your family. For bringing you here," he said, smiling again.

"Uh . . . no. That's okay," I replied uncertainly. "I'm . . . uh . . . enjoying it." I hurried out of the room. "Bye."

What did he mean by that? I wondered. He's just like my family, I finally decided. Totally nuts.

That night, we ate in the hotel dining room. I hoped to see some other kids at dinner. Some *normal* kids. Kids who couldn't tell a red hawk from a turkey buzzard. But we were the only ones in the dining room.

Mr. Dove was our waiter. Maybe he was the cook, too. Did anyone else work here? I wondered.

Ben and Andy couldn't stop talking about how

many birds they'd seen. They were so excited. "There are *thousands* of birds here!" Andy declared.

"No. Millions!" Ben corrected him.

Mom and Dad held hands all through dinner. They couldn't wait for us all to explore Mockingbird Maze in the morning.

I tuned out. I'd never been so bored in all my life.

Later, I was in my room, trying to get to sleep. I closed my eyes. I listened to the wind blow through the trees. I tossed and turned for hours. I twisted my covers into knots. No way could I fall asleep in Cuckoo's Nest.

The wind began to pick up. I heard flapping. Must be the awnings over the windows, I thought.

Then I heard a cry. My eyes popped open. I glanced around the room. It was flooded with moonlight. Shadows flitted on the bed, the floor, everywhere.

I threw back the covers and tiptoed over to a window.

I gasped!

The sky was thick with birds!

They circled in front of my room. Cawing and cackling.

An enormous crow landed on my ledge.

It stared at me with its bottomless, black-hole eyes. Then it pecked at the glass.

It's trying to tell me something, I thought.

A weird thought. But the whole thing was so weird. Why were the birds flying at night? Why were they circling in front of me? Cawing and chirping so demandingly?

They really did seem as if they were trying to communicate.

With a shudder, I pulled the curtain, hurried back to bed and slept with two pillows over my head.

The next morning, Andy and Ben woke me up at dawn. They insisted that I come with the family into Mockingbird Maze.

"I might as well," I said, yawning. "There's nothing else to do here." That was as enthusiastic as I could get.

The five of us ate a hurried breakfast. Then, armed with notebooks, bird books, and binoculars, we stepped out into a gray morning. The sun hadn't climbed over the trees. The morning dew still glistened on the grass.

What am I *doing* here? I asked myself, shaking my head unhappily. I hate birds. I *hate* them!

To our surprise, we found Mr. Dove at the entrance to the maze. He wore blue denim overalls, and he carried the hedge clippers. His round face was red and sweaty. I guess he had gotten an early start pruning in the maze.

“Good morning, everyone.” He grinned at me. I hope you enjoy the maze. Lots to see. Lots of urprises.”

He chatted with Mom and Dad for a few minutes. Andy and Ben started chirping at me. ‘Cuckoo! Cuckoo! Cuckoo Kim!” They think hey’re a riot, but they’re just dumb.

A short while later, we stepped into the maze. The tall hedges cast dark shadows over the path. [already felt lost!

We took about five steps — and stopped.

“Oh, wow!” I cried out. Standing in front of us was a huge hedge sculpture. Five people carved out of hedge. And the five people were *us*!

“Mr. Dove — !” Dad called. “What *is* this?”

We turned to see him grinning at us from the maze entrance. He waved the big hedge clippers. “All part of the program,” he called. “Part of the program.” He disappeared.

Dad shook his head. “What an odd bird,” he muttered.

“Dad — *please!*” I begged. “Stop with the bird talk!”

We admired the hedge portrait for a while. I’m not sure why, but it gave me the creeps. Why did Mr. Dove do it? What did he mean, it was part of the program?

The questions repeated in my mind as we made our way through the twisting maze. Everyone else oohed and aahed over all the birds. There were hundreds of them. All different kinds. All chirping and cawing and crowing at once.

I had to hold my hands over my ears. It was deafening!

These birds are all chirping at once because they're trying to tell us something. That thought flashed through my mind again. That's totally crazy, I told myself. And I pushed the thought out of my head.

I shouldn't have.

I should have paid attention to my growing fear.

But now it was too late.

We stepped into a narrow tunnel — and came out the other end into a round structure. Dome-shaped. Made of metal wires.

It took us a few seconds to realize we had stepped into a cage. A giant bird cage.

"Wow — this is awesome!" Andy declared.

"What a great maze!" Ben agreed.

Then the wire door snapped shut behind us.

Andy's smile vanished. "Hey — how do we get out?" he cried.

"You can fly out," a voice replied. Mr. Dove appeared from a trapdoor in the cage floor.

"Huh? What do you mean?" Mom cried. She grabbed Dad's arm. "What's going on, Mr. Dove?"

"All part of the program," Mr. Dove replied. "All part of the program. I want you to be happy birds."

"Excuse me? Happy *birds*?" I demanded.

"It's a very old trick I learned," Mr. Dove said. "Quite easy. If you get the hedge sculpture right. Quite easy. And now you can join your feathered friends. You'll be happy. I want you to be happy."

Before we could say anything, Mr. Dove raised the hedge clippers. He pointed them at Mom and Dad. And clicked the blades together twice.

"Nooooo!" I wailed as I watched Mom and Dad shrink away — change shape — and flutter up against the cage wall.

"I turned them into lovebirds." Mr. Dove beamed. "Now they'll be happy."

"Noooo!" Another horrified wail escaped my throat as the hedge clippers clicked twice more. And as I stared in shock, not believing it, not believing it — but seeing it — my brothers were also changed into fluttering, chirping birds.

"Two mockingbirds," Mr. Dove said. "They'll like that."

He turned to me.

"No — please!" I begged. "Please don't turn me into a bird! Please!"

He smiled. "Of course not, Kim. I owe you a favor. I know you hate birds — right?"

"Please — !" I repeated. "Please — !"

"I said I'd help you pay them back," he said softly.

"No. Please — !" I begged. "Please don't — "

My family chirped and twittered, fluttering across the cage excitedly.

"I want you to be happy, Kim," Mr. Dove said.

Then he clicked the hedge clippers and changed me, too.

He changed me into — a cat.

ALIENS IN THE GARDEN

Thick, black clouds rolled across the sky as I walked toward the park. Lightning flashed and thunder rumbled in the distance.

Forget the park, Kurt, I told myself. Nobody will show up in this weather, anyway.

More thunder. Louder now. That did it. I turned around and started for home. As I hurried around the corner, I spotted Rocky up ahead of me.

I stopped — and wished I could disappear.

Rocky is a dog. A mean, vicious dog with ratty brown fur, sharp yellow fangs, and killer eyes.

I held my breath and crossed my fingers that he wouldn't come any closer. And I got lucky. Rocky sniffed in the gutter for a couple of seconds, then trotted away.

I let my breath out in a big whoosh.

"Yo, Creep-o!" a voice roared from behind me.

I sucked in my breath again. "I should have

known," I mumbled. Wherever Rocky goes, Flip won't be far behind.

Slowly, I turned around and faced him.

Flip is Rocky's owner. Flip is fourteen, two years older than I am. And he's huge, with the same ratty hair and yellow teeth as his dog.

It's hard to decide which one is meaner.

"Where do you think you're going, Kurt?" he demanded.

"Home," I told him. "A storm is coming."

"Ooh, a storm!" He sneered and pushed me backwards. "Gonna go hide under the bed?"

Flip's favorite sport is picking on me. He pushed me again, harder. I almost fell. "Get a life, Flip!" I yelled. "Go sniff gutters with your mutt!"

Flip's eyes narrowed. He clenched his big fists. You should have kept your mouth shut, I told myself. You're in major trouble now!

Just as Flip dove for me, a shaft of lightning split the clouds. Thunder boomed. More lightning flashed, and then rain poured out of the sky.

"Aah, you're not worth getting soaked for," Flip growled. Instead of pounding me to dust, he shoved me aside and took off.

Saved by a summer storm! I'd lucked out after all.

Upstairs in my bedroom, I changed into dry clothes. I could hear the wind howling outside. I ran to the window and crouched down in front of it to watch the storm. As I did, I saw something whiz past outside. Another lightning bolt split the sky. It zapped the flying object and lit it up.

I stared hard at the object. It looked like a toy spaceship.

I mashed my nose against the windowpane to see better. There! It hovered low over the backyard garden. Wobbling back and forth. Out of control.

I craned my neck to watch. The object spiraled down . . . down . . . down . . . then — *splat*! It nose-dived right into the middle of a berry bush.

I kept my eyes on that bush until the storm finally blew itself out. It wasn't a long storm, but it was one of the heaviest I've ever seen. When the rain slowed to a drizzle, I ran outside and sloshed my way into the garden.

Disaster area! Ripped leaves and broken branches covered the ground. Slimy green vegetable guts dripped down the fence. Mud slithered into my shoes and oozed between my toes.

I squished over to the berry bush and stooped down. Bloodred juice splattered onto my fingers as I pried some branches apart.

There sat the object, stuck nose-first into the ground under the bush. Wisps of hissing steam rose up from it.

I cautiously reached down and touched it.

Warm, but not too hot. The mud made a sucking sound as I tugged it loose.

I wiped the object on my shirt and stared at it.

Some kind of spaceship, for sure. Made out of metal. Cone-shaped, with three little wings at one end and a tinted window at the other. I couldn't see inside.

But it's definitely not a toy, I decided. It's too solid. And it survived the storm *and* the crash.

An awesome thought suddenly hit me. Could the little spaceship be real?

I always figured flying saucers and alien spaceships had to be huge. But I'd never seen one. How could I know for sure that I didn't have one in my hands?

I tucked the ship under my arm and hurried to the park to show it to my best friend, Jenna. I knew she would show up. Jenna loves going to the park. She practically lives there.

As I sat down on a bench, Flip burst out of some bushes and landed in front of me. Guess my luck ran out.

"Hey, Creep-o, what's that?" he asked, grabbing for the spaceship.

I tried to push him away, but he yanked me straight off the bench and tossed me into the grass.

The ship flew from my hand and landed nearby.

Flip stared at it. His mouth hung open for a

second. Then he shook his ratty head and bellowed out a laugh. "A toy spaceship? Aren't you a little old to be playing with toys?"

As I struggled to my knees, Flip reached for the ship. I knew he'd try to smash it, so I made a grab for it.

In a flash, Flip had me in a headlock. His arm squeezed tighter around my neck. I tried to pull it away. The muscle felt like a stone. His arm didn't budge.

I gasped for air.

Flip let out another laugh.

But his laugh turned into a shriek. To my surprise, his arm dropped from my neck.

I sank to the ground. Flip shrieked again.

I sucked in air and stared up at him.

He held his face with one hand and hopped up and down, screeching in pain.

As I gazed at him, a blue light zipped past my eyes and hit Flip on his bony knee. Sparks flew from his skin. He roared and dropped to the ground. Then he rolled over, leaped up, and ran off.

Saved again! I thought. But by what? Where did that blue light come from?

I sat up and glanced around.

And gasped.

On the ground near the ship stood three small aliens.

Aliens? You're seeing things, Kurt, I told myself. Flip's choke-hold cut off your air and messed up your brain.

I glanced away. Shook my head to clear it. Blinked hard and rubbed my eyes. Slowly, I glanced back at the ground.

The aliens still stood there, not much taller than the grass. They wore puffy silver suits and round white helmets with shaded visors.

Whoa! Not only had a real spaceship crashed into the garden, but it had real aliens in it. Awesome!

I stared hard — and saw that each alien clutched a tiny gun in its hand.

Ray guns. Ray guns that shot a painful blue light!

I'm toast now! I thought, jumping to my feet.

But instead of zapping me, the aliens shoved the guns into their suits. Then they tilted their heads way back and gazed up at me.

I crouched down on my hands and knees. I stuck my face real close to one of the aliens and squinted into its visor.

A weird face with bright-red hair growing all over it. Beady little eyes. A button nose and a smile on its tiny mouth.

I heard a faint squeaking sound. I stared harder. The alien's lips flapped. It's talking! I realized. An alien is actually talking to me!

I grinned. "Hi, I'm Kurt," I told it. "Listen, thanks for zapping Flip."

All three aliens grabbed their helmets and cringed.

At first I didn't get it. Then I realized the problem — my voice. I'm at least a hundred times as big as these little guys, I told myself. My voice is killing their ears.

"Flip is a total bully," I whispered. "I really owe you one. I mean, you saved my life!"

I peered at the first alien again. It just shook its head and shrugged. It couldn't understand a word I said.

"Hey, Kurt what are you doing?" a voice called out from behind me. My friend Jenna's voice. The aliens stood still as she dropped onto the ground beside me.

Jenna gazed at the aliens. Then she slowly glanced at me. "Please tell me you're not playing with dolls, Kurt."

"They're not dolls," I whispered. "They're aliens."

"Alien what?"

"Alien aliens," I told her. "From outer space."

She rolled her eyes. "Give me a break!"

"Keep your voice down!" I whispered. "It hurts their ears."

"You're kidding, right?" Jenna glanced at the aliens. "Hello down there!" she cried.

The aliens grabbed their heads and cringed again.

Jenna gasped. Her green eyes grew huge.

"Kurt!" she whispered. "Please tell me you've got a remote control somewhere."

I pulled the pockets of my shorts inside out. "No remote, Jenna."

"This is unreal!" she murmured. But I could tell she believed me now. "How did they get here?"

I pointed to the ship. "The storm knocked it out of the sky, into my garden."

"Wow!" Jenna gazed at the aliens. "I never thought I'd see anything like this! I mean, there's actually life on another planet somewhere!" She bent lower and squinted closely at the first alien.

"Don't make any sudden moves," I warned. "It's got a mean ray gun. They all do. Flip tried to choke me — and they zapped him."

Jenna grinned. "If they zapped Flip, they're definitely good guys." She inspected the alien again. "I wonder where they're from."

"I don't know, but I bet they want to go home," I told her.

"After meeting Flip, who wouldn't?" Jenna muttered. "Can the ship still fly?"

Before I could answer, the aliens suddenly stiffened.

I glanced up. "Uh-oh! Flip's back!" I warned. "And he brought Drake along for company!"

Flip and his cousin Drake were tearing along the path toward the bench. Drake carried a bat. With a wild laugh, Flip vaulted the bench and landed near the spaceship.

The aliens scattered.

"Ready for some fun?" Flip roared to Drake.

Drake snickered.

"Leave them alone!" I shouted.

Flip laughed again. "Hey, Creep-o, didn't your mother ever teach you to share your toys!"

Two of the aliens scurried off in opposite directions. Drake darted after one of them, whacking his bat on the ground and laughing.

"Cut it out!" Jenna cried. She chased after Drake.

I spotted the third alien running for the ship. It tripped over a twig and fell on its face.

Flip snatched it up in his fat hand. "You're dog meat!" he snarled at it.

He pinned the alien's arms to its sides and began to squeeze.

He'll squash it! I thought. They saved me. Now it was my turn to save them!

I made a desperate leap. I crashed against Flip's knees, knocking him to the ground. The alien popped from his hand and tumbled end over end through the air.

I stretched my arms out as far as I could and caught it inches from the ground. It struggled to its feet on my palm.

"Kurt's got one!" Flip shouted to Drake, scrambling up. "Forget the others. Get Kurt!"

Drake and Flip charged at me. Jenna jumped on Flip's back, but he shook her off easily.

I slipped the alien into the pocket of my shorts — and ran!

I dashed along the path, scuttled through some bushes and into a clearing. As I sprinted up a grassy hill, I heard Flip and Drake crashing through the bushes after me.

I put on more speed and charged down the other side of the hill. Then I doubled back.

Gasping for breath, I crawled through the bushes again. At the edge of the path, I peeked out.

And froze.

Flip's dog, Rocky, stood on the path, his killer eyes glaring straight into mine.

My heart hammered against my chest.

Rocky's lips curled back. His yellow fangs dripped saliva. He lowered his huge, shaggy head and snarled. He pawed the ground. Snarled again.

And sprang at me!

I cried out as a blue light zapped through the air. It caught Rocky right between the eyes!

The dog yelped and dropped to the ground at my feet, looking dazed.

The blue light meant only one thing — an alien close by. I glanced around and spotted it, caught in a thicket of thorny branches.

"Thanks again!" I whispered, reaching into the bush. The tiny spacesuit ripped as I tugged the alien free. I quickly dropped it into my other pocket.

Still dazed, Rocky whined meekly as I stepped past him and bolted down the path.

"Kurt!" Jenna cried when she saw me. "Hurry!"

"I've got two of the aliens!" I gasped, running up to her. "We've got to find the other one!"

"I did," she told me. "It's in the ship. Maybe it's trying to get the spaceship working."

"Let's hope it can." I dug the other two aliens out of my pockets and set them in the open hatch of the ship.

They waved at me, then hurried inside. The tiny hatch closed.

A loud, angry bark made Jenna and me spin around. Rocky had recovered and was charging toward us. Flip and Drake raced behind him, shouting, "Get the aliens!"

I stooped down next to the spaceship. Tiny red lights flickered on, but it didn't move.

The barking and shouting grew louder.

The spaceship still didn't move.

I had to do something! I grabbed it off the ground, cocked my arm back — and *hurled* the ship as high into the air as I could!

The ship soared upward. Higher . . . higher.

Then the nose dipped.

Jenna and I both gasped.

The spaceship began to spiral down.

Rocky chased after it, barking wildly. Flip and Drake cheered.

I groaned and started to cover my eyes. But

then I saw a puff of smoke from the back of the ship. Then another. The little spacecraft leveled off — and began to climb.

"Yes!" I cheered.

Flip and Drake stared with their mouths hanging open.

More smoke billowed. The red lights twinkled. The ship kept climbing. It rose higher and higher, until all we could see was a silver dot in the sky.

"Unreal!" Jenna kept muttering as we hurried out of the park. "Real, but totally *un*real!"

"Flip and Drake still can't believe it," I said, snickering. "They're both back in the park, gaping at the sky."

She laughed. "Too bad the aliens couldn't have zapped them one last time."

"Yeah, and it's too bad they couldn't have stayed a little longer." I stared up at the sky, too. "One thing is for sure — I'll never forget them."

"I'll bet they never forget *us*, either." Jenna pointed at an ice cream truck down the street. "And I think we deserve a reward for saving them, don't you?"

"Definitely." I dug into my pockets and pulled out some coins.

I also pulled out a tiny scrap of silver material.

"Hey! It's a piece of a spacesuit," I told Jenna. "It must be from the alien that got caught in the thorn bush."

Jenna squinted at the scrap. "It's part of a sleeve, I think. And there's something on it. Something colorful."

We forgot about the ice cream and ran to my house. I found my magnifying glass and peered at the scrap through the lens.

"What do you see?" Jenna asked.

"I'm not sure." I closed one eye to focus better. "It's a rectangle," I told her. "With stripes going across it. Red and white stripes. The upper left-hand corner is blue. And it has a bunch of white stars on it." I counted them. "Fifty stars."

"Weird." Jenna frowned. "I wonder what it means."

"Me, too," I agreed. "Maybe it's some kind of symbol. A flag or something. From the aliens' planet." I sighed. "I guess we'll never know."

"Let's go get that ice cream," Jenna said.

I tucked the tiny cloth rectangle into my pocket and followed her out the door.

THE THUMBPRINT OF DOOM

"Let's go swimming in the lake," I suggested.

"Trisha, you already said that. Can't you think of anything else to do?" Jeremy asked. "Harold doesn't want to go swimming. He's afraid."

I was afraid too. Afraid that this was going to be the most boring summer of my life.

Usually I go to sleep-away camp in the summer — but not this year. This year I thought it would be fun to hang out with my best friend, Jeremy.

I thought wrong.

I didn't know his cousin Harold was visiting — for two whole months. Nerdy Harold. Ugh.

We're all twelve, but Harold seems a lot younger. Probably because he's really, really short. The total opposite of me and Jeremy.

"What are you afraid of, anyway?" I asked Harold, tightening my ponytail. We were walking around the block for the third time, trying to decide what to do.

"Yeah, what *are* you afraid of?" Jeremy asked.

"Fungus."

"What?" Jeremy and I shouted together.

"Fungus," Harold repeated. "You know, those tiny plants that live in the water. The ones that are so small, you can't see them."

"So what about them?" I asked.

"Well, I don't like things I can't see," Harold mumbled.

I'm doomed, I thought, staring at Harold. This really was going to be the worst summer of my life.

"How about the movies?" Jeremy suggested.

Harold said okay, so we headed for town. We had walked halfway down the block when I spotted her.

"Look," I said, turning to Jeremy. "There's the new girl. Her family moved in last week. Mom says she's our age. Let's go say hi."

I stared at the girl as we walked over. She was really pretty. Her long, shiny black hair hung down to her waist, and her skin was a beautiful olive color. She wore khaki shorts and a matching T-shirt.

"Hi!" I called when we reached her yard. "You're my new neighbor. I live over there," I said, pointing out my house.

"I'm Carla," she introduced herself, striding across the lawn in her bare feet. "We just moved in."

Carla glanced at Jeremy, then at Harold. She had the brightest green eyes I'd ever seen.

"I'm Trisha. This is Jeremy and Harold. We're going to the movies," I said. "Want to come?"

"I'd really like to," Carla started. "But I can't. My horoscope says I shouldn't go anywhere today."

"You believe in that stuff?" I asked.

"Well, I'm kind of into it. I'm pretty superstitious."

"You mean you're afraid of black cats and stuff?" Harold asked.

"Harold is only afraid of things he can't see," I told her.

Jeremy shoved his elbow into my side. Carla didn't seem to notice. She continued, "Well, I'm not afraid of black cats. But some things. Have you ever heard of the Thumbprint of Doom?"

"The Thumbprint of Doom?" I repeated. We shook our heads no.

"Well, if someone puts it on your forehead," Carla explained, lowering her voice to a whisper, "you're doomed! Something horrible will happen to you in less than twenty-four hours."

"Do you *really* believe that?" I asked.

"Yes," she replied. "Yes, I do. It's the thing I'm most afraid of."

"We — we have to go," Harold stammered. "We're going to be late for the movie."

"Okay. See you around," Carla said. The three of us hurried away.

"Boy, was she weird," Jeremy snickered.

"Totally," I agreed. Then I waved my arms over my head and started shrieking. "Oooooo! The Thumbprint of Dooooom." I jabbed my thumb onto Jeremy's forehead, hard.

Jeremy chased me down the street trying to give *me* the Thumbprint of Doom. Then we both raced after Harold. We tackled him to the ground and gave him the *Double* Thumbprint of Doom!

The next day, Jeremy and I headed down to the lake to go rowing. Harold decided to stay home — to read the dictionary. He says he wants to finish it by Christmas. He's already up to the *P*'s; I convinced him he was way behind schedule.

"You get in first," I told Jeremy when we reached the lake, "and set up the oars." Jeremy had a hard time slipping the oars into the oarlocks. They were about a hundred years old — rotted and warped.

The old wood creaked and groaned as I slid the boat into the water. I started to jump in — when I heard the scream.

A terrified scream.

"Trisha! Noooooo!"

I lost my balance and fell into the lake.

I fumbled for the side of the boat and pulled

myself up, gasping for air. Then I threw myself on the shore.

"Are you okay?" It was Carla.

I couldn't speak. I nodded.

"Hope I didn't scare you," she said. "But you can't ride a blue canoe on Tuesday!"

"Huh?" Jeremy cried, helping me up.

"It's bad luck," Carla said. "A blue canoe on Tuesday is bad luck for Wednesday."

"Carla, you scared me to death," I sputtered. "I don't believe in those weird superstitions. *And I don't believe you did such a stupid thing,*" I muttered under my breath.

While I wrung out my T-shirt and poured the water from my new sneakers, Carla apologized. Then the three of us headed home. I wanted to be mad at Carla, but I couldn't. She was convinced that she had saved my life.

"Hey! There's Harold," Jeremy pointed out on our way back. Harold was walking down the street, dodging from tree to tree. I'd seen him do that before. He was trying to avoid the dogs — if there were any.

"Hey! Guys! I finished the *P*'s!" He ran up to us. "Isn't that great, Trisha? I finished the *P*'s!" Then he shot his arms out and — he shoved me hard!

I fell to the ground and scraped my knees.

"HAROLD!" I screamed. "What did you do that for?"

"You were going to step on a crack! See," he said, pointing to the sidewalk.

"So what!"

"It's bad luck, Trisha," he explained. "Step on a crack, break your mother's back."

"Since when do you believe in superstitions?" Jeremy asked.

"Since we met Carla," Harold said, smiling at her. "I think she makes a lot of sense."

This was *definitely* going to be the worst summer of my life, I thought.

But I didn't know how right I was.

A few days later, Carla stopped by the baseball field to watch us play.

It was the bottom of the ninth, we were one run behind, and I was up at bat. We already had two outs, so I was really nervous. The game was all up to me.

I planted my feet in the batter's box and waited for the pitch. It flew past me. So did the next one. Two strikes.

"This is it, Trisha," I told myself. "Concentrate!"

My eyes were glued to the ball. It was coming — a fast ball. My favorite pitch!

I started to swing and —

"TRISHHHA!" Carla ran out onto the field. "Don't!" she shrieked, waving her arms high in the air.

The ball whizzed by me. "Strike three!"

"Carla!" I screamed. "What is your *problem*?"

"It's thirteen minutes after one o'clock on Friday the thirteenth," she said in a rush. "You can't hit a ball now. It would be a disaster!"

"Thanks, Carla," I grumbled. "Thanks a lot."

Carla and Harold left right after the game. Jeremy waited for me to collect my stuff from the bench. Then we walked home together.

"I can't take it anymore," I complained. "Do you know what Carla did to me yesterday?"

Jeremy shook his head no.

"She forced me to walk around the fire hydrant seven times — backwards."

"Why?" Jeremy asked.

"I don't know *why*, Jeremy. All I know is she's driving me crazy. Those superstitions are ruining my life."

Jeremy shrugged.

"We've got to show Carla that superstitions are totally dumb, Jeremy. We've got to. The question is *how*?"

Three days later, I knew how. I had a plan to cure Carla of her superstitions forever. It was sneaky. But it was good.

Friday night after dinner, Jeremy, Harold, and I stopped by her house.

"We're riding over to the Jefferson Field fairgrounds," I told her. "To check out the new carnival. You've got to come!"

Carla stood in the doorway, holding open the screen door. "Tonight?" She narrowed her eyes. Thinking. "No," she finally said. "Not tonight. The stars aren't right."

We begged and pleaded, and finally dragged her out of the house.

By the time we reached the fairgrounds, the sun had set. Jefferson Field sparkled in the dark with thousands of colored lights. They decorated a huge Ferris wheel. And a giant roller coaster. And they lit up the midway.

Carnival music blared everywhere. Bells rang out every time someone won a game.

"Wow! This is great!" Jeremy cried as we walked through the midway, tugging Carla behind us.

I spotted a small, dirty, white trailer in the back. A sign hung over the door. MADAME WANDA SEES ALL. HAVE YOUR FORTUNE TOLD.

"Come on!" I turned to Carla. "Let's see what Madame Wanda says about your future. Bet it isn't as scary as you think."

"No," Carla refused. "I'm too scared."

"We'll go in with you. It'll be a laugh. Bet she tells you some wild things."

Carla shook her head no.

"I'll stay out here with Carla," Harold offered. "You two can go in." Harold was scared, too.

"Harold is afraid of the future," Jeremy whispered to me, "because it's another thing he can't see!"

"We're all going in," I declared. And with that, Jeremy and I pulled Carla and Harold into Madame Wanda's trailer.

It was very dark inside, and a sweet odor filled the room. Incense, I guessed. Soft, eerie music surrounded us.

A cold green mist swirled through the air. It sent a chill down my spine. I turned to Carla. She shivered, too.

In front of us, a single candle glowed on an old table. Our shadows shifted on the walls in the flickering light.

It really was scary in here.

"H-hello," I stammered.

No answer.

I took a step forward and heard a moan.

A low moan.

My heart began to race. I glanced at the others.

Harold stood frozen in place. Jeremy looked frightened, too. In the dim light, I could see his eyes nervously dart around the room. Carla didn't move.

The moan grew louder. "Let's get out of here," I whispered.

I turned to leave. But a breeze — from nowhere — snuffed out the candle, plunging us into darkness.

We screamed.

And then we heard the voice.

"Come forward," it called from a darkened corner. We inched up. My legs trembled. The moaning grew closer. Closer.

"I — I want to go," Carla groaned. She bolted for the door, but a hand suddenly reached out and grabbed her.

Madame Wanda.

The woman struck a match and lit the candle. "Sit!" she commanded.

We sat.

She took her place at the table. She was dressed in a shiny black gown, and on her head she wore a dark-green turban.

I studied her face. Purple veins shot through the whites of her eyes. I couldn't stop staring at her eyes — and those lips. Dark, dramatic lips.

She grinned at me and her lips parted. Her dark eyes glowed, as if seeing right through me.

I jumped up, but she yanked me back down.

She stared deeply into our eyes. "Who will go first?" she asked slowly.

A trickle of sweat dripped down my forehead. I grabbed Carla's hand and raised it in the air. "She will!"

Carla snatched her hand back, but Madame Wanda reached out and seized it. Carla's hand trembled in Madame Wanda's.

"Do not be frightened," the fortune-teller said.

"I am only going to reveal your future. Nothing more."

Madame Wanda held Carla's hand tightly as she peered into her crystal ball. I glanced around the table. Jeremy and Harold sat perfectly still — statues with eyes glued to the crystal ball.

"Ahhhhh. I see something," Madame Wanda murmured. "Yes. It is becoming clearer!"

And then she gasped.

We all jumped.

Madame Wanda's face filled with horror. Her eyes bulged wide with fear. "No! No! I don't *believe* what I see in your future!" she cried.

"What? What is it?" Carla screamed. "Tell me!"

"I — I cannot. I have no choice! I cannot allow you to grow old and suffer!" Then she dropped Carla's hand — and pressed her thumb into Carla's forehead! "I have given you the Thumbprint of Doom!"

"Noooooo!" Carla shrieked. She knocked her chair over — and hurtled out of the trailer.

We all leaped up and ran after her. We found her leaning against the trailer. Gasping for breath. "The Thumbprint of Doom!" she murmured. She rubbed her forehead.

We laughed.

"Don't be afraid. It was all a joke," I explained. "We just wanted to show you how dumb superstitions are. Nothing bad will happen to you. You'll see. It was all a joke."

"Yeah," Jeremy added. "We paid Madame Wanda this morning. We paid her to say all that and press her thumb on your forehead."

"I know. I know it was a joke," Carla replied calmly. "I *knew* that woman couldn't give me the Thumbprint of Doom."

"How did you know?" I asked.

"Because only I have the power!" Carla cried. "Why do you think I believe in this stuff? Because I *know* it's all true! I know it's true — because I have the power! That's why I'm frightened of it. And now I have no choice. You know my secret. I have no choice."

Then Carla dived toward us. And before we could move, she pressed her icy thumb on our foreheads. "I've given you all the Thumbprint of Doom!" she cried.

I shrieked in horror. Carla grabbed my sleeve with an iron grip. I struggled to pull free, but she held on.

"Let me go," I cried. "Let me go!"

Carla threw back her head and laughed — a wicked laugh. She yanked on my arm. And a burning pain shot through my body.

With a burst of strength, I ripped free — and we ran.

We ran from evil Carla.

We ran from the carnival.

We ran to our doom.

* * *

Carla watched the three kids run off.

"That was a very mean joke, Carla," Madame Wanda said, stepping out of her trailer.

"They started it," Carla replied.

"How long do you think it will take them to realize that you have no powers? That you were just playing a trick on them?"

Carla giggled. "They'll figure it out after a day or so. Then maybe we'll all have a good laugh about it," she said. "I'm going to explore the carnival now. What time will you be home?"

"About ten," Madame Wanda replied.

"Okay," Carla said. "See you later, Mom."

R.L. STINE is the author of the series Fear Street, Nightmare Room, and Give Yourself Goosebumps, as well as the phenomenally successful Goosebumps series. His thrilling teen titles have sold more than 250 million copies internationally—enough to earn him a spot in the Guinness Book of World Records! Mr. Stine lives in New York City with his wife, Jane, and his son, Matt.